PRAISE

"A Wild West cyberpunk dystopian science fantasy novel as if written by Raymon Chandler and oozing style and substance. You wish you were as cool as *Bloodmetal*."
—Paul Jessup, author of *Glass House*

"Apparently, Gene Wolfe and Steven Erikson had a lovechild and it grew up sexy af."
—Jonathan Wood, author of *Broken Hero*

"If weird western fantasy fiction mashups are your thing . . . get *Bloodmetal* on your to-buy list pronto."
—Lori Hetler, *The Next Best Book Blog*

"*Bloodmetal* is a whip smart mix of swordfights, gunbattles, and political intrigue. A wholly unique blend of weird western and weirder science fiction that's overflowing with incredibly cool ideas. Darin Bradley can always be relied upon to write intelligent, thoughtful, mind-blowing novels, and this is his best one yet. I loved it!"
—Josh Rountree, author of *The Legend of Charlie Fish*

BLOODMETAL

by

Darin Bradley

Underland Press

This book is published by Underland Press, which is part of Firebird Creative, LLC (Clackamas, OR).

Why does my mouth taste like ball bearings?

Edited by John Klima
Book Design and Layout by Firebird Creative
Title Treatment and map by Stoney Wayne Bass

This Underland Press trade edition has an ISBN of 978-1-63023-073-9.

Underland Press
www.underlandpress.com

BLOODMETAL

For Leslie. Ad astra.

Ap - Lian
Dhialt
The Thacrol Nations
Mendi Territory
Tulan
Nuhrven Baruul
Karlande
Nidal
Silangarde
Levuwes
Naredesh
Great Salt Wastes

CHAPTER ONE

Carsand stared into the tiny, gold rosette embedded between this woman's eyes, and he wondered if death came different from an alien implant. He remembered that much, at least—that she could kill him with it. Trick his own brain into doing the job for her with illusions and phantasms. She was inspecting his eyes, which she'd unveiled by parting his eyelids with her slender fingertips. Or he was still into his poppy, and none of this was real.

If she did split his head with some strange torque from the blood-metal filament behind her tiny transducer, she was likely to get his brains all over herself.

Carsand thought he might survive after all. She didn't look like the kind of woman who'd avail her face of his brains.

They never gave *him* any fancy gold transducer. They just buried the bloodmetal filament in his head and waited for it to take root. There wasn't much of a scar anymore.

"Do you know who I am?" the woman said. She had a voice like a courtroom verdict.

He tried to sound charming. "I don't believe that I do."

"Do you know where you are?"

He gave the idea a try. Nothing. "No, ma'am."

She studied him. She had eyes like chipped flint and severe, arched brows. She either had a silk scarf on her head, or she had the straightest, blackest hair he'd ever seen, and he'd been in Baruul for two months.

Ah, yes. Baruul.

"Wait," he said. "We're in Baruul."

"He'll live," she said. "Take him."

It sounded like she had two additional pairs of feet, and the four hands she took him with were decidedly less delicate than the fingers she'd lent to his eyelids. These new arms and legs got him up off whatever he'd been lying on. The smell of old poppy hung in the air, like he'd set fire to a florist's shop and then passed out for a few weeks.

He watched her pluck things from low tables cluttered with plates of old food and bottles of wine in various states of consumption. He recognized the cut of her dress—long and black, reaching almost to her boot heels, and sleeves that disappeared into the cuffs of her matching gloves. He knew clerics that dressed like that, but they didn't have bloodmetal filaments in their heads. The hem of her dress winged her around the room as she shoved things into a satchel: a necktie, a belt, his hat. She didn't disturb the glass pipe beside the flattened pillow.

Right, these were all his things.

Damn, but he stank, too. No, wait. His other selves did. He looked at each in turn, holding him up by the arms. They each cut the same mirthless, military profile.

"I hate to be indelicate," Carsand said, "but I think we all need a bath."

"Shut your mouth," one of them said.

Dammit, which one?

Carsand recognized the steel blazon studded into their leather armor. The royal seal. He looked next at the pistols on their hips: burnished stocks and upraised tracery on the barrels. The plugs of bloodmetal behind the firing pins were worth enough to buy every poppy in this temple. They had swords with the same indulgences across the quillons and on the pommel. Expensive weapons, which the king paid for.

His eyes looked at the glass pipe on the pillow as if drawn by magnetism. A force that could get him out of these men's grasp and across the room if he just asked it nicely enough. An attraction he couldn't deny. That's what he'd been doing. Some oblivion with that pipe and an elegant cluster of Barular who waited on him in tailored muslin. They had everything he wanted, in the bed and out of it, men and women both. Carsand wasn't too particular. He was glad to remember he had habits.

"Knights of Silangarde," he said. He'd rather have been staring into that woman's rosette again. These venal sons of bitches. He didn't have any bribe to suit their tastes, and even if he did, they'd probably muster the house knights in the first hardscrabble border demesne they came across, just to make those guys beat the hell out of him instead of doing it themselves. Because they could.

Why *did* he recognize that woman?

"Do you have a second mouth to shut?" the other knight said.

Carsand had gone as far from Silangarde as he could get, and now these people were here. Something had gone wrong.

The woman turned, and her heels were loud on the flooring as she brushed past the knights. Did he know someone who wore that dress before her?

"Bring him."

They dragged him through the lamp-lit hallway, and clouds of burning poppy wafted through the louvers in the doors. Poppy temples didn't have windows. Their devotees didn't take kindly to bright light.

The knights held him in the parlor while she negotiated with a steel-haired Barular woman behind the counter. Courtesans and masseurs and people without any use to their being that Carsand could determine lounged on chaises and sofas, unashamed of the suggestive drape of their muslin wraps. There were legs and asses and suggestive mounds of flesh everywhere. Even the knights availed themselves of the view. The collected Barular stared at them.

One of the knights shuffled. "What are they looking at?"

Carsand's begloved captor showed some form of identification to the woman behind the counter, and she received Carsand's sidearm and sword for it. He assumed he carried them for a reason. An important one, since he had a royal license, working with the crown and its bulldog artifexi.

Oh, hell. That was it. She was an artifex. An Inquisitor who found hidden things, or hid them herself, with the power of her brain and the filament inside it—a physical congress with metal that could think. Or at least listen, in his case.

That's what all the Inquisitors did, in those long black gowns. Even the men. Twisting the world with their *interferences*.

"You're wearing full armor in a poppy temple," Carsand said. "You get around much?"

The knight glared at Carsand. "I don't traffic in savage countries."

Carsand laughed, and his head went bright with a jolt of pain. "Barular architecture alone renders Karlande little more than a brick shithouse. Let alone the mathematics they—"

The knight cracked a gauntleted fist across Carsand's face, and he was back in sweet darkness.

She had either set Carsand's brain on fire, or she had revived him with smelling salts. He didn't much care which, as the goddamned difference was hard to come by. He was back in the searing light of his bad decisions whether he liked it or not.

His eyes did the watching for him while his brain cooled. It took him a minute to realize she was tucking a small jar into her reagent bag across the room. She snapped the bag's leather jaws together and joined them with a gold clasp. He felt dizzy, like the room was rocking.

"Where are we?" he said.

The room smelled like old tobacco, and there were assorted carpets and chairs with cabriole legs and an Ap-Lian changing screen in the corner. There were a couple of holes in its wicker panels. She poured a glass of wine from a decanter on the sideboard. The liquid sloshed in it.

"In a transduction conveyance," she said.

"A trans—" Carsand lifted himself onto his elbows and looked out the leaded window. He could see the linked cars in an arc trundling behind them across the hard-packed road.

"You mean a train," Carsand said.

She looked at him like an insect. The cowl of her dark hair trembled in the train's motion. "Spare me your vulgar nomenclature."

"What's its name?" Carsand said.

"Elsabet."

"You know her?"

"Of course I know her."

He lied back down on the sofa. "You two go a lot of places together?"

She laced her fingers around the glass, and the transducer between her eyes caught a flash of wild light.

"You wandered out of range," she said.

"Why does my mouth taste like ball bearings?" he said.

"I gave you an elixir to weaken the poppy's grip on your body," she said. "Otherwise, you won't move your bowels for days. It's quite unpleasant, I'm told."

"Since when does the Consortium care about my bowels?"

"It doesn't. I'm kind."

He glanced at her, looking for humor. He'd seen more expression in a garden statue.

"Don't you need your reagents for yourself?" The light was still overly bright, so he drew the lace curtain across the window.

"I can spare a few."

He pinched the bridge of his nose. "So, you came all the way to Baruul to care for my bowels in a train—"

"Transduction—"

"Conveyance. Yes, I know. A transduction conveyance named Elsabet fit for the king."

She stared at him. He hadn't seen her drink any of the wine yet. She held it as if she needed an adornment, something safe to hold, even through her gloves. He'd seen an artifex once too far gone on his own reagents to know he had a bare-handed hold of a recalcitrant farmer's rusted plowshare. He gave himself the blood poisoning with an interference he powered too long through his transducer. He was trying to burn the man's entire field with the power of his mind, but holding on to that metal ploughshare, he cooked himself like a holiday pig. The farmer just stood there. Burnt alfalfa, burnt artifex. It seemed like it made a kind of sense.

Carsand would've used lamp oil and a torch to burn a field, but whatever.

He didn't see that kind of thing too often, though. Most of them took precautions, like her—gloves and masks and all kinds of things. They didn't care much for over-conducting the energy of the cosmos. Especially the old ones, who were more bloodmetal than brain, constantly uncapping their transducers and injecting ever more and more of the wet, red metal into the holes in their heads.

"I came because my superior asked me to."

He squinted at her. How old was she? Not as old, on closer inspection, as he might have thought. Somewhere in her twenties? Still sharp enough at all this to be in control of the foreign passenger in her mind.

"And who is your superior?"

"The prime minister, of course."

Carsand swallowed. Lathael. The prime minister had been guilty on more than one occasion of making unpleasant use of the filament in Carsand's head. It burned Carsand up that he couldn't do anything with the damn implant. They'd put it in too late. He hadn't grown up with it like a proper artifex. He couldn't talk to its sensitive metal, which they liquefied into aether and then precipitated into the alien stuff with its sensitivity to thought. Probability. The bloodmetal existed between states—what was real, and what could be. He wasn't sure where they got it. Or why it liked bonding with brains.

So this woman did the prime minister's work, and the prime minister did the king's. The Consortium and the Crown got along smashingly.

They had dragged him out of his sweet den. The darkness where he'd been hiding from the greatest trespass ever visited upon him.

"And who, pray tell, are you?" Carsand asked.

"Moiren Sile."

"You don't take the dead king's surname?" he asked.

"I do not need King Aklave's beneficence. My family carries rank sufficient to my needs."

"Well, then, could you please stop standing there. I find it aggrieves my recovery."

She arched a sharp eyebrow. "Anything else?"

"A drink wouldn't be untoward, under these circumstances."

She turned to her sideboard and settled her glass in a depression intended, he supposed, to keep it from falling over in the train's motion. The whiskey decanter came heavily out of its own niche when she lifted it.

"How did you find me, anyway?" he asked. "I was well out of range of your relays."

"The relays had nothing to do with it," she said. She handed him the tumbler and took a seat opposite his sofa. She sat as if her spine had been fused. "You handled the task for us."

"Me?"

He saw a touch of a smile, at his expense.

"You climbed upon the tables in the poppy temple, besotted with delirium, and announced to everyone that you were a *wizard*. You were adamant that someone inspect the scar where we implanted your filament."

"Son of a bitch."

"Quite naturally, the proprietress informed the authorities of your indiscretion. I imagine you could have lived out what money you had left before we would have found you. You might even have effected your own expiration, much to everyone's annoyance."

He stared into his whiskey. "Do you know what the prime minister cost me in Naredesh?"

"It isn't my station to know."

"Well, there are plenty of relays you can interrogate. They know."

"I do not conspire with puppets. They are only extensions of our greater will." She smiled again. "Not unlike you."

He drank as much of the whiskey in one swallow as he cared to, which was probably more than his usual volume, sitting across from an Inquisitor like this. She watched him, and he didn't say anything else, so she left the room. It occurred to him quite abruptly that the whiskey had not been pure, and the sofa took him back beneath the light once again.

He watched the Salvation monk pace the meditation labyrinth outside the prime minister's study. The monk was a Katarine, by the look of his robes. A getup not dissimilar to the cassocks Moiren and the other Inquisitors wore.

There were panes of stained glass leaded into the window. They turned the monk occasionally green, blue, and red as he moved along the labyrinth. Carsand remembered when the prime minister would chase the monks out of that garden if Carsand and Naetan had done well enough at their lessons. If Naetan had, at least. No one seemed to care if Carsand learned anything or not. He was collateral, after all. A foster locked safe here in Silangarde so Carsand's father wouldn't join the effort to bring Westreign back under Naredal rule.

Mostly Carsand never paid attention. The tutors always made fun of his accent, so he didn't bother with their foreign, Karlander ideas.

He and Naetan would chase each other through the labyrinth, pulling up its stones and hurling them at each other in an idiotic game seemingly universal to boys everywhere. He hadn't seen the prince in five or six years. Not much reason to anymore, he supposed.

The prime minister opened the heavy office door. It squealed against his efforts, and he closed it carefully behind him. He was a tinier and even more bookish old man than Carsand remembered. He looked like somebody afraid of disturbing the furniture.

He turned his liver-spotted head and stared at Carsand. That same look he'd given when the boys broke a window, or stole a dessert, or got caught with any of the house staff. A dead, blue gaze the color of an iceberg crevasse. Carsand was suddenly very aware of his hands in his lap. And the shackles binding them.

"So, that was fun, was it?" the prime minister said.

"Prime Minister," Carsand said. "Lathael."

Lathael's soft shoes whispered him across the room, and he took the seat behind his desk. He looked even smaller sitting down. The books on the shelves behind him seemed like giant editions for bigger men.

"You murdered one of my knights in Naredesh," Lathael said. "In addition to costing me a good measure of valuable time."

"Had to be done," Carsand said. "That knight was a threat unto my person."

Lathael looked at him like he was simple. "Of course he was. That was the point. If you'd come when I summoned you, we wouldn't have had to go to such a bother."

"I didn't *want* to come," Carsand said. "I have business in Naredesh."

"Yes," Lathael said. A slurring sound. Something he was sparing Carsand out of the side of his mouth. A charity. "I'm quite aware. But I can't have one of my operatives gallivanting about Naredesh when the empress is being so belligerent along our border."

Carsand leaned forward. He felt a chill in his own gaze. "The king's border houses keep *crossing* the border."

"Yes, well," Lathael looked at some notes on his desk, "that's the nature of a border, isn't it? A line of excitation between two differently aggravated bodies?"

"That's semantics."

Lathael looked up sharply. "Since when did you know anything about semantics?"

"I read," Carsand said.

Lathael narrowed an eye. "*When* do you read?"

"That's beside the point. What in God's good name was so damn important that you needed me? Again?"

Lathael looked back at his notes. "I have an agent, in Oliniron, suffering the machinations of a rival family. I need to you to stop it."

"How?"

Lathael gave him the stupid look again. "Why would I care *how*?"

"Well, what have they done?"

Lathael pushed a pile of documents across his desk. "You can read on the road. Let's just say my agent is more loyal to his highness than his relatives, and they want his holdings. *Do* something to make them quit."

"And what is the name of the offending family?"

"The Astafos."

"I . . . know that name."

Lathael studied his work now. He was finished with Carsand. "No, you don't. You were never good at heraldry."

"My things?"

"Moiren has your sidearm and your crest. Pray do not lose them again."

Carsand jiggled the chains on his restraints suggestively.

Lathael looked at him. "Oh, get out of my office. And do not look to cheat death a second time. You are quickly outgrowing your value to the crown."

CHAPTER TWO

Camorenne Astafo really hated the light in Silangarde. It was just so very *present*, bouncing off the city's white stone architecture from every angle with a damnable regularity. It was nothing like her family's demesne back in Oliniron, where the trees and mountains had something to say about where, precisely, the sun might beam its ghastly brilliance.

It was one of the only things she missed about her home.

When Emille, her maid, drew back the curtains, it was as if the entire city invaded her chambers—*and* the fog of last night's wine.

"Emille, really, must you open them so *abruptly*?"

Emille curtseyed against the wall. Even her blonde hair was too bright for Camorenne's liking. The dark fabric of her customary livery, though, was a relief. The girl muttered something in Naredesse.

Bevry entered the room like a schoolmaster, a silver tray perched atop his gloved fingers. "In Karlean, Emille, if you please."

He kept his other arm deferentially behind his back, and he passed a slow, judgmental look across Emille. He was always on about the poor girl, demanding she play her part the way he did—and his father before him, and his father's father before him. A butler by blood. A tradition that demanded propriety, even if the hired help wasn't up to the task.

"Bevry, must you start already? Leave the girl be. And what are you doing in my chamber so early? I haven't dressed?"

Emille coughed quietly into her fist against the wall. She hadn't propped Camorenne properly against her headboard. Even the girl thought the intrusion was untoward.

"My apologies, madam, but you've received a letter from your brother, and he has marked it most urgent."

"Fine," she said. "Leave it on the bureau."

Bevry bowed, deposited the letter, and *removed* himself. Camorenne couldn't think of any other way to describe how he moved about the place.

"Pay him no mind, Emille," Camorenne said. She leaned forward as the girl situated her more comfortably. "He really does mean only the best."

"Yes, ma'am."

Camorenne never really begrudged the servants their way of doing things. Back home, father had been hiring them since Karlande conquered Nidal. Camorenne had grown up listening to them twitter in their native language when they thought no one was listening. In Westreign itself, she understood, ethnic Naredals had such a harder time getting by than all the Karlander settlers, so no one begrudged them whatever happiness they could find—least of all the aristocracy. One had to sympathize with an entire generation that fell under Karlande's great sword. Those who had stayed put in their native land had every right to preserve their culture, even if they were Karlanders now. Provided they switched their loyalty to the newly minted province of Westreign.

She really did think it was gauche of the king to name his new provinces that way. Eastreign, Westreign. As if they weren't territories but chores on a ledger.

Emille brought tea on a tray from the hallway, and she retrieved the letter while Camorenne arranged herself. Ricarde really had actually marked the envelope urgent. She pulled it out of its sleeve and read over it while Emille began brushing a dress on its stand in the corner.

"Well," Camorenne said, "dear Ricarde seems to have secured an invitation. For me. A gala quite out of my reach."

She looked at Emille. Ever since she'd arrived in Silangarde, Camorenne hadn't had much luck carrying out her brother's schemes. It seemed everyone knew that the Astafos were out of favor with the prime minister. That was not an easy blemish to rid oneself of, and it made it interminably difficult to discover anything verifiable about the Sedas and their mysterious favor with the crown.

"He reminds me of the urgency of my task," Camorenne said. "He provided numbers from the ledgers to clarify what I'm costing the family."

"Ma'am," Emille said, in that way that meant nothing more than *Yes, I hear you speaking.*

Camorenne held her tongue. It wouldn't do to speak ill of her brother in front of the girl. Lord knew that would get back to someone eventually.

"Very well. We shall drink someone else's wine this evening. Oh, and remove that necktie from the floor there. I don't even recall whose it is."

Emille abandoned the dress and moved into action.

"And retrieve my Tulani corset. That contraption ought to serve well enough tonight."

"The boning still needs repair, ma'am."

"Oh, damn," Camorenne said. "Does that stay still come loose?"

"Yes, ma'am."

"Well, we'll make do."

The lanterns were a surprise. She could see footmen beside each coach in the long line of them waiting to deposit their nobility at the doors to the hall. The footmen held their lanterns aloft on poles and encouraged the drivers to let their passengers out now, rather than jamming up the already dark-and-confused procession at the doorway. Women clutched their hats and men gesticulated their displeasure as their escorts apologized and guided them into the building.

"But why is it so dark?" Camorenne asked as a footman approached her door.

"I don't know, ma'am," Emille said. She sounded as unconcerned about the dark building as she might be about, really, anything. Camorenne didn't actually know what properly interested the girl.

When the young footman opened the door to her coach, Camorenne adjusted the offending stay in her corset—Emille had done the best she could with a needle and thread—so that it would quit stabbing her, and allowed herself to be disembarked.

"What in Salvation is going on?" Camorenne demanded.

"Begging your pardon, ma'am," the footman said, closing the coach's door behind Emille, "but there's a dispute with the artifexi who power the hall. They aren't working tonight."

That was a disappointment. The hall was a beautiful thing, specifically outfitted with the strange equipment artifexi used to animate their various conveyances. She glanced over her shoulder. Aevas Castle, atop its great stone-of-silangarde mound in the heart of the old city, was still aglow in the dark like sunlit scrimshaw. Obviously the artifexi didn't care to take their dispute all the way to the king.

"This way, ma'am."

Camorenne followed him, and Emille stepped quietly into place behind her. Candelabras and chandeliers winked behind the great society hall's windows as she tried not to trip on the hem of her dress. It reminded her a bit of the occasional get-togethers Mother would throw back home. Few houses ranked like hers could afford custom service from a live-in artifex, so she remembered those parties like dazzling memories, full of soft, orange light and indistinct shadows in the corners of smoky drawing rooms and drafty dining halls. Camorenne had come to prefer the lavish events one could expect in the capital. When one could get an invitation.

She dismissed Emille when the footman left them in the foyer. The girl wandered off to the edges of the great room, where other ladies' maids sat on upholstered benches, sipping wine they didn't customarily get to enjoy and trading gossip about the women they served. Camorenne adjusted her damnable corset again and pulled the first glass of something off the first passing tray she saw. Even with all the candles, it was difficult to determine exactly what was what, or who was who.

This wine was clearly not from Naredesh. It seemed her hosts were doling out the cheap stuff to the masses. No doubt she could find something better than sour Karlandi wine from some hinterland region she'd never heard of.

She saw the hosts receiving guests from a too-long line of shuffling nobility, listening to one name after another. A clerk nearby recorded the names of everyone who cared to log their attendance. Camorenne decided to skip the ceremony. The aged couple in their formalwear wouldn't know who she was anyway. They were doubtless some business connection of her brother's that he'd managed to cajole into giving her an invitation. She decided instead to eavesdrop, which was easy enough to do in the dim light.

୶

After four or five glasses of unimpressive wine, Camorenne decided it really wasn't all that bad. Neither was the gala, for that matter. The ambiance made a bit of a masquerade of the whole affair, which made it easier to avoid her rivals who would otherwise have made a big show of refusing her company to anyone who might see and take note of their demonstrable loyalty to the prime minister—and whoever he happened to favor at the moment. She saw them, tenderly nursing drinks that they didn't feel they should overindulge, standing in puffed and preened groups doing nothing particularly at all while their husbands gathered elsewhere, smoking and discussing their frustration with the artifexi growing continually too ambitious for their noble tastes.

The servers threading through the crowds around the gambling tables, she noticed, were serving cut-glass tumblers of whiskey and brandy, rather than wine. She abandoned her glass and stepped up to the table between two people and watched a gambler at work. An older man. Head full of silver hair. Not doughy or weak-chinned like so many his age. Certainly younger than her father.

He caught her eye and gave her a wink before he threw his dice onto the patterned baize. There were polite, mild-mannered cheers when his roll went well, and the attendant pushed a pile of coins at him. When the dice came back to him, he gave Camorenne another glance, and threw again. Another victory. A server came around with the drinks she wanted, so she plucked a glass of whiskey from his tray. The gambler caught her eye and gestured that she should join him.

A game was finally afoot.

She had to turn around to shove the damnable stay in her corset back into its place, but she did it quickly, and she adjusted her hat with her off hand as she joined him.

"Well, now," he said, "might you be a good luck charm?"

Camorenne didn't see anyone nearby waiting on him, man or woman, so she lidded her gaze and gave him a smile.

"Let's find out," she said.

"Indeed."

He tossed the dice again. Another stroke of luck. He was becoming popular with those betting on him.

"It's settled then," he said. "The lucky Lady . . ."

"Camorenne."

"Camorenne?" He enunciated her name slowly. "I don't believe I know your family."

"Camorenne Astafo."

"Ah, the Lady Astafo."

"Lady Astafo is my mother. Camorenne, if you please."

"Very well, Camorenne. I am Davo Murel."

"Lord Murel," she intoned, inclining her forehead politely.

He pointed at the table. "Care to make a wager?"

"I'm just here for the drinks."

"And the company, I hope," he said.

She leaned closer to him. "Not particularly."

He laughed. A real laugh, not some gentleman's courtesy noise. There was a bit more candlelight in his eye when he looked at her again.

"Present company excluded?" he said.

She went to work on her whiskey. "We'll see."

"So your family is in mining?" Davo asked.

The air out on the balcony was crisp, but at least it smelled less of bodies, and tobacco. A few others milled about scattered lanterns and braziers full of imported sandalwood and sassafras. Camorenne quite liked the fragrance. A pair of airships circled the sky over Silangarde, their great balloons lit like small moons. Camorenne had never even seen one moored on the ground—tickets were for the extravagantly wealthy, or powerful. She'd heard the ships' artifexi didn't even own them, they were so expensive to build. Instead, they powered them for their respective orders, who footed the bill and paid them for the service.

Davo handed her a tumbler of liquor as he joined her. She accepted it with a glance and then continued surveying the city. The plumes of chimney smoke arising from the new city, beyond the old wall, she imagined, smelled far less pleasant than this balcony.

"You know Oliniron?" she said.

"Parts, yes," he said. "I make most of my money in shipping. Moving heavy metals costs quite a bit, you can imagine."

"Yes, of course."

"I make sure I'm the one charging for it."

She held her silence—better to let him reveal whatever he cared to about himself.

"But I don't believe I've seen you at many of these events," he said. "And I've been coming to them for years now."

"I've only been in the city six months," Camorenne said.

"Really? Doing what, exactly?"

Spying. Digging for information. Snooping. She wasn't quite sure what to tell him.

"My brother's work," she said. "Liaising with his connections here in the capital while he maintains the estate."

"Splendid," he said. "Then I shall look forward to your acquaintance more often."

Camorenne wasn't quite sure how to reply to that. She'd been marked ever since she arrived. She was surprised, in fact, that he would chat her up like this. But perhaps that meant the tides were shifting in her favor.

"In fact," he said, "I believe it's been fifteen years or more since I found myself in the company of Oliniron nobility. Here at least."

That got her attention.

"Oh, and when was that?"

"Well, the fundraiser for Lady Seda's orphanage, I believe. Quite an event. Twice as lavish as tonight's party. Are you neighbors, the Astafos and the Sedas?"

Camorenne tried to keep a pleasant look on her face. She bought herself a moment with a sip from her glass. More whiskey. At least he was paying attention to her tastes.

"In fact, we are," she said.

The Sedas' land had once been the Astafos, some generations back, until bloody disputes between their respective orders of house knights rendered the manicured lawns and evergreen topiary the rightful property of the Sedas.

Unless the current Lord Seda failed to produce an heir, according to the Courts. She'd been only a child when her father won that petition, here in Silangarde, at the Courts of Saint Levine.

"But I wasn't aware her ladyship had anything to do with an orphanage."

"Really?" Davo said. "How surprising. I'm to understand they built it directly on the property. Is it remote, your territory?"

"Quite," she said.

"It must be tucked away behind some mountain or something," he said absently.

"What *sort* of orphanage?"

"Oh, some sort of religious thing. Something sanctioned by the church for the very most unfortunate young people."

He realized he had her attention.

"I'm sure I still have the correspondence, back at the residence. If you're interested."

She drank her whiskey straight away.

"Quite."

"How *does* this thing work?" Davo asked. Angrily. But not at Camorenne. It sounded more like he was angry at his chamber than at anyone in particular.

"It's from Tulan," Camorenne said. She added her own fingers to the effort to get her corset off—and quite out of their way. Davo had already asked his valet to retrieve his social notebook, from the days when he might have attended Lady Seda's fundraiser. This was all exactly what Ricarde had sent her here for, and Camorenne would prefer to browse the notebook at her leisure, later, with a sated Lord Murel resting on his bed. And she would sate herself in the effort, while she was at it.

"It doesn't function like any corset I've ever seen," he said through quickened breath.

She'd left him in only his collar and tie. His shirt had been much easier to get off, and they'd not bothered with all the details before they got to work on her considerably more complicated attire.

"Can't I just rip it off and buy you a new one?" he said into her ear, still clutching at the corset's fasteners.

Well, that was an idea. But she didn't relish the idea of traveling back across town to her apartments without one, even if she would be in a coach most of the time.

"Damnnation," she said. "Emille, dear, get in here!"

Davo took a step back, and Camorenne spun on her heel and stomped off toward the door. Her boots made angry work of the floorboard—she hadn't gotten to taking them off yet, and Emille opened the door and matched her lady's stride as if they had practiced the maneuver. She spun Camorenne around and went about undoing the corset without asking for instructions.

Camorenne watched Davo from across the room. He'd never seen anything like this, she was sure of it, and the way he clenched and unclenched his fists meant he wouldn't be terribly difficult to please at all.

The corset fell away into Emille's ready hands. Davo's gaze fell after it.

Emille spun on a heel and disappeared back through the doorway. Camorenne and Davo met somewhere in the middle of the chamber, and the remainder of what they were wearing fell away. They got to work on his mattress, in the dim lamplight—a not dissimilar brightness from the gala. Something bright enough to work by, yet not so bright as to chase all the mysteries from the bedroom.

And her friends wondered why she preferred Silangarde.

There came a shout and a thud from outside the door. Davo stopped immediately.

"What was that?" he said.

Camorenne tried to enlist the help of her legs to anchor him in place. "Who cares? Let your valet see to it."

He ignored her, and the sound of banging footsteps, of someone running *toward* the chamber, reached them across the room.

Davo extracted himself from the bed and swirled a jacket around his shoulders. Camorenne buried herself in his bedding. He opened the door, wide, and she could see Emille and the valet beyond. A third man hung between them, clutching his belly.

"What is this?" Davo asked.

"Begging your pardon, sir," the valet said. "He got in through the window in the study. If it hadn't been for this maid, I think he would have visited harm upon your person, or her ladyship's." He glanced at Camorenne in the bedroom.

"Well, why is he bleeding on my rugs?"

"Because, sir, the maid stopped him."

Emille held up the offending stay from Camorenne's corset. The pale baleen dripped with the man's blood.

Davo turned and gave Camorenne an astonished look. Camorenne only shrugged. The girl was within her rights, protecting her mistress.

"Well," Davo said, turning back, "we'll see that you're rewarded, young lady."

Emille curtseyed, the bloody stay still upright in her hand like a trophy.

"Get him to a surgeon," Davo said. "And stay with him. I should like to see what all this was about in the morning."

"Of course, sir."

Davo closed the door. Camorenne smiled. She liked a man of his word, and Davo looked like he was on his way back to the bed to keep it.

Camorenne lowered the society paper she was reading and looked at Bevry over its edge. He was still standing there, his tray perched upon his gloved fingers.

"Well, Bevry," she said. "What is it?"

She knew it irritated him that she subscribed to *Katarin's Gazette*. It would have bothered Father Aomed, too, back home. Such a sacrilegious use of the saint's name, but Camorenne didn't care.

"I trust you had an enjoyable evening," Bevry said.

"Quite."

"The hour of your return was most irregular. Should your brother ask about the operation of this house—"

"You shall tell him nothing," she said. "Would you have taken notice were it he, here in the city, returning as he pleased without a by-your-leave from *his* butler?"

Bevry moved his lower lip. It was as close as he got to a facial expression.

"There now. I should think not. That will be all."

"Of course, madam."

He bent at the waist and swiveled his empty tray to leave.

She went back to her paper—there would be a write-up on the gala—along with the rest of the city's latest social gossip. Davo's journal hadn't contained much on the Sedas' orphanage—only its name: The Holy Sanguinary Academy for the Lame and the Orphaned. The library at the College of Saint Mira would have more. She would need to spend some time there.

How had they never heard of the orphanage? And why in Salvation was it in *Oliniron*, on *her* family's hereditary estate?

She put down her paper. Bevry had also delivered a note from Lord Murel.

It seems our guest last night took exception to one of the Murels entertaining one of the Astafos. It's quite clear it was me he intended to harm, not your ladyship, though he won't say who filled his purse. We'll let the courts sort the rest of what he does, or doesn't, have to say.

This was new. She'd tell Ricarde. He wouldn't have an opinion about how she went about gathering information. Indeed, she imagined he'd applaud it, but he would send some of the household guard if he decided the state of things in Silangarde warranted it. And why not? The fuller her household became here, the more legitimate her presence would become.

She picked up the paper. That suited her just fine. She preferred a permanent installation in Silangarde. Returning to Oliniron just wouldn't do. She wasn't her own woman in her family's presence, where she paid visits on rivals and waved at men pulling ore from the mountains and drank so much damnable tea because *that was what one did*. With enough information of her own, Camorenne could ensure that these apartments stayed on the family's ledgers. Permanently.

CHAPTER THREE

They rode three days from Fort Terone just to get here. Because Ashre needed the mountains—talking on the wind was easier the higher up you could get. Or so she said. Couran didn't know how it was done.

He looked out across the grasslands. He couldn't imagine a relay tower anywhere in this country, unless some enterprising artifex had rigged one up in the brains of some of the wandering bison. Who knew how Ashre was keeping a hold on anyone's filament harmonic out here? The middle of nowhere. Not a relay for days

Or maybe she wasn't. Maybe she was standing up there, on that promontory, looking out over the same plain and the same bison and the same strident sky, just waiting. Waiting for someone to find *her* harmonic. Maybe she didn't want to talk to anybody. She never told Couran much about what they were doing and why. Only what he should be doing and *because she said so*. Somebody had probably done the same thing to her when she was an apprentice. It's a thing that happened in the great tradition of passing on the Restoration. Get used to taking orders. Artifexi of Couran's kind couldn't always wait for answers before working their interferences. They weren't much of an order. More of a tradition really, restoring balance to the equilibrium of energy—including the disruptions caused by the other orders of the Gnostic Accords with their schemes and designs and grand plans to learn whatever they could about the cosmos. The Restoration usually had to be pretty quick on its feet.

So, working without all the information they might want was a skill to cultivate. And Ashre was good at cultivating it for him.

Couran adjusted the brim of his hat for a better angle against the unkempt sunlight—it was full of moving dust. He turned to watch Ashre up there behind him. It had taken her hours to climb that high, especially with her limp. Now she stood there. Her copper hair beneath the brim of her hat like a pennant snapping on the wind. She didn't move. She hadn't moved for hours.

Couran liked Fort Terone better, even if the locals hadn't been overly fond of the transducer in his forehead. His money was good at the inn where he'd elected to drink until Ashre came up with their next move, so they left him alone. It usually went that way. People were easier around the other order of artifexi because they all wore cassocks and shrouds and regalia. The Restoration had no uniform to speak of. They looked like everyone else. Except for the gunmetal transducer between the eyes that said they sure as hell weren't. It made people uneasy. Only the Chaotics, the Unheard Order, garnered more suspicion than the Restoration, but no one was even really sure where they were.

At least in Fort Terone he'd had a mattress, and somebody else cooked the food.

The horses weren't satisfied with the small patch of shade he'd found between a few mesquite trees, and they stamped their feet to let him know it. He pulled the rifle out of its scabbard on his saddle and cocked it, just in case they'd found a snake or something. But when he walked over and looked, there wasn't anything in the grass but grass. All the better. The horses didn't like the sound of the rifle. Neither he nor Ashre, nor anyone in the Restoration, for that matter, had the money or the license for bloodmetal firearms, so they used conventional gunpowder. It usually worked well enough, but it was loud as hell, so he didn't blame the horses.

He stomped far enough away from camp to not rile the horses any more than he had to. He needed to shoot some game if they were going to have any kind of a decent meal later—*if* he could find something to shoot.

He squinted into the scrub, but he knew that was no good. His eyes hadn't been right ever since the first bloodmetal implantation when he was a kid. The implantation that, if successful, would have landed him a career with the Consortium. But he was no different than at least half of everybody who went through the implantation. In fact, he was luckier than most. Getting out with dim eyesight was a lot better than how some ended up.

It was better to be out here with Ashre, collected by the Restoration, than left to a life of service to the successfully implanted artifexi—who were sworn by the Accords to look after their failed brothers and sisters. Couran's father had at least done him the courtesy of paying the Restoration its price to take him in—before he told him not to bother being his son anymore.

Couran relaxed and reached into the hollows of his mind. He exhaled slowly, and the partition he'd learned to keep between his own mind and the filament came gently away. The filament stirred deep in Couran's consciousness, awakening to his needs—*their* needs. It came upon Couran's brain like a welcome friend, and the two of them took a look into the scrub together—a heightened pair of sensate symbiotes.

Couran could feel his transducer warming as the bloodmetal bent the wavelengths of light and air before them, sharpening the view, highlighting details, peeling away shadows. He hadn't eaten any reagents, so he'd probably get a bloody nose out of this, but that wasn't too awful. Provided he didn't keep at it for too long.

He *saw* the grasses and the animal prints and the full measure of the light, like something liquid—like plants swaying under water. The way fish moved in any such direction that pleased them since the water didn't seem to much care.

And there it was. A rabbit in the scrub. Couran didn't see any young around it, so he put the rifle to his shoulder and he and his filament stopped being two different things, and the transducer stacked their thoughts and bounced them around inside itself until it had stacked enough of them, like resounding echoes, to actually do something about the state of things, and it released its slippery harmonics, between how Couran's world was and how the filament's might be, and when the trigger gave way to Couran's finger, he and his bloodmetal ceased being two different ideas and became, instead, a single somebody really good at shooting rabbits.

Couran dressed the rabbit. There wasn't any kind of creek nearby, so he salvaged what he could of the ends and sliced them up with the cooking knife and situated everything in their stew pot over the campfire. Since he couldn't wash the entrails, he buried them far enough away that some scavenger wouldn't harass the horses over the meal. It wouldn't be dark for another hour at least, especially in such flat territory, but he'd rather not start cooking in the dark. They were running out of salt. He'd need to find or trade for some more.

He checked, and Ashre was still up on the promontory. Staring. He put the horse's feedbags over their heads and pulled his jacket off the saddle. Back at the fire, he wasn't sure if he was staring at the same herd of bison out on the plain or some new group of wanderers. They weren't moving around as much now—settling in, he imagined. He figured they must know, in their animal way, how long until the sun would drop behind the mountains at Couran's back.

There was nothing to hear. The wind had died down, so the scrub hunkered in its pyramidal clusters motionlessly. He could see where the deer and the javelinas had pruned the shrubs by grazing on their upper and lower branches at different rates. It looked like there was some gardener at work out here, fascinated by imposing geometry on a land that would never see a right angle. The prickly pear paddles looked afflicted with some disease where their predators had gnawed on their soft flesh. He would see if any of their fruit was soft enough for breakfast in the morning.

He ate his portion of the stew alone, staring at the fire. There were clouds blocking the moon, and when he looked at anything other than the flames, all he saw was nothing. He waited later than usual to lie fully back on his bedroll. The clouds had feathered apart like a threadbare garment, and Couran could stare at the stars behind them, which somehow made it seem darker.

He woke up, and Ashre was staring at him from across the fire. She chewed steadily on the meat in the stew—it had still been tough, despite how long he'd cooked it. Ashre's eyes were red beneath the wide brim of her dark hat, and he could tell by the way she clutched her bowl that her joints hurt. They had reagents for that in the saddle-bags, so he started to get up.

"Leave it be," she said. "I've already had some."

He watched her in the firelight—a sharp-featured specter against the darkness. She had her kerchief tied loosely around her neck, and shadows pooled in the hollows of her throat as she chewed. The inflammation around her eyes made them look larger than usual, and he could see the whites like beacons. She had dark eyes even in the full sunlight. No doubt she'd been chewing roots and sipping tinctures all day up on the promontory, cooling off her brain while she was at her work.

"You didn't shoot it on your own," she said.

He put a fingertip to his upper lip. He thought he'd wiped away the blood, but he brushed flakes of it out of his stubble. It'd been a few days since he shaved.

"No, mistress."

"Well, you know what I have to say about that."

"Yes. I'm sorry. I thought you'd want something other than tack when you came down."

"You're right. I did, but that's not your decision to make."

"No, mistress."

She set her bowl down and stood up, palms planted on the small of her back. She arched her spine, and Couran could hear things pop. When she slid her hat off, her hair looked redder than usual in the firelight. It'd come half loose of its braid in the wind all day. She still didn't have any gray to it, which is something he'd seen her check just about anytime they came across a mirror.

She rubbed at the flesh around her transducer and pinched the bridge of her nose as she straightened out. He waited.

She looked out at the darkness, and he wondered if her vision, unlike his, could make anything out of it.

"We're going to Dhialt," she said. "North."

"Yes, mistress."

"I've had word from Adwar."

He heard the faintest trace of her native Naredal accent in the sound of her brother's name. She'd mostly rid herself of it, and he hadn't heard her speak Naredesse in years, but that was still her country, no matter how much time they spent in others. If her implantation hadn't gone poorly, like his, then she would have ended up in the Order Entropic with her brother. One of the Field Men—those who stared at the ground and plumbed the planet's secrets, not unlike her afternoon up on the rocks. They wielded such power, so much more than the other orders, but they so rarely used it. Not unlike the Restoration. Couran wondered if Ashre still carried a touch of that potential within her.

"There is someone we need to join. A Displacer."

Couran wanted to ask why. He always wanted to. He wouldn't be an apprentice much longer, and then he could. Until the Restoration called him away somewhere, and he could no longer travel with Ashre.

He tried not to think about that.

It seemed like she heard him. She turned and planted her gaze on him, hands on her hips.

"It was good stew, and I needed it."

"Yes, mistress."

"So go ahead. One question. Because that was thoughtful."

He thought about it for a moment. "Where will we find this Displacer?"

Ashre lowered her arms and kicked her bedroll out flat. "She's at the Enclave. Sealed up in a wall."

They rode north, the ever-rolling plains at their left, and the escarpments and early peaks of the Thachrol Nations to their right. Some days brought them upon a rogue rock formation or weather-worn butte where there should be only grassland, but they mostly only saw slightly curving variations of the horizon. Ashre rode ahead of him, and she seemed to know exactly where she was going—like she always did. They rode mostly in silence, watching the bighorn sheep and occasionally catching the shadows of soaring golden eagles. Ashre at least identified things for him. He scribbled notes in his journal with the battered pencil he could never keep sharp. He hated that. He liked a sharp pencil.

Ashre boiled them juniper-berry tea whenever they found a creek to rest beside, and she squeezed the jelly from the aloe vera plants into her mug.

She usually concealed her pistol with her jacket, but on the day when she hoisted a booted leg over her saddle and swept her garments back to reveal the shining weapon and its varnished stock, Couran wondered what they were headed into. The plants around him looked a little different this morning. A species he didn't recognize—thin, pointed stalks in tight clusters. Ashre, he noticed, didn't collect any of them.

He laid the rifle across his saddle as they rode that day.

The creek they were following became a river, and it snaked its way between a line of bluffs Couran couldn't see the end of.

"This all used to be an ocean," Ashre said ahead of him. There wasn't much of a wind, but she had her stampede strap cinched up tight against her chin. She turned to give him her profile as she talked, but she wasn't doing it for his benefit. He could tell she was surveying their surroundings.

"This is the last of the mountains, then the grasslands cover everything we can see."

Couran wasn't sure what to do with this information, but he wrote it down anyway. "How do we know, mistress?"

"The Entropics tell us. There are papers on it you can read at Saint Mira."

"Are we going to Silangarde?" he asked.

She ignored him. They moved fully between the cliffs framing their passage, and Couran thought he could smell smoke. But then it was gone. Nothing.

"The Dhiallen live almost entirely underground, in the salt mines they have carved from the dead ocean. They let the Mendi roam the surface freely, and they pay them to caravan their salt down south."

Couran had never met any Mendi. He had only the stories he'd collected in the saloons and inns they'd stayed in as he was growing up in Ashre's care.

"But the Mendi have their own trades," she said, "this far south."

"Like what?"

They rounded a curve in the channel, and she reined in her horse. Couran took his place beside her. It was a standard procedure she'd taught him. Remaining behind her could indicate seniority between them, which wasn't always a tactical advantage.

"Wax," she said.

He followed her gaze. There was an entire operation at work along the riverbank and up into the slope of the cliff wall. Men were stamping piles of those thin, pointed plants into stone ovens dug out of the riverbank. They'd reinforced the walls with baked mud and plant fiber, and the smoke he smelled earlier curled out of stick-rimmed vents. Others were trekking back from the river with buckets on their shoulders, which they emptied into the steaming piles. Burros stood around dumbly, some burdened with bushels of the plants, some without. Beyond the ovens, at least a dozen more men were digging what looked like a new course for the creek while a few others stood around a large boulder, seemingly suspended by some unseen force against a jut in the cliff wall. They poked at it and leaned on levers they'd shoved under the stone, but it wasn't doing anything.

A few of the men closest to them stopped their work at the boilers and stared at Couran and Ashre. By the strange cut of their clothing, Couran assumed these were Mendi. He saw sidearms on at least a few of them. Further down the river, well away from the steaming pits and the dry riverbed, women in long skirts stood beside cured leather tents and stared at the newcomers. Even from here, Couran could see the gold glinting anywhere they could find a place for it on their arms and heads.

The men, four of them, came up to Couran and Ashre. Two of them in front, two alongside the river. They were closest to Couran, and he was glad the mouth of the rifle barrel was already inclined in their direction.

But they all had guns. Whatever method they'd used to elect a speaker, Couran couldn't tell, but he stepped up to his duty and brought his fingers to the brim of his hat. Ashre gave him a nod in return.

"You speak Trade?" she asked.

"We aren't accustomed to trespassers in this territory," he said in kind.

Ashre didn't say anything for a moment. She looked around like a foreman evaluating their work.

"I don't believe you all are the rightful stewards of this country. Are you?"

He smiled, and his teeth were stained with . . . whatever they chewed out here. Couran had no idea. "We have something of a charter with the landowners," he said. "I don't believe you do."

He looked at Couran. Couran did his best to return a level stare.

"Why don't we just leave you to your business. We didn't mean to interrupt a day's work," Couran said.

"I know this puppet game," the Mendi said, looking back and forth between them. "You two are Restoration, and you're too young to be at it on your own, young man, which makes her your mistress."

Couran didn't say anything.

"So, it might be best if you didn't pretend at equality and let the adults do the talking."

"We just want passage," Ashre said.

The foreman said something in Mendi, and the others chimed in. They had a good conversation for a few minutes without moving.

"We might like you to stay here," he said. He didn't even glance at Couran.

"I appreciate the invitation, but our errand is pressing."

The Mendi slowly put his hand on his gun. Ashre didn't move.

"And if I insist," he said.

"I wish you wouldn't."

He said something else to his countrymen, and got a few quick remarks in exchange.

"And what means do you have of paying for your passage?"

"You're trying to move that boulder."

He turned around and looked at it, as if he'd forgotten they had a boulder problem.

"And you want to divert the river to power that paddle bellows between your wax boilers."

Couran studied all the wood-and-mud equipment Ashre was talking about. He had no idea how she'd divined all this just by looking at it. They had never talked about Mendi, or wax, or a river-powered bellows before.

The Mendi turned around slowly, and he took his hand off his gun.

"It'll take you weeks to move that rock, if you can do it at all," she said. "Which, judging by its look, you can't."

"You will move the boulder?"

"Get your people out of the way."

He spoke to his men in Mendi, and they moved back to join him. When the leader gestured Ashre onward, she nudged her horse forward. Couran made sure he waited long enough that she could maneuver the animal without kicking his own, should the need arise, then he started after her. The lead Mendi walked alongside Ashre, and he shouted and gestured at the other workers. Everyone stopped what they were doing and watched the procession through the camp. Couran looked in one of the boilers as they passed—the water, barely high enough to cover all the plants they'd shoved into it, was scummed with waxy, white bubbles. And it smelled like an outhouse.

When the Mendi decided they'd come close enough to the boulder, he stopped and gestured at it.

"By all means," he said.

Ashre gave the boulder a good stare. Couran watched her while she worked. His own filament could feel hers stacking harmonics in her transducer. A single drop of blood fell from her left nostril, and everything felt tight to him, and when she released her interference, his filament could hear the air singing.

The rock came loose with a crunch, like a bad tooth in a pair of pliers, and it skidded into the river, and the ground beneath them all trembled for a moment. It had mostly plugged the river, and they all stood there in silence. The water pooled behind it and then, as designed, started filling the Mendi's sluice and moving on about its business.

The leader looked at her, and Couran imagined he wanted her to stay now more than ever, but he didn't look at her like he thought that was very possible anymore.

She wiped the blood away with a gloved finger.

"We'll also need some salt for our trouble," Couran said.

On the Dhiali grasslands, they saw caravans of Mendi drovers and their escorts moving salt loads in long sequences of straining wagons. Ashre gave them a wide berth.

They were still a day or two out when a storm began gathering in massive fists of empurpled clouds. Couran had hoped they wouldn't encounter one, but the Dhiali plains in springtime were a playground for tumultuous weather. Uprooted plants rolled or jumped or otherwise fled the storm on the cold wind dragging the clouds through their swirling course.

Couran and Ashre took shelter in the ruins of a salt mining town. It was clear that the entrance to the mine had collapsed, so Couran figured it must not have been producing enough to make repairs worth the trouble. The Dhiallen must've climbed out of their subterranean tunnels and apartments and simply moved on.

The gently sloping mine entrance was large enough for the horses, so they nestled in as close to the piled rubble as they could. Ashre stood by the entrance and pointed out the hatches where the miners would have descended to their homes, and the rain blew sideways outside. Couran had never seen such hail, and when a stone bounced its way into the mine and rolled up against his boots, he pulled out his journal and wrote down the ice's measurements.

He could only see Ashre when the lighting flashed close enough to make a silhouette of her against the raging sky. His filament was quiet as he watched, so he knew she wasn't interfering with anything. She was just standing there, watching the rain.

No one rode out to greet them at the Enclave. Couran had only ever seen sketches of the place, and those had resembled some antique travelogue—somebody fixated on ruins and crumbling estates.

But they were pretty accurate. He knew most of the Enclave was underground—a lesson learned, perhaps, from the order's Dhiali hosts. These ruins looked like they had been blasted by stormy winds. They had been frozen and cracked by winters that sealed the Dhiallen underground and drove the Mendi into caves for months. The architecture wasn't antique. The order had built the stone out-buildings themselves, maybe a hundred years ago, and eft them to the whims of the surface.

Which, Couran understood, was very like them. This place was how the Displacers got their name. *The Enclave Displacement*, their order was called, named for the effects of this place on an artifex's mind, given enough time. Their eldest, most powerful artifexi were more architecture than human—and what human they were was mostly surrendered to the filaments they steadily fed with more and more cured aether, the fluid out of which they precipitated their strain of bloodmetal. Displacers turned themselves into *places* where they could simply be, meditating on the nature of the universe and bending their minds to the secrets of the cosmos.

Couran didn't entirely understand it all.

Sitting atop his horse quietly, waiting on commands, Couran studied the little cottages and towers and walls that led nowhere—sharp, white stone, almost like stone-of-silangarde, against the deep contrast of the Dhiali sky. He even saw a stone staircase, sagging and worn upon its treads, that went nowhere at all.

His filament hummed at him, and he realized there were interference harmonics at work.

Ashre spoke up immediately after. "She's this way."

Couran followed her between and around the aboveground wreckage of the Enclave. The further in they moved, the more aware he became of the Displacers around him. He couldn't tell where they were, but they were there. In places, he saw discarded trowels and piles of bricks and stones in what looked like abandoned reconstruction projects. The evening sky deepened upon them. They would need to camp somewhere in these crowded, empty buildings. The horses were unfazed.

"Lantern," Ashre said ahead of him. It was warmer here than it had been further south, which he thought was strange. She had her jacket coiled up on the saddle behind her, and he could see the hair clinging to the sweat on the back of her neck. The white tracery around the collar of her dark shirt reminded him that it had been a while since they'd been able to wash. The sweat that came and went left these delicate lines like evidence of tides come ashore.

Couran fished the lantern from their gear and got it lit. He handed it over when she reached for it.

"This way," she said.

It was getting harder to see where they were going, but he could feel whatever wavelength was drawing her through the Enclave. He hadn't seen a single entrance into the earth below.

She reined in before a segment of wall. It was crumbling on both ends, but it stood over his head for a good stretch in its middle. Ashre looked around until she found a suitable place to hitch their horses, then she led him stomping back through the tall grass and stopped before the wall. There were pickaxes and metal pails of hardened mortar leaning against it. This had been repaired recently.

Couran waited patiently while Ashre stood there. After a moment, she hefted two pick-axes and handed one to him.

"Mistress?" he said.

She pointed the pick-axe at the wall. "Now we dig her out."

CHAPTER FOUR

They really weren't all that different, this priest and Fabienne. They both negotiated with the laws of the universe—he with his prayers and censers of incense, she with reagents and interferences. There was a reverence to both pursuits, and she appreciated the serenity inside this chapel. It was a shed compared to the enormity of Saint Katarin's Cathedral in Silangarde, but out here in mostly rural Oliniron, such a monstrous edifice would feel like a cheap effort—like a human attempt at scaling all these towering mountains. Their bared, snow-capped peaks were closer to God than any architectural masterpiece would ever be.

Still, whoever had built this chapel had done so tastefully. The wooden pillars spiraled up into the clerestory, lifting the eye to the light spilling through its windows. The sunbeams lanced through the smoke from the priest's incense, and it was easy to watch those perfumed clouds swirl—like they were trying to go someplace, swimming through the air in God's house.

She knelt when it was her turn for the eucharist, and the priest muttered his bit in Old Karlean as he settled the holy wafer on her tongue. He could almost be one of her old instructors back at the academy, from before she'd graduated. A balding man in the strange clothes that identified his station. Like priests themselves, her elders in the Consortium rarely left the comfort of that remote campus in Eastreign. Instead, they sent people like Fabienne into the hinterland to do the order's dirty work.

She unbowed her head and made her way back to the rear of the chapel. There weren't many other worshippers, but they all watched her, like some apparition come to their sanctuary. She did her best to ignore them.

෯

After the last of them had left, she approached the altar, where the priest and his boy were folding things and tucking them away in their holy nooks.

The priest glanced at her under his unkempt brows.

"Lady D'Aklave, I presume?"

She curtseyed and extended one of her black-gloved hands. "Father Tomas?"

He shooed the boy through the doorway leading into the chapel's secret interior, where their rooms were. Like an actor sending his partner backstage.

He took hold of her fingers and brought her knuckles to his lips. "So glad you could make it."

The two of them looked like a painting. The very image of dark versus light. He a glowing, white-gowned vision in the chapel's pouring light—she, a figure in black, from her stiff collar to the hem of her dress. Her hair was so blonde as to be almost white, like a cascade of smoke from a snuffed candle.

She retracted her knuckles with a smile. "Of course. Such a lovely service."

"I'm touched you rode all the way from Talve to see it," he said, gesturing to a side door away from the altar.

She took the cue. The heels of her boots sounded somehow quieter than they should have across the aged flooring. As if she'd learned to mask the sounds she made, just as she masked everything else about her person.

"The Consortium sends its regards. We're only too happy to visit. Our special relationship with the church means everything to us."

The doorway led them through a short, curtained corridor and into a simple sleeping chamber. There were four sleeping bunks niched into the walls, and a single window with a view of nearby Mount Whatever It Was—undoubtedly, the pride of the local landscape. The altar boy was stuffing a few items into a knapsack. A much younger boy, maybe five or six, sat on the lowest bunk, staring at her as she walked in. He was clean, and his clothes were good.

Father Tomas stepped in behind her.

"Anything I need to know?" she asked over her shoulder, eyes on the boy.

"No, he is a quiet boy."

"Good," she said, turning to face Tomas. "That will make the journey back more pleasant."

He handed her a scroll with the church's signet seal. "Here's the bill of sale, if you'll please convey it to my brethren at the academy for safekeeping."

"Of course," she said.

She turned back to the boy. The Church's latest acquisition—property she must convey safely back to Talve. She wondered who his father might be. What sort of annoyance the boy had turned out to be to earn himself a seat in her coach back to a new life as merely a memory.

"Come along, child," she said.

The boy got up silently and accepted his knapsack. He took her hand when she reached for him. She turned her gaze back on the priest, his pure, white vestments only a cheap illusion back here, where the deals were done.

"Anything else?" she asked.

"May God watch over you on your journey," he said.

She looked down at the boy and gave him a reassuring smile.

"Please, father," she said. "Let's not kid ourselves."

The boy was a strange traveling companion. Fabienne had expected she would have to entertain him as they passed two days in her dark coach, with its leaded windows and Ap-Lian leather cushions—a gift from the Consortium during her tenure here in Oliniron. The boy simply sat there, looking out the windows. At the inn, he ate when she told him to eat, and back in her room, he slept when she directed him to sleep. It was not an unpleasant evening, as such went.

The road through Talve was carnivalesque. Saint Simion's Day was in two days, and the Talveans were draping multi-colored pennants and bunting everywhere. A few had already painted their faces and were carrying drinks around in the streets. It was an assault on the eyes, given the ordinarily rustic mountain town with its already-claustrophobic wooden gables. The boy watched everything through the window without a word.

Outside of town, a pair of Lord Seda's household knights stopped them at the gates to his estate. They passed only a cursory glance at Fabienne and then bowed away. They knew better.

Her driver skirted the main pathway to the manor and instead followed one of the groundskeeping roads around and away, until the house disappeared behind one of the mountainous slopes that crisscrossed the demesne. It took them another hour to wind their way through the labyrinthine roadways the Salvation Church had paid for when they built the academy—decoys to keep anyone canny enough to slip onto Seda's land from finding their way.

The Holy Sanguinary Academy for the Lame and the Orphaned rose up before them suddenly, as if it had been waiting and now stood to acknowledge their arrival. The aspen trees pulled away from it, and the carriage made the slow half-circle along the gravel road and around the gibbering fountain, then it came to an ominous stop before the great double doors.

The Academy had been the late Lady Seda's gift to the church. A use of the family lands to bring honor to Oliniron Salvation. The prime minister had been impressed. The donation won the Sedas his enduring favor.

And now Fabienne would deliver unto them the Church's latest acquisition. Which was good. She needed to check on the Consortium's stake in this religious charade.

As she crossed the academy's sprawling lawns, strangely bereft of children of any kind, Fabienne could feel the interference in the air. It drew her, as if by magnetism, toward the wild undergrowth at the edge of the tended grounds. She walked with a fast, steady stride—even without the interference navigating her in, she knew exactly where she was going.

The trees began rising around her, and the heavy material of her dark cassock knocked aside the undergrowth like a plow. Even these woods knew better than to restrict Fabienne's movements. The air thrummed with the ongoing interference, and the bloodmetal filament in her brain hummed back at it, like two creatures calling out.

She stopped abruptly before an exposed stone ridge. The place was silent. Talve's peaks imposed in the distance beyond this small piece of budding mountain. She put her gloved hand into a niche in the rock and wrapped her fingers carefully around the device installed there. It was a tube of clear glass, wired at each end into the complex system of mirrors it controlled. There was a single drop of aether in the glass, suspended in fluids its creator wouldn't divulge. Kam, whom she would visit later, designed the device to disguise this entrance. The aether inside the glass would never be drawn into a proper filament. It would remain in its semi-fluid state, attuned to the action of drawing and redirecting energy to alter how things looked, or what anyone knew about them. The very roots of power behind the Consortium's particular interference skill set. It wasn't as *intelligent* as a proper filament. Kam had trained it to do only this thing. And it did it well. It was highly illegal according to the Gnostic Accords—the agreements that bound all artifexi, and therefore everyone else, thanks to the rulers who didn't want to earn the artifexi's ire. Except in Baruul, whose rulers largely didn't care what artifexi thought and instead made plenty of money by employing sorcerers, who were really just artifexi without bloodmetal implants—technicians who tuned and monitored bloodmetal-powered devices.

Fabienne turned off the device, and the stone in front of her opened up. It revealed a short passageway to a sun-glimmering woodland. Beyond, the bunkhouses where the "orphans" lived were dark, fuzzed by junipers that no one bothered to trim. The orphans themselves were hard at work in the field, their delicate fingers suited so perfectly to the cultivation of *delirium shade*, the poppy-like blossom from which she would draw ingredients for the Consortium's ambitious reagent. The plants were the Consortium's entire stake here. The full reagent would finally give them the strength to overpower the Gnostic Accords and finally realize the true scope of their power. Their coming rule. Adult fingers always snapped the fragile flowers they needed.

The plant's cultivation had been banned by the Gnostic Accords more than a century ago. The Consortium took pains to keep Fabienne's operation clandestine, though she hardly suspected anyone was looking too closely out here in middle-of-nowhere Oliniron.

Her filament echoed the silenced interference in her mind, letting her know the universe was finished reshaping itself for now. She needed to be sure the illusion was still operating. She switched it back on, the rocks closed before her, and her brain once again harmonized with the illusion.

She strode directly in, swallowed whole by the stone. The woods were quiet again, still as death.

The device disguising Kam Glimjeld's chateau on a hillside overlooking Talve worked much the same way. Fabienne deactivated it to make sure he hadn't put in some additional safeguard that she wouldn't see and would therefore trigger upon her entrance onto his grounds. She wasn't quite sure who he was hiding from. The Consortium knew where he was, and if there was anyone he should be worried about regarding his sorcery, it was them.

Her superiors made it a point to always know Kam's whereabouts, ever since his expulsion from the order. Few knew the nature of his crime, but it had been sufficient to warrant the death of his filament via the introduction of toxified aether. By necessity, he had turned to sorcery to effect his interferences, though Fabienne had no idea where he got the bloodmetal to work with. He was the first person they contacted back when the Salvation Church was building the academy and prepping the reagent fields. He'd been planted in Talve ever since, and he had been her first stop when she first arrived to take over the next phase of the operation.

His butler opened the door some minutes after she knocked. She was quite sure that Kam already knew she was here, but they had to go through these motions nonetheless.

The butler didn't say anything. He never said anything. He simply made room and bowed, his formal livery swinging stiffly with the motion. He was tall, like the rest from the Thachrol Nations, like his master waiting inside. It lent a severity to their motions that made their adoption of Karlandi manners look mechanical.

He had a bloodmetal device of his own, affixed to his forehead and buried in his skull with tiny spider-like wires. It was a proximity device—she measured it almost reflexively the first time she came here, and the sleeping bloodmetal in the device whispered with its fatal suggestions, should he wake it up by wandering too far.

"Good evening, Jern," she said, stepping inside. The door latched silently when he closed it. Fabienne found it more unnerving than had it resounded with some giant, metal lock.

"Is he in the library?" she asked.

Jern bowed.

"I'll see myself in."

Kam lit his house just like Aevas Castle in Silangarde. He had created a system of bloodmetal-induction that kept the lamps upon his wall burning without any fuel. In Silangarde, an artifex would be regulating the power and the system's operation in the castle—someone was always on shift. Here, Kam had put his skills to use for his own benefit—no supervision necessary.

She didn't bother knocking on the carved wooden doors to the library. Kam wasn't nobility, so she didn't owe him any obeisance. And anyway, she was mildly irritated he had summoned her. What could be so important that she needed to come all the way up here?

He was sitting on one of the sofas near his fireplace—a decidedly Olinire thing of masonry and inlaid timber. He'd gone to many pains when building his house to make himself look like a manorial Olin lord with ancestral holdings. This house could have been some lord's hunting getaway, perhaps. A place to go and be away from his responsibilities back at the demesne. Kam even had antlers mounted in most rooms, in this case directly over the mantel, as if he spent his time out on this mountain hunting things.

He had a book before his face in one hand, a wine glass in the other. Fabienne thought he looked like he was posing for a portrait.

"You sent for me?" she said, standing barely inside.

He turned to her. Despite his Karlandi aspirations, he looked every bit a Thachrol—full, styled blonde beard, a head of cascading hair. And then there were the tattoos. Everywhere.

"Come in," he said, adjusting his angle on the sofa.

She couldn't read Thachrol script, but she knew that all those lines, filling his face, covering his neck, repeated the nature of his crime against the Consortium across his entire body. His expulsion had been a shame to his clan, who had held the favor of their king for boasting an artifex under his allegiance. Like any other Thachrol exile, they documented his crime, stripped him of his clan, and condemned him to the Glim—the clanless.

She resisted the urge to roll her eyes. Yes, he cut an intimidating profile—his fine clothes aside—but *her* filament still functioned. She could trap him in a world of illusions faster than he could grab her. It annoyed her that she had to humor him like this.

She moved soundlessly across his carpets and took the other sofa. She sat as stiff as the boards around her, at the edge of the cushion, her gloved hands folded primly on her knees, like an obedient concubine. Whatever it took to finish this and get back to the Academy to sleep in her own bed.

"How was your pilgrimage? he asked.

"Life-changing," she said. "I'm a new woman."

He smiled, and she could see wine staining his mustache. "Well, as many churches as you've seen . . ." he paused for annoying effect, ". . . it must have been some service."

"Kam, why am I here?"

"So forward, Lady D'Aklave. Very well. I've brought you here to change your life."

"Didn't I just tell you I'm a changed woman," she said.

He laughed. "How true. Such wit."

She didn't say anything, so he took a drink of his wine and set it on the table between them. The fire popped in the hearth.

"I would like you to alter the nature of our relationship," he said.

"We don't have a relationship. You hide my orphanage, and I let you live up here."

He jerked at that. "*Your* orphanage? Please, where were you when *we* were building it. You're just it's custodian."

"Fine, what manner of relationship did you have in mind?"

He let the fire burn between them.

"You are going to help me compromise the Consortium's precious reagent."

She didn't move. "To what end?"

"To the Consortium's end. Their reagent will not give them the edge over the Accords to take over the continent. It will, instead, be their entire undoing."

Fabienne felt something filling her chest. Not fear—finality.

"Why would I do this, Master Glimjeld?" she said.

He leaned forward and summoned Jern with a bell.

"Because," he said, leaning casually. Nothing about his posture looked affected now. He was comfortable. Jern led someone into the library. Fabienne turned.

"I have your sister."

Fabienne stared at her. Aisabelle. Her older sister. A slightly taller, slightly blonder version of herself, down to the same dark, whirlpool eyes. She was in a dinner dress, presumably one Kam had made for her, and, like Jern, she had a device clinging to her forehead. Fabienne hadn't seen her in at least ten years, during one of her rare visits back with her family. Their father had been successful enough in his leather goods trade that the Consortium had taken his bid to be an investor seriously. Seriously enough that he gave them Fabienne and they turned her into an artifex. He'd squandered his money, though, and last she knew, Aisabelle was a penniless servant somewhere. She stared at Fabienne, her expression unreadable.

"I've been searching for her for quite some time," Kam said. "Since the day you first came here, and I determined who you were. It took more time than I expected, I'll admit."

"Kam," she said. "If I tell the Consortium—"

"You won't. You will cooperate, or Aisabelle will pay the price, one piece of her at a time."

She stared at him for a moment.

"You want to destroy the Consortium," she said.

He got up. "Not *entirely*. You see, I didn't think the threat of your sister alone would be sufficient to motivate you into an alliance with me. Do you know what I stole from the Consortium to warrant all . . . this?" He gestured to his face.

"No."

"I stole their most valuable asset. The secret to creating bloodmetal."

He extended a hand to her. She put her fingers into his palm slowly.

"And I'm going to give it to you, my dear, for your cooperation."

CHAPTER FIVE

Carsand watched from the porch of his hotel. They were everywhere—Talveans in varying states of sobriety paying homage, he guessed, to Saint Simion. Famously inebriated among the Salvation Church fathers, Simion had somehow earned a pass on all the exhortations against alcohol and excess and ended up with a day on the holy calendar all his own. The faithful were out in form, going to and from the various saloons, public houses, taverns, and hotels serving up drinks in Simion's honor. They looked like floating things, like debris in the river, bobbing as they moved drunkenly in their brimmed hats and layered skirts. There wasn't a hint of an interference light in town as far as Carsand could see, so everyone wobbled and collided and went darkly about the muddy avenue under the incapable glow of oil lamps and torches.

An errant streamer slapped him wetly across the neck. It felt like getting licked by a horse. He jerked it free and stepped into the mud, glancing around for more streamers.

The Talveans were mostly miners, he observed as he walked. Some had done themselves up in finery for the evening, but many were still wearing the leathers and smocks they used to pick ore out of the mountains. The town *looked* like a mining town. Its avenues were narrow, and the timber buildings climbed directly up, several stories, rather than spreading out and giving the townsfolk a little room to move. The gables were severe—the rooflines steep and stabbing into the night sky. Carsand imaged it helped with the snow in the winter, keeping it from piling too heavily on the roofs. Everything felt *hunched*. Carsand wanted to be about his business with the Astafos and get out of here. The issue of Lathael's constant yanking on Carsand's bloodmetal leash was a larger matter that warranted some further consideration.

Most of the people here weren't obviously armed. That was good. He didn't figure these people for the fighting type, but he gave a patrol of household knights—Lord Seda's, by the look of them—a long measure out of the corner of his eye as he pushed his way into a saloon. They looked a little under the drink themselves.

Inside, the place was festive. People were laughing and slapping and grabbing at each other. Some in their seats, some in others' seats, their glowing faces made ghoulish by the lamps on their tables. Carsand leaned against the bar to give them a good look, but nobody was doing anything but drinking and flirting.

"What are you having?"

Carsand turned. The bartender looked tired. Balding and mustached. His Naredal accent was palpable. So, he probably didn't own this bar. Another migrant laborer, pouring drinks for someone else making a lot more money tonight than he was. A countryman.

"*What can you offer?*" Carsand asked in Naredesse. He took his hat off and set it on the bar.

The bartender looked at him a little more softly. "*Whiskey mostly. It's what they like. Some wine—it's Karlandi,*" he warned.

"Whiskey, then," Carsand said.

The bartender refused Carsand's coin, but he accepted his toast. Carsand was glad for it. The intel from Lathael that he read on the journey from the ruling province didn't say very much about the local populace, just the nuances of the Sedas and the Astafos and who had owned which tracts of land at which point. If Carsand needed some leverage, or some good, old-fashioned civic agitation, he knew now where to start.

A trio of Knights of Astafo moved into the bar like a cold front. Despite Lathael's barbs, Carsand made it a point to know his heraldry—especially before he arrived wherever Lathael decided to send him. He recognized the Astafo blazon on the men's uniforms. They wore semi-ragged tabards over leather armor that looked like they could use a tailor. Perhaps things were growing a bit stale at Astafo Manor, including the coffers.

But they were wearing swords. The sight of the three men dropped the volume in the saloon, and the revelers leaned further into their lamps as if they might leave the knights in the darkness, locked out of their fun like restless spirits in the night.

Carsand got the bartender's attention.

"All these knights—Sedas and Astafos—are they always patrolling the town like this?"

The bartender glanced at them. *"Not usually. The Astafos technically have no authority outside the family's lands, and Lord Seda rarely uses his men to enforce much of anything."*

"Are they out for Saint Simion's?" Carsand asked.

"They're out for something," the bartender said.

He was right. They were clearly looking for something, and trying to look casual about it. They hadn't moved toward the bar, so they weren't here for a drink. It looked to Carsand like they were waiting for something, just taking up space inside the doors.

"Lord Astafo is a coward!" the shadows shouted at the three men.

"Who said that?" one of the knights shouted back. They looked like three pieces of some animated clock, all facing the same direction and making tiny little bodily movements while they waited for some alarm, and then they would do some dance to announce the hour before retiring back into their own darkness.

"He can't even hold his lands!"

The crowd were all looking around, too, trying to pin somebody down who they couldn't clearly see in all the bodies. Carsand could tell the speaker was moving—the shouts had come from two different areas.

When the first knight drew his sword, the crowd convulsed like a giant muscle. They heaved away from the doors, bumping into tables, moving like water.

"Show yourself!" the knight shouted. Carsand pulled his cloak away from his sidearm and rested his hand on the stock.

When the second and third knights also drew their swords, Carsand stepped away from the bar and unholstered the weapon.

"Put your swords away before somebody in here gets hurt," he said. The crowd gave him their attention for a moment—the latest player to take the stage in this strange play.

The first knight advanced on him, so Carsand took aim over the man's shoulder, pulled his trigger, and the bloodmetal pin expelled the bullet with a silent violence that belied its constant interest in doing exactly this, as it had been trained. The bullet cracked like a whip, and the distinct sound of a powder-free gun stopped the knight.

Carsand pulled the royal crest out of his pocket and brandished it. Even in the dim light, its polished metal edges and enameled fields were unmistakable.

"In the name of the king," he said.

"These Seda agitators are insulting our lord," the knight said.

"Then go home and tell him about it," Carsand said. "I'm sure whoever you planted in here to say that will be glad to get back before I figure out who they are."

The knight said nothing. He surveyed the crowd, and they surveyed him right back. Waiting, like animals, to take their cues from the bigger animal's movements. He put his sword away, and they moved off. With a royal crest like that, Carsand could go straight to the king and tell him what Lord Astafos men are doing. That would be much worse than any embarrassment they suffered surrendering to Carsand's will.

The tide of drinkers ebbed back into its original place, and their volume climbed. As if nothing had happened. He turned to sit back down, only to hear sudden shouting out in the avenue, even over the sound in here. He took several long steps to the windows. The patrol of Knights of Seda and the three Astafos were charging each other in the street, weapons drawn and screaming. But Carsand didn't see any pedestrians immediately around them.

So he went back to the bar for more whiskey.

Carsand escorted himself out of the saloon a few hours later. He'd actually gotten bored of drinking whiskey, and the bartender—Andro, Carsand learned he was called—was too busy to stand around and fill Carsand in on all the nuances of the local politics. It was just as well. Carsand's work here convincing the Astafos to stop harassing Lathael's pet, Lord Seda, would begin in earnest tomorrow, so it was probably best if he quit while he was ahead.

If he was actually ahead. He wasn't quite sure. Andro had been pretty generous with his whiskey. The rest of the patrons were less interested in curtailing their religiously sanctioned imbibing. If anything, it seemed like they were just getting going. Carsand hadn't been to the Oliniron Province very many times, but they'd never failed to surprise him with their consumption. So far from the heart of civilization in the ruling province, there wasn't much to do but work and drink, and they gave their all to both endeavors.

The festivities were going just as well out in the avenue, despite the chill of mountain air at night. People were sitting or lying prone everywhere. Some singing reverential hymns, others bawdy drinking songs. Carsand saw a priest lumbering along, his boys doing their best to stay upright in the mud while balancing the ungainly trophies of the faith. The incense didn't do much for the general state of perfumery in the avenue. The procession stepped over a man lying face down in the mud without a hitch.

As he moved away from the center of town, he could begin to see the mansions of the wealthy glinting on the hillsides surrounding the town. Lathael had provided him a map to memorize, so Carsand dredged up the local layout and moved off in the direction of Astafo Manor, intent on having a quick look at what its hillside lanterns would reveal about the place at night.

He shouldn't be here. He should be back in fucking Levuwes with the empress, getting drunk in her marbled lounges on delicate Naredal wines instead of Oliniron's punchy whiskey. He should be in her bed later, telling her stories of what he remembered as a noble son in Nidal before King Aramos yanked it out of her hands and renamed it Westreign. He still *would* be there if Lathael hadn't started yanking on his filament to get him back in Silangarde. When that didn't work, and Carsand killed the knight who came to retrieve him, he'd had no choice. If Lathael had become convinced that Carsand was a greater liability than an asset, he wouldn't stop until the risk was eliminated. *One* assassin Carsand could handle—he got lucky, he hadn't been drinking that night. But Lathael had more effective means of ridding himself of problems. The knight was just to annoy him.

He shouldn't be hiking up a Talvean hillside to spy on some bullshit nobody who'd pissed Lathael off. He should be with Ladre. Maybe he could just burn down Astafo Manor and be done with the whole affair. Back in Levuwes by winter.

He got as close as he dared to the grounds. He could see the Astafo house knights patrolling the wrought-iron gate. A good stone wall—no doubt simply scooped off the mountain and assembled there on the spot—swept away from the gate and disappeared into tangles of pine and spruce trees. He would need to create a distraction if he was going to get close enough to look for a break in the wall. He unholstered his pistol and took aim at one of the perimeter lamps further away from the gate.

"What *are* you doing?"

Carsand whipped about, gun raised. He saw a very tall, very stiff man in a green cassock with a hooded lamp. His gold transducer glinted between his eyes even with the light cast away from it.

"Who the hell are you?" Carsand said, and realized with the saying of it he'd had more whiskey than he'd realized. He definitely didn't quit while he was ahead.

"I'm Adwar Challant of the Order Entropic," he said. He lifted the lamp to get a better look at Carsand's face. "Are you . . . Carsand Raleis? And are you drunk?"

Shooting the lamp probably wasn't among his best laid plans, Carsand realized. And furthermore, this man also had a Naredal accent. Apparently, Talve was lousy with his countrymen.

Carsand lowered his pistol.

"Come with me," Adwar said. "We should probably talk."

"Your filament is essentially a signal beacon out here," Adwar said, leading Carsand through dark ferns in a cluster of aspen trees. They looked like they were watching him with their dark knots, eyes up and down upon him as Adwar's light swayed in his hand.

"When I detected it, I was quite certain that filament wouldn't have been Fabienne D'Aklave up here so close to Astafo Manor," Adwar continued, "and really, there shouldn't be any other bloodmetal in Talshire. So, you were hard not to miss."

"I know how the damn thing works," Carsand said, slapping at plants, "but I wasn't told to expect somebody like *you*. What were you doing out on the mountain at this hour anyway?"

Adwar stopped and turned. The lamplight made his silver beard look gold. "I am an Entropic."

"Right," Carsand said. He followed Adwar obediently when he started walking again. Most people called the members of the Order

Entropic "Field Men," because it seemed like that was mostly what they did—stand in fields and stare at the ground. Carsand gathered there was more to it than that. Entropics rarely worked interferences, as the particular sensitivity of their filaments to whatever kind of energy it was they worked with meant their work was *very* powerful. And very *disruptive*. Carsand knew there was something in their Gnostic Accords about the Entropics and protecting the balance of energies, but that was about it. Who knew what secrets deep underground Adwar had been spying on? Or what he could do with them if he wanted to.

Adwar stopped. A cabin seemed to simply stand up before them in the darkness.

But the Order Entropic was important. The empress hosted their campus in the forests of Naredesh, and she spared no expense for the pursuit of their research—or their comfort. They repaid her with their clandestine knowledge in droves, and they made sure to buttress her rule however they could.

Carsand reached forward and tugged on Adwar's vestments as the door clicked open. "So, is this how you know me? The Order?"

"Yes," Adwar said over his shoulder and waved Carsand into the darkness.

"Well, I don't remember you," Carsand said.

"Of course, you don't," Adwar said, a voice in the darkness.

An oil lamp came alive nearby. The cabin was large inside, if a little sparse. Carsand turned and looked back out the door. Had something this big really been hiding in the shadows? He had half a mind to go back outside and check, but Adwar was watching him, so he refrained.

There were tables against all four walls, each piled with neat pyramids of loose dirt in different shades. There were weights and measures and decanters, and pieces of copper and brass atop piles of documents and leaning against rows of books. Against the far wall, an ornate telescope stared out the window. It looked Ap-Lian by its embellishments.

"Some tea?" Adwar asked, stoking a small stove.

Tea with a wizard in the woods. Why not?

"That sounds fine."

He took one of the two chairs in the center of the room. The furniture, the windowsills, even the cut of the flooring and the walls was simple. Clean and straightforward, not at all like the curls and arches common to all the wooden architecture Carsand had seen down the mountain in Talve.

"Did you build this place yourself?" Carsand asked.

Adwar returned with two porcelain cups on a wooden tray. "In a manner of speaking. I *created* it, you could say."

Carsand tired of artifexi constantly telling him how to articulate things. He sipped his tea, set it down, and then spread his arms.

"Well, what in Salvation are we doing here, Mr. Challant?"

"Technically, it's Lord Ch —"

"If anyone should be calling anyone lord around here, it's you, so let's get to it."

Adwar gave him a good stare. Carsand figured that an artifex of Adwar's stature and seniority didn't often have to put up with flippant noblemen, even if they were in exile.

"Indeed," Adwar said.

Carsand leaned forward. "Why did you *create* a cabin, on a mountain, in backward Oliniron, next to Edmon Astafo's demesne?"

"Because the Consortium is unbalancing the Isostasy of Energies."

Carsand made a face. God, he hated how they talk. "The Isos— . . . right, the Accords. So that's it. That's enough to bring you out here?"

"We're not sure what the Consortium is doing, or why they're doing it, but we know they're doing it in alignment with the Salvation Church, which certainly means the Crown as well. And with the Consortium's campus nestled so cozily in Eastreign, you can see how this confederation doesn't sit well with the custodians of Empress Ladre's rule back home."

"So, you're babysitting."

"In a manner of speaking. I am waiting. It is important to allow events to develop. There is a philosophy dear to the hearts of the Entropics, which states that every event is dependent upon those that came before it, and it, in turn, determines what comes after. Phenomena do not simply occur. If you begin watching the reactions early enough, you will know the final waveform early enough to affect it."

Carsand stared for a minute. "So that's what you people do? Watch *waveforms*?"

"In a manner of speaking."

"Of course," Carsand said. "And you live *here* in the woods?"

Adwar set his tea down and folded his hands in his lap, as if attending his own interview. "I have quarters in Astafo Manor, but his lordship has also done me the courtesy of allowing for this space. I prefer the solitude when it can be arranged. All of which is, I assume, what *you're* doing here."

Carsand leaned back. "It's complicated."

"Oh, I don't think so. Not really. Let me see. You were in Levuwes, quite besotted by the empress, who was, in turn, quite taken by you, forgoing any other lovers, or suitors, in your favor. You lived a life of freedom, indulgence, and comfort in the shining halls of the capital, and then suddenly you didn't. So perhaps you were working for King Aramos as an agent, only King Aramos annexed your father's province by ripping it directly out of the empress's benevolent fingers, at great cost, and ruining the lives of the native Nidali. So, you wouldn't be working for him. Am I about getting it?"

"In a manner of speaking," Carsand said.

"Your father retained rule of his lands after swearing fealty to the king, but that wouldn't be enough, so he surrendered a son as collateral. An heir, in fact. So, what bidding of the king's you do, you do under duress, summoned at his whim by the stunted filament sleeping in your forehead. Pedir Seda is beloved by the king; the Astafos are not, which would explain why we're both here."

"I don't *want* to be here," Carsand said.

"Oh, that we've quite established."

"What does the empress think happened to me?"

Adwar regarded him curiously. "What part of anything I just revealed to you would you think we hadn't already told the empress? She knows precisely what happened to you, and she isn't happy about it. She's looking for you."

"She shouldn't do that. The prime minister is a dangerous man."

"Lord Raleis. While we both know that the empress is beautiful and charming, you have quite missed a few things if you don't know just how dangerous she also is."

Whatever that meant.

"The question is, what are you doing here, and how can I help?" Adwar said.

Carsand didn't expect that. He made a note to add Adwar to his list of aggrieved Naredals to muster if things started going south on this mission.

"I'm to deter the Astafos from their persistent inquiries into the state of Seda's affairs. The secrets of his success. How he won in the courts when he seized some of their lands."

"That's an impossible request," Adwar said.

Carsand shrugged. "Unless I kill them all and burn down the manor."

"The prime minister wouldn't waste an asset like you on such a fruitless task. No, you are some kind of bait."

"What do you mean?"

"The prime minister knows how persistent, and distributed, the Astafos are. Even if, as you say, you literally burned down the manor, the kingdom wouldn't be rid of them. So, whatever you are here to do, it's to motivate the Astafos to hoist their own petard."

Carsand held up a hand. "Okay, even if I didn't have a million other questions, let's dwell on this one for a moment. I have no idea *what* I'm supposed to do to the Astafos."

Adwar smiled at him. "Which is where I come in."

CHAPTER SIX

Camorenne traced the cathedral's sweeping lines with her finger, curious if she could feel any sort of relief between the ink from the woodcut and the paper. The Church of Saint Mira was the most holy place in all Salvation, and she still hadn't attended services there. She hadn't attended services anywhere in Silangarde, for that matter. Her station would make it easy enough to attend. She should. She would make time for it.

"Emille," she called, "Let's go to service at Saint Mira's this week, shall we?"

"Ma'am," Emille called from the next room, doing something with Alessandre, Camorenne's cook.

That settled, Camorenne went back to her newspaper. There was a piece on Saint Mira's about some artist of King Aklave's, someone hired to create the "Taboo Grove" on the campus of the college. The poor man went mad, it seemed, and died in one of the King's gilt guest rooms. She skipped ahead a bit. There were statues of incest, adultery, murder. There were statues dedicated to gluttony and gossip and even some addressing witchcraft and bestiality. The Grove served as reminder of those sins that the faithful should avoid, should there be any question.

She would most certainly need to make time for those. She'd already told Emille to prepare attire for the city today. She was taking the girl with her to library at the College of Saint Mira. It was time she uncovered some more details on Lady Seda's Holy Sanguinary Academy for the Lame and the Orphaned.

She folded her paper and summoned Bevry with the bell upon her table. He glided dolefully into the sunny parlor, as if he'd been waiting just outside.

"More tea, ma'am?" he said.

"No, Bevry. Thank you. Arrange a coach within the hour. Emille and I are going to tour the college this afternoon."

He bowed. "Of course."

"Oh, and have you found anything out about bringing some of the household knights here to the capital?"

"I have, ma'am," he said. "I'm afraid it's quite irregular—against the law even. Knights from houses beyond the city aren't permitted in the capital. The possibility of threat against the king's person is too great."

"Damn," she said. She was counting on some extra security from the knights back home. "I'll have to get creative."

"Indeed."

She waved him off, and he backed out of the light.

"Emille!" she called, straining her neck as if she might see around the corner without getting out of her chair. The girl's muffled response told Camorenne she was still at some other chore. Emille had learned long ago when she was actually being summoned and when Camorenne simply wanted to shout at her instead of changing rooms for a proper conversation.

"Let's get dressed, dear," Camorenne said. "Oh, and bring a knife today."

The chamber she'd been directed to in the library was so quiet that Camorenne could actually *hear* Emille at her embroidery. The punching sound of the needle through her cloth was quiet, but it was there. Camorenne watched her for a moment. The girl entertained herself silently next to the window, absorbing the dim sunlight that came through the old glass like a complacent housecat. She couldn't read Karlean, of course. What else was she to do while Camorenne studied the social records? She looked up now and then when one of the attendant monks padded past the doorway—moving like cats themselves through the dark, woody paneling of the library's winding interior.

Camorenne went back to the volume she was working on. There'd been several mentions of Lady Seda's party in various records of the day, most of them compiled by the courtiers whose job it was to keep up with who was throwing which engagements where—so the crown could tax them for the privilege. That was definitely one of the Crown's cleverer tricks—getting the nobility to invest in currying favor and improving their relations.

The party was fifteen years ago, just as Davo had said, and it was held in Daedo Hall—an even more impressive venue than the one Camorenne had just attended. Daedo Plaza was nestled in the shadow of Aevas Castle, where it reaped many of the overflow benefits of such proximity to the king's home. Mostly Mira Scholars from the college lived there, and its ancient, rounded cobblestones and splashing fountains created an air of quiet in the heart of the old city.

It would have cost a fortune. So how had the Sedas paid for it? Or even why? She checked and rechecked the entries, but there didn't seem to be anything more than the fact that, yes, there had been a party, yes, the Sedas granted a portion of their lands to the Salvation Church, who had autonomy within that zone and were not subject to the Sedas' local rule. It had been only a few years later that the Courts finally ruled in Pedir Seda's favor over the land dispute with her father. Were the two so directly related? It seemed an awfully high price to pay since Seda ceded more land to the church in the donation than he'd won from her father in the courts. Was this all that she'd be able to send to Ricarde?

Details. Lists of names. Announcements of titles. Dances danced. Food consumed. Wines distributed . . .

She double-checked. This entry recorded the wine the Sedas had served at their ball. The other records hadn't bothered mentioning it. There were several varietals in the list, all common—all wines she'd had before. But, there, at the bottom, CAMPANILE NORTH in careful handwriting. Camorenne looked up, but she didn't see the room around her. She was seeing every conversation she'd ever had about Campanile North—the most sought-after bottle in all of Karlande. Indeed, it was quite possibly the only bottle in Karlande that people beyond its borders paid attention to. She'd never had it. She'd never met anyone who had it—because it came exclusively from the Campanile Vineyard in Eastreign, which was nestled directly below the campus of the Eastreign Consortium for Inquisition Mechanics. The vineyard got all of its funding from the Consortium, and they were the only means of acquiring any, which they mostly reserved for favors from kings and crime syndicates, like The Shroud, who produced most of the artifexi's reagents, and then sold them on the side to people who only wanted them for their recreational effects. People like Camorenne.

But the Consortium had sent its wine to Lady Seda for a party under Aevas Castle celebrating a land grant for a hidden orphanage to the Salvation Church. She scratched her notes furiously. This was something Ricarde could use. Somehow.

Emille cleared her throat at the window. Camorenne looked up at her sharply, annoyed.

"Ma'am," Emille said quietly. She nodded at the doorway.

Camorenne turned. She hadn't heard anyone approach, but there was a gentleman there now, smiling slightly and holding his hat by the brim against his chest. He didn't look like much to her. A worker, perhaps, or a messenger.

"Lady Astafo," he said, as if he were amused by it.

Her delivery. "Ah, yes. Do come in."

He moved through the doorway without a glance for the intricate and priceless carvings in the panels around them.

"Won't you sit?" she said.

He inclined his head slightly. "I won't. This will only be but a minute. The money, please?"

She pulled a small silken purse out of her satchel. It chimed as she handed it, and its concealed coins, over to the stranger. He slipped it under his cloak and it disappeared into some pocket. His hands reemerged with a small leather box, which he settled on the table beside her.

"And what is it called?" she said.

"It's new," he said. "Just entering distribution in the city."

She would have to remember to thank Davo. It was his connection that she was using to buy these reagents. They'd never gotten much back in Oliniron, but even here in the city, she wasn't sure how to find her way into the reagent market. After all, the artifexi nominally didn't want everyone using up all of their reagents, so the king obliged them by making the trade nominally illegal.

She couldn't resist setting up the introduction in a library owned by the Salvation Church. Which, she assumed, was the reason for the expression on this man's face. No doubt he more commonly sold his wares in taverns or private chambers.

"It's called 'petal,'" he said. "You steep it, like a tea. Its effects are quite . . . relaxing."

"It sounds delightful," she said. "Is it actually made of flowers?"

"Does it matter?" he said.

"No, I suppose it doesn't."

He bowed again and winked at Emille. "Ladies," he said, and was gone.

Camorenne looked at Emille. The girl was staring at her with a flat expression.

"Oh, don't be like that," Camorenne said. "You look just like Bevry."

Camorenne stood outside the leaded windows of the pub. The place was packed, and the jumping lamplight and imperfect glass gave the revelers a watery, swaying look. Men had their shirtsleeves rolled, hats on tabletops like extra guests at a party, and the women had their blouses pulled down over their shoulders against the heat of the place, despite the chill in the air outside. The last time she'd tried to spend time in a pub, alone, her station had betrayed her, and all she did was chill the atmosphere in the room.

She moved on, dodging oncoming pedestrians in slow motion as carts followed their clomping horses down the avenue. The street was bright where the lamps from the artifexi's network shone—a steady, unflickering light that, out here, she found somewhat unnerving. Bevry had been livid at the idea of her spending the evening out in the city by herself, but it wasn't his decision, and she secretly enjoyed barbing him like this. Emille needed some time to do something other than be a lady's maid for an evening, too. She might be in a pub herself, for that matter, where she would be welcomed. One of the working family. Just an honest girl looking for a break among her people.

Except for her accent, of course.

Camorenne ducked into a tea house instead and ordered brandy with her pot of tea. There were a few others, people of station by their dress, around her, but no one worth any social effort. She finished her drink and left.

Back outside, her mind wandered, back to her work for Ricarde, back to what she'd learned about Lady Seda. How she would amuse herself without company back in her town home.

"Excuse me, ma'am."

She looked down. There was a pauper at her feet. He had milky eyes and skin like crumpled parchment. He gestured with a cupped hand at something over her shoulder. She turned, and there was a street vendor, grilling meats and twisting off hunks of bread for the people in his line.

She looked back at the pauper.

"Please, ma'am."

She stared at him for a moment. She wasn't feeling particularly charitable. However, she had absolutely nothing else to do.

"Oh, all right," she said. "Wait here."

She stepped into the line and realized that she needn't really have told the man to stay. It irritated her that she sounded stupid. But she could eat, and it would be novel to do so out here along the avenue. Her father used to buy her snacks from the street vendors during the festivals in Talve. St. Simion's was her favorite. So much color, and everybody drunk all over the place.

She brought the pauper a bread bowl and a ladle full of greasy-looking stew. She held her sausage away from him as she handed it down, as if he might snatch it out of her hand.

"There now," she said. "All better?"

"Thank you, ma'am," he said. He took it reverently, in both hands, like a supplicant receiving a blessing.

"Very good," she said, straightening up. She stared at him for a minute. What more should one say in a situation like this? She decided it was better to just walk off.

Nothing really captured her interest as she slowly made her way back home. The traffic was thinning, and lights were beginning to go out in upper-story windows. It probably was best to be getting back. She could undress herself this evening. Get drunk on sweet wine and read until there was no energy left to stay up.

When she saw the cluster of men on the other side of the street from her door, she thought they were embracing each other. Perhaps sharing some secret. She stopped, and peering through the light spilling upon the trio, she could tell they weren't embracing but struggling for dominance. Two of them trying to get a better hold on a third.

"Silangarde trash," one of them said. He had a clear southern accent, like hers.

There was a shift in the balance between them, and an arm flashed. One of them fell with a scream, and the other two ran off, the soles of their shoes slapping against the street. They didn't spare her a glance.

Camorenne approached the downed man trepidatiously. Perhaps she should get Bevry? But then she was standing over him, and he was only a boy, a teenager, and there was blood spilling between his fingers where he had them clutched against his side. He looked at her through bared teeth.

"Help me," he said.

Camorenne's heart raced.

"Oh dear."

The surgeon tied his final stitch, bandaged the boy, and collected his fee without a word. He'd said very little since his arrival after Bevry reluctantly fetched him at Camorenne's request.

"He should rest," the surgeon said. Then he gave Camorenne a stiff bow and was gone. The boy laid very still on the sofa in her parlor. The knife had gotten him in the belly, but the surgeon didn't think his attackers had done any real damage. Camorenne supposed she would find out one way or another. No doubt he was still in the grip of the poppy tincture the surgeon gave him before he began his work.

Bevry and Emille stood behind her like decorative statues, staring at the boy.

"Emille, fetch a blanket. Bevry, I'll sit with him. Go give me that look from another room."

"Ma'am," the two said in unison. Camorenne was surprised they hadn't wakened the cook so she could be part of the spectacle as well.

"Well now," she said after they'd left. "You've had quite the evening, haven't you?"

He stared at her for a moment, like he was trying to remember how to speak. "Thank you," he said. "Ma'am."

She got up and poured herself a glass of brandy. "Well, I couldn't very well leave you bleeding on my doorstep, now could I?"

Emille walked in with a blanket and arranged it over him. His eyes stayed with her the entire time, and they followed her like pups all the way back out the door. Emille wasn't that much older than this boy. She suppressed a smile.

"What is your name?" she asked him.

"Kedrick," he said. He was eyeing her brandy.

"Do you want some?"

"I think I do," he said.

She arranged a glass for him and set it on the lowboy beside the sofa.

"All right then, Kedrick," she said, realizing she'd found her evening's entertainment after all, "what happened between you and those other boys?"

"They weren't boys," he said. "They were older. Your age."

She decided not to take offense at the attachment of old to a sentence also bearing a reference to her person. "Why did they stab you?"

He drank some of the brandy and winced. "Because they knew I was there. They'd been following me. We . . . don't agree."

"About what?" she said.

He stared at her for a long moment, but he didn't give her the same look he gave Emille. He looked at her like a judge. "About . . . how to run The Shroud."

She stared at him. "The Shroud. You all, the three of you, are members of The Shroud."

"Yes, ma'am."

"You're telling me that you, you there, and those two men disagree about the management of a criminal organization?"

"Yes."

Surely this boy was teasing her. But it wasn't common, especially here in the capital. Nobility garnered more respect here than it did back home.

"What is the nature of your disagreement."

He managed to sit up with only the slightest grimace. "Well, ma'am, you see, they're from the south, like you, and I'm with the organization local here in Silangarde. All the provinces disagree with each other these days. Things are starting to break up, and they're making attacks like that in secret wherever they can. Nothing large, or we'd draw the attention of the Knights."

He certainly didn't sound like he was trying to deceive her. "And what were you doing out there anyway?"

He picked up his brandy again, and she thought she could see some color coming back to his cheeks. "Following you, ma'am."

Her shoulders went tight. "Following *me*? Whatever for?"

"I was ordered to. You gave food to that old man. I saw you."

"Never mind that," she snapped. "*Why* were you following *me*?"

"Because I want to be your friend."

Camorenne thought that might be the most ridiculous thing she'd ever heard. From a teenage boy claiming to be a part of the country's most powerful crime syndicate, no less. She didn't say anything. She just gave him a look.

"Well, I mean, not you specifically. It's where you're from that interests the leaders. You're new in the city, your family is controversial, and you're looking for friends yourself."

She would need to tell Davo about this. It was a bit much. "How do you know all that?"

The question confused him. "It's The Shroud. We know everything. If we're friends with you here, then you'll be friends with us back in Oliniron."

"Where you hope to . . . *shake up* . . . the Olinire Shroud."

He was relieved that she finally got it. "Yes, you see? And it turns out, you actually are nice, so maybe you'll be *my* friend, and not just The Shroud's."

She leaned away from him. This could be an incredible resource. She'd need to be careful, however, as The Shroud were notoriously dangerous, and the last thing she would want is to end up as a hostage brokered back to her father. But if The Shroud knew *everything*, and she'd done them a favor by saving the life of their young recruit—or so she chose to believe—there was an opportunity here she couldn't ignore.

"So, do you think we'll be friends?" He glanced at the door as if he might see Emille there again.

"We shall see," she said.

"Can I stay here tonight?" he said. "Please?"

She got up and poured them both more brandy. "You're a bit forward, but I like that in a friend. And I need somebody to drink with, so, yes—you can stay."

CHAPTER SEVEN

"But what were you doing in there?" Couran asked.

Ashre gave him an acidic look.

". . . ma'am," he added.

Couran had arranged a fire in the old building's small fireplace after Sovi led them to it, following her extraction from the wall she'd sealed herself in. She'd emerged from it like a ghost—a woman wrapped in twisting layers of white linen, veiled but for her eyes. Couran had never met a Displacer in person before, but he knew they all dressed like that, men and women alike. It was something to do with purifying their passage through this life. She'd pulled the linen away from her face, though, once they'd settled next to the fire, so he guessed maybe there were allowances for normal living here and there.

Sovi accepted a small bowl of tea from Ashre; she gave Ashre a long look before she bowed over the bowl. "Thank you," she said quietly.

"Welcome," Ashre said, just as quietly, her gaze also lingering.

Ashre was always quiet, as if she'd scarred her voice in the long business of always having something to say about the world. Couran felt like he was back in his father's chapel, sitting between his mother and his aunt and listening to their hushed voices reciting holy things in ancient languages he didn't know.

Sovi looked at Couran. It wasn't very bright inside this ruined structure, but he could tell how dark her eyes were, darker even than Ashre's, which already had the bewitching habit of sucking the light from any conversation and secreting it away. She looked like she might be the same age as Ashre, maybe a little older. She was Mendi—he could tell, if by no other means, by her relentless gaze. He'd heard before that Mendi didn't look away. That was something for Silangarders and courtiers in Naredesh who didn't have good reasons to actually keep talking to each other. He found he couldn't help but lower his gaze.

"I was meditating," she said. "An immurement. It's a regular ceremony among our order. We each of us subsist with the aid of our transducers and become less human and more still, like the buildings themselves."

She gestured around them. "Even this decrepit structure houses a Displacer. He has been here for years, more architecture than man now. We are guests within him."

Couran looked around at the chipped stonework and warped timbers. There was roof enough to keep them dry, but that was about it. He wondered which wall the man was entombed within, and then he realized that, actually, he didn't care for the idea.

"I'm sorry for the disturbance," Ashre said.

"All is excused," Sovi said. "The circumstances necessitate that I spend my time out here helping you, rather than in the walls. For now."

Ashre inclined her head and drank her tea.

Sovi cut a glance at Couran, and then back to Ashre. "How much does he know?"

"Little," Ashre said. "He knows what he needs to."

Sovi smiled then, and Couran relaxed slightly. No one had been doing much smiling since they'd met a few hours ago.

"You're still that way with him," Sovi said.

"It's our way," Ashre said. There was more tension than usual in her jaw.

Couran leaned forward. He wasn't accustomed to making camp with other artifexi—there had only ever been visits from members of the Senior Council, who would meet them someplace to bring them bloodmetal to expand their filaments. And those artifexi almost never said anything anyway.

"Do you know me, ma'am?" Couran said.

"I have known your mistress a long time." She looked again at Ashre, who was staring into the fire and toying idly with the kerchief around her throat. "We communicate often."

Couran thought about all the times he was left to himself while Ashre stood on rocks and cliffsides and stared at nothing, communing, it seemed, with the universe itself. Who else was she communicating with? He was forbidden from using his transducer to communicate with anyone but Ashre, and they rarely did even this.

"When you were a boy, the three of us traveled together for a time, though I didn't look like this then. I wore other attire for clandestine purposes. You had just become her ward, and our respective orders had shared interests for a time. The world was still full then. We were young, and there were universes of interferences yet to unfold at our behest."

"It didn't turn out that way," Ashre said.

Couran looked, but she was still watching the fire.

"No, I suppose not," Sovi said. "But your mistress has kept me informed as you've grown. I know you much better than you know me, Couran."

Couran wasn't sure how he felt about that. And did Ashre really communicate with others about him? That seemed so . . . *unlike* her.

Sovi let an awkward pause drift between them.

"So, he doesn't know enough," she said.

That got Ashre's attention. She and Sovi locked gazes like they might see who could pull the light right out of the other's eyes.

"He deserves to know," Sovi said.

Sovi had touched some nerve between them. Ashre sat like one of Saint Mira's garden statues. Staring perpetually with only the semblance of human movement.

"We're going to Eastreign," she said. She dropped her hand away from her throat. She was softening the way glaciers do. A thing felt, but otherwise imperceptible. A way she preserved her strength, for both of them—she and Couran—all those nights in the middle of nowhere.

Couran didn't say anything. He wasn't supposed to say anything unless Ashre invited him to. It was the longest-running part of his training. Learning how little the world needed to know to protect the Restoration's efforts.

Eastreign. Home. He hadn't been back since Ashre collected him from the Consortium, when his bloodmetal implantation had first damaged his vision and rendered him officially useless as an Inquisitor. His father paid the Consortium's fee to extract the boy, into the hands of the Restoration, and that had been the end of it. He wasn't much use to the family as a warden wandering the world to right the wrongs of other artifexi in the Restoration. His father made it clear, through Ashre, that he needn't overly concern himself with making it back to his ancestral homeland. Couran's brothers could more than take care of the family's affairs without him.

"We're not going anywhere near your father," Ashre said.

"Where *are* we going," Sovi said. It wasn't a question.

Ashre gave her an irritated look. This wasn't how things were done. "To the Tower of Tehruz," she said.

"That is a Traebit place," Couran said. "A legend. No one even knows where it is." He immediately lowered his head. "I'm sorry, mistress."

A stiff moment passed. "It's all right, Couran. You may speak freely."

He looked back up. "Their entire civilization peaked before the Karleths even organized as tribes."

Ashre sighed. "The original Strangemen were Traebits, which is why we're going. And *I* know where it is."

The Strangemen. The ancients who'd discovered the secrets of bloodmetal.

Sovi leaned forward, and her headscarf caught the light from the fire. It glowed like a mummer's screen for an instant. "We're going to speak with a Strangeman. With the filament left behind following his death."

Couran looked at them both in turn. "I'll assume that's why you're joining us. Because I don't know how to talk to dead people."

Sovi laughed. Across the floor, Ashre snorted and looked away.

"This Strangeman is going to tell us why the Consortium is secretly cultivating a banned reagent at a hidden orphanage owned by the Salvation Church."

He looked at Ashre. She nodded.

He wasn't sure what to say. He didn't have much choice about what they did, after all. He stood up and retrieved one of their lamps. "All right then. I'll see the horses properly tucked in."

Both women were gone when Couran woke up. One of them had stoked the fire in the crumbling hearth and packed it with fresh tinder, so that was one less chore he'd have to do, at least. A simple pleasure. He wondered which of them had done it for him. Had Sovi unlodged a softened part of Ashre? Something subtle enough to make waking up and starting his day a little easier.

Probably not. Ashre had her way. He didn't see her deviate from it often.

He checked his and Ashre's horses in the decrepit lean-to where he'd left them overnight. Both animals were cheerily munching on the overgrown Dhiallen grasses. He made sure they had enough lead on the hitch-line he'd roped across the posts between them. He looked around. The buildings and pieces of buildings stood ceaselessly all around him. A gray-white city of bones. A place built just for the sake of building it, not for actually being a place. He wondered if anyone had ever inhabited these dwellings. Properly inhabited them, not just sealing themselves in the walls. And was there only one Displacer per building? That didn't seem very efficient.

He marched back to their temporary abode. There was no sign of either Ashre or Sovi. He retrieved their cooking gear from the saddle-bags where he'd set them by the doorway—there was no actual door, of course. He would check these ruins later for clean water to refill their constantly dwindling supply. They had enough nettles for him to make another pot of tea, but there wouldn't be much left over. Jerky and brick bread for breakfast. The tea always made it a little easier to eat.

He wondered where the Enclave even was. The campus at the Eastreign Consortium was so massive, it dominated the mesa it sat upon. One saw it miles away. Out here, though, he'd seen only the strange architecture. Perhaps it was underground, like the Dhiallen themselves. He knew the Displacers took their name from the Enclave—what it did to a person living and sleeping and meditating constantly in their sepulchral retreat, constantly in the dim presence of silent others, always reading each other's minds and thinking about existence. Interfering with their thoughts and perceptions themselves to iron out a smoother, cleaner existence. He wasn't entirely sure what they could do to others with those talents, but he did know they lived an awful lot longer than anyone else.

The Enclave Displacement. That was the name of Sovi's order. A tribe made strange by their sanctuary. He was suddenly glad his father hadn't had any interest in seeing him into their number. There wouldn't have been any political advantage in it anyway. The Displacers weren't nearly as active as the Consortium was in the halls of Aevas Castle—or the Entropics in Empress Ladre's columned galleries and arcades.

He looked up when Sovi moved past one of the gaping windows. She was leading a horse of her own. Couran couldn't imagine where she would have gotten it. Surely, they wouldn't raise their horses underground?

She entered the structure a few moments later, unmasking her face. "Good morning, Couran."

"Ma'am," he said. "There's tea."

She picked up a cup and let him pour for her. She was smiling at him, and he wondered if he'd rather go back to everybody not smiling all the time.

"Where is your mistress?" she said.

"I don't know, ma'am," he said. "I never know."

"Sit with me," she said.

He poured himself some tea and sat across from her by the hearth. She watched his every move, as if she were studying him to give some report later on.

"Does it bother you, not to know?" she said.

"No, ma'am," Couran said. He forced himself to meet her relentless gaze. She was pretty, he realized. The same way a brushfire or a thunderstorm was pretty. Something barely beheld, certainly not considered. He guessed she was pretty the same way Ashre was.

"It's not long, now," she said, "until Ashre will release you from her tutelage. You know that, don't you?"

"Yes, ma'am."

"And then you won't be plagued by not knowing. In fact, I imagine you and Ashre will communicate even more via transducer then than you do by word now."

He didn't say anything.

"The Restoration and the Displacement have different philosophies regarding the knowing of things," she said. "We believe knowing more is better. Knowing is existing. I would prefer you know more."

"It's our way," Couran said.

"I know, but you'll need your own way, too, not just the Restoration's, and not just Ashre's."

He nodded at that.

"She's not far," Sovi said. "I doubt she ever has been very far from you, even when you didn't know where she was. Go ahead, listen to your transducer. You'll see."

"But I'm not permit—"

"I give you permission," Sovi said. "I rank highly enough to do so, as established by the Accords. Even the Restoration abides by that."

The tea should offer him protection enough to listen to his transducer. They drank it this way every morning, in case something unexpected happened, to minimize the effects on their bodies should they need to suddenly interfere. He wouldn't interfere with anything, he would just listen.

He slipped slowly into a tighter union with his filament. The edges of things blurred and also became sharper, and the silence of this place roared at him. Sovi's transducer was a singing thing right next to him, a trumpet on a castle wall, so he took a minute to learn her song well enough to ignore it.

The area outside, beyond this building, opened up to him, and he could feel the gently humming harmonics of the Displacers in all these walls. They were so quiet, so barely there. He wondered how they could be thinking of anything in that state.

And there was Ashre, maybe one hundred feet away, sitting on a stone bench behind a roofless chapel. She was still, communicating with someone. No doubt receiving instructions and orchestrating their next moves in the unending game of keeping the balance. Whoever she was talking to, they were very far away, he could tell by the exertion she and her filament were making together. She'd be sore when she rejoined them.

He slipped back into his own mind, and the filament went gently back to simply being there—to being part of him.

"You see?" Sovi said.

"She's going to need stronger tea," he said.

Couran thought they would slowly find themselves climbing the foothills as they made their way southeast toward the Dhiali border, but the earth began to fall away before them as they approached the foothills. He made a note in his journal. Most of the plains were on some massive shelf, looming over the center of the continent. It fell down and away before it began to rise into the mountains of the Thachrol Nations that extended all the way through central Karlande—through the heart of Silangarde itself. Ashre led their column silently onward. It always seemed to Couran like she'd seen everything already and was doomed to keep repeating experiences, perhaps for his benefit. Sovi mostly kept to herself in her position ahead of him. He wondered if she was present with them half the time, or if she was pitching her mind across some distance, pondering some deeper thing in a place beyond her brain.

He noticed the bison on the sloping plain easily because they were the largest, darkest things he'd seen for days in the expanses of pale grass and wrinkled scrub. He knew about bison. Ashre had taught him. A species critical to the lives of the Mendi, who hunted them and made use of their hides and meat, which they traded freely with the Dhiallen, who mostly preferred not to acquire their own meat up on the surface. Massive animals. Difficult to hunt, and capable of squashing a man on a horse with ease. There must've been thousands of them, moving like slow schools of fish through the green below, shifting about as they took their time deciding where best to graze, only to abandon the idea and move on a few feet more.

"We'll ride around the herds," Ashre said over her shoulder.

"Yes, mistress," Couran called back. He cinched the stampede strap on his hat up under his jaw. The rifle was loaded in its scabbard in front of his knee, but he wasn't sure if it would be any good to them. Mostly likely the gunfire would cause more trouble.

Ashre led them steadily on, veering off to their right, and bringing the late afternoon sun into an awful angle of attack on their eyes. Couran could see a river down in the distance, flashing at the sun where it curved its way through the hollows at the bottom of the Thachrol foothills.

Ashre stopped her horse at the head of her column. Sovi and Couran came up beside her. She was staring at the warped horizon with the same look she wore when communicating via her transducer. Both present and not.

"What is it?" Sovi asked.

Ashre moved her jaw to one side, as if she would shake her head, but the motion ended there. "A feeling. An imbalance."

They sat their horses in the quiet, listening to the distant sounds of the bison and the wind in the grass.

"Couran, make for that horseshoe bend in the river. We'll make camp there and ford in the morning."

"Yes, mistress."

"I'll be along. Go on."

Couran nudged his horse, and Sovi moved to follow him. He imagined she knew as well as he did when Ashre wanted to handle a thing by herself.

Maybe there would be fish in the river. He could cook something decent for their dinner.

Sovi didn't nudge him awake. She jerked him straight into union with his filament with an iron grip on his mind. It felt like a lucid dream, a thing he could wander through but would ultimately turn out to be unreal. The entire world was vibrating, and he felt like he was standing inside a thunder cloud. He could tell she was interfering with Ashre's brain. Severely. He realized Ashre was up, standing like a figurehead on the prow of some ship. Her back ramrod straight, her transducer blasting and pulling power from the thunder around them in crashing waves and throwing it back into the darkness, where it split the chaos swirling around them. Sovi, he realized, was mitigating the movement of so much power in and out of Ashre's head. She was keeping his mistress from cooking her own brain.

And now she was doing it to him. He'd never felt so much of the cosmos moving through his head, and neither had his filament. They were experiencing it together, both innocent and awash in the very forces of reality.

Help her. Sovi told him.

Couran moved himself forward—was moved forward, it seemed. He could never tell who was in charge when he engaged with his filament. It always felt as if things were just happening—the right things at the right time—and he was merely a witness to them. He stood beside Ashre, and the rippling probabilities she and her filament were enforcing on the world, made everything seem as if they were moving through glass.

Only up close did he realize that Ashre was deflecting a stampede. The thundering darkness wasn't a storm—it was a legion of the deadly bison pounding down upon them, and she was stealing the energy of their movement and using it against them so they wouldn't crush them—and their horses, who were in a full panic and straining in leaping jerks against their leads.

He'd never attempted anything this powerful. He couldn't even speak to Ashre, ask her for help. Her mind was a whirlwind of energy harmonics moving in and out. It was like screaming into a hurricane.

Whatever Sovi was doing to his brain, he knew he was suddenly capable of more than usual. He could do more than exchange balances of power and move objects around, or slip someone else's interference back into nothingness, where it belonged. Preserving the balance. He thought at the stampeding animals. He sifted through the piling and piling realities his filament could unfold, feeling for those ones he knew would take, the probabilities with the most heft—the highest chance of unfolding in their favor. When he found the harmonic, he latched onto it. He thought of nothing else. All those years Ashre forced him to spend meditating in the woods, or beside a campfire, or in a cold river, finally paid off. He was nothing but a creature who understood only the diversion of these animals, like a wedge of iron shoved into the earth and forgotten for all time. It's all he ever was, ever could be. He held the thought, held the position, for eternity. He aged, and his life slipped by him, and the wives and children that other men his age would grow into and live with shriveled up and died like burnt chaff. Kingdoms fell, and armies crumbled, and even the stars began to wink away.

Until it was gone, and Sovi yanked him out of the vision to keep him from plunging into inescapable madness. He was dizzy, and confused, and his ears and nose were wet. Sovi was on the ground with Ashre, and her white wrappings were striped with blood—Ashre's blood.

"Calm the horses," Sovi said, quiet and stiff.

He thought he said *yes, ma'am*, but he wasn't sure. He moved away, and in a daze, slowly brought the panicking horses back to their senses. He cooed and whispered and showed them his palms as the last of the bison crashed through the river and rumbled into the hills. He couldn't see them. What moon there was had sheltered behind a bank of clouds, as if it didn't want to fully see what was transpiring on the plain beneath it.

How had Sovi done that? How had *he* done that?

He felt Sovi's strong palm on his shoulder, and it jerked him out of his reverie. He could barely see her by the falling light of their small fire.

"She'll be all right, but we won't hear from her until morning."

Couran nodded.

"Are you all right?" Sovi asked.

He nodded again. "Yes, ma'am. What you did . . ."

She dropped her hand. "I'm sorry about that. There wasn't time."

"What happened?"

"Someone spooked the bison," she said.

"Some . . . *one*?"

Her jawline swiveled to stare off into the darkness. "Ashre was right. We're not alone."

CHAPTER EIGHT

Fabienne watched the knights stab each other next to the baker's stall. Townsfolk spilled around them calmly as they went about their errands, ducking sword strikes and stepping over stumbling combatants. Neither of the two orders of house knights seemed to be really giving this skirmish their best efforts. No one had died yet, and the melee had held at about ten knights, give or take. She also hadn't seen any reinforcements hurrying down the slopes from the manors. It looked to her almost like they'd scheduled this exchange. If any of them drew their pistols rather than slapping at each other's armor with their swords, she would intervene. Ostensibly, she was supposed to intervene now, given the Consortium's arrangement with Pedir Seda, but she didn't particularly feel like it. The entire sustained conflict was pointless, and she was only here long enough to shepherd the cultivation of *delirium shade*, and then she'd never be back in these hinterland mountains again.

But if they started shooting, that would cause an actual disruption, so she chewed the boiled roots that would keep her brain cool if she needed an interference to make the world go dark for them all. The reagents made her feel lighter. It wasn't unpleasant, so she leaned against a patio timber and watched, collecting glances from the townsfolk.

Eventually, the knights unthreaded themselves from each other. They looked ridiculous, smeared with the perpetual mud of the avenue, and they shouted obscenities at each other as they sulked away. One of the Astafo knights gave her a long look as he peeled away from the scene. She returned it without blinking.

᪣

Fabienne needed to check on her relay, and when she received the dispatch from The Shroud for a rendezvous, it only made sense to head up the mountain to the tower. She rented a horse from the livery beside the hardware outfitter and rode slowly out of town. Consorting with The Shroud wasn't something one did down here in Talve, even if one did enjoy certain social privileges.

It would take her most of the day to reach the tower, so she'd need to sleep there overnight. Part of the charm in making this semi-annual trek was to be sure the staff was keeping her quarters ready for her at all times. She could check on the relay remotely with an interference, of course, but she needed to verify its health visually. The filament in its head wouldn't tell Fabienne much about how the relay was eating, or if it was cutting itself. They often did, living isolated and bored like that.

The sun was falling behind the surrounding peaks when she reached the tower grounds. One of the Consortium's construction teams had infiltrated the area and erected the tower before she was born, given Talve's proximity to the Oliniron capital in Ae Darde. The tower was strong enough to survive the snows up here, built from roughly hewn stone the architects and laborers could find at this elevation. It wasn't a huge place. Forty or so feet high, with scattered attendants' cottages at the edge of the encroaching trees. There wasn't much as far as surrounding land went, this high up the slope, but the groundskeeper did what he could with the ferns and other plants that thrived up here, just below the timberline, out of direct sight down in the valley. The gate to the garden was ajar, which would be a demerit.

She saw the cook step out of the kitchen and toss a bowl of refuse into the bracken. The woman saw Fabienne approaching slowly, still astride her horse, and dashed back inside. A moment later, the only footman (who was also the butler) hurried through the tower's front doors to meet her.

"Madam," he said, a little out of breath, reaching for her reins.

"Osmond," she said stiffly. "The garden gate is open."

He bowed his graying head. "I'll see to it immediately."

He'd never lost his Eastreign accent, even living here so long. Fabienne figured it was because he never went into the town—that was the porter's job. So, he only ever spoke to the rest of the staff who'd been sent here from service at the Consortium campus.

"Have the girl draw a bath," Fabienne said as she stepped down out of her saddle. "I'll see the relay later, after a meal."

"Of course, madam," Osmond said. He bowed again as he led the horse to the small stable hewn out of the cliffside. She shouldered her own satchel and reagent portmanteau across the small grounds and through the door Osmond had left open. The place had never stopped smelling of varnish, which the builders had applied liberally to protect the timber that filled the tower. She wouldn't have to check on the cook—she'd already seen Fabienne and was, no doubt, at work on what passed for impressive fare up here. Osmond would see to the girl. She imagined the porter and the groundskeeper were off doing something useful. And there were all the family members. She would give everyone until at least tomorrow to get everything in order for her observation. She could do them at least that small kindness.

The place had the feel of a museum—of something preserved. Ruins from the ancient Karleth empire, perhaps, or a segment of ancient wall left behind by the Traebits before King Aklave conquered them and created Eastreign. There were old places like that tucked in Silangarde, nestled up against dwellings and restaurants, with ropes and attendants who would let you in for a tour for a few coins. Oliniron had largely only ever built things out of timber, so she didn't think there was anything more than a hundred years old anywhere in the province.

The tower was solid, and it allowed the relay and the staff to live in relative comfort. The Consortium saw to their every need—indeed, the needs of every relay in every dwelling they had across the continent. The attendants didn't have much, especially compared to the luxuries the Consortium bestowed upon the relays, but they didn't have to worry about much either, living out their rustic lives, sharing their holidays and feast days and birthdays. Having their children and their arguments and their tribal initiation whenever a staff member had to be replaced. And every now and then, an artifex would arrive, like nobility back from some long campaign, filling the ghostly role of manorial lord or lady in the flesh, and the attendants would suspend their small lives, and the entire world became about pride of purpose, lest they be found lacking—and therefore kicked out. Fabienne found it best not to try to befriend them. She felt it made their world make a little more sense.

It was a rustic place, clean, with a sense of mountain space, despite the closeness of the walls and staircases. It was lit largely by candelabra—wax was easier to get in Talve than oil—and it was free of rugs and tapestries to help control pests that would get in and wreak their havoc upon the wood. The carpenter had built most of the furniture himself, upholstered with the animal skins he bought off the region's trappers.

She could hear creaking in the framing of the floors above her, likely all the way up to the relay's chamber, where it paced and napped and did what it did to pass the time. She preferred her chambers on the first floor, where it was warmer and she had solid earth under her feet.

When she reached the end of the shadowed hallway, her door was closed, as it should be, and it swung inward silently. What remained of the day's light fell through the leaded window onto the furs folded on the bed and spread across the floor. She could hear the girl struggling with the water for the bath, and the cook in the distance, shouting for important ingredients. Outside, the groundskeeper closed the garden gate and skulked away from Osmond.

She let them work. Their little world, thrumming awake from its long sleep since her last visit.

"So he's a . . . 'relay'?" the agent asked.

"*It's* a relay," Fabienne said.

She wasn't sure what she'd been expecting of a member of The Shroud. The cartel was so large, so powerful, that it was rumored to be extending its reach beyond Karlande. The Consortium was in something of a marriage of convenience with The Shroud in order to acquire all of the rare and difficult-to-cultivate ingredients that would ultimately go into the Consortium's new reagent. And there was the partnership with the Church to keep all these clandestine alliances nominally legal enough to keep everyone out of the Courts of Saint Levine, should Karlande's expansive web of peers become restless with the thing, or use it as an excuse to put a new royal dynasty in place— perhaps one more aligned with their interests. Most of this she knew from hearsay and a few official briefings before she left Eastreign for

Talve. She'd never consorted with The Shroud themselves before. That business had been for her superiors.

But here was one. He'd handed his bowler and overcoat to Osmond as if he were any regular butler. Poor Osmond hadn't quite been sure what to do when the man handed him his gunbelt. Powder and bullets, she'd noticed. The Shroud wasn't known for investing a lot in agents that had a habit of dying and needing replacing all the time.

This agent was smaller than she expected. Short, perhaps forty, with a passable sense of fashion and a slightly weak chin. If she'd found him clerking behind a counter in a bank, she would have thought him perfectly within his element.

"Does he have a name?" the agent asked. He was standing just inside the door, looking around the small parlor where the relay spent most of its hours, as if checking for traps before committing fully to the room.

"Probably," she said. She sat primly on the edge of a deerskin sofa and folded her gloved hands upon her knee. "We're encouraged not to fraternize. It's not allowed to share its name with me."

"Why not?" the agent asked, apparently satisfied with the rustic décor and apparent lack of assassins. He took the sofa opposite her. Osmond came in bearing a tray with brandy in cut-glass tumblers. She waited him out while he arranged the drinks on the table between them.

"Attachments are dangerous," she said. Osmond tip-toed over to the relay, whispered in his ear, and then bowed. The relay was simply sitting and staring into the fireplace with his back to them, almost as if he hadn't noticed them enter the room.

"Relays are important to our work," she said, "and sometimes they are expended in the line of their duties."

"You just . . . use them up?" the agent asked.

"Often there isn't enough time to prepare them to ingest the proper reagents for interferences of significant magnitude. The consequences can be fatal."

He leaned back and squinted. He suddenly took on the disposition of an inquisitor himself, which amused her. She allowed herself—and him—a small smile

"And *what* do you need them for?" he asked.

"Relays are hosting bloodmetal," she said. "Though they haven't the training to interact with it directly. They're inert, but the bloodmetal isn't. They allow us to be in places we really aren't, when we need to carry out interferences remotely."

"You people are truly vile," he said.

That really made her smile. "Elevated philosophy coming from someone who buys, sells, and kills other people."

"Yes, well," he said. "We don't put on airs about it."

"More important than the relay's name, I should think, is yours," she said. She'd checked the relay earlier, before the agent arrived. It was fine. Dull and obedient, and apparently not abusing itself. Just another middle-aged man sitting in a tower on a mountain in the middle of nowhere. When she'd interfered with it, its bloodmetal was similarly content, nested in the relay's brain and not doing much of anything but taking in the surroundings. Bloodmetal was like that. It took its cues from its host.

"Reginald," the agent said. "It should have been in the correspondence."

It probably was, but she preferred to make him say it.

"Just Reginald?" she said.

"Just Reginald."

So, somebody clever enough to be of use to The Shroud with no family resources to his name. Notable.

"And *why* are you here, Reginald . . .?"

"I'm here because your order asked me to be here," he said.

That got her attention. "Indeed?"

"Yes. Listen, could you have your cook send up a plate? The climb up the mountain didn't afford much time for dinner."

"In a moment," she said. He may have been her senior, but she was lady of this tower, for what it was worth. She controlled the schedule. "Why meet with me in person to deliver a message? Surely there are easier ways to communicate."

"Your superiors didn't trust an interference to update you. Something about rogue listening devices and unstable elements in the region."

The Consortium knew about Kam and his apparatuses that could allow him to intercept wavelengths of interference. And there could be others, but usually they sent one of their own couriers only when they needed to communicate about something more significant than logistics.

"Quite," she said. "But why you?"

"Because we were already on our way back from the ruling province. And given our arrangement . . ."

"We?" she asked.

He sighed and rolled his eyes, as if he'd already done his part. "The Shroud have grown too large, too differently established in each province. Silangarde Shroud isn't Oliniron Shroud. In fact, the two houses, if you will, won't even share the same roof for much longer."

"The Shroud is fracturing?" she asked. This would have an enormous impact on the orders of the Gnostic Accords. The Shroud had a chokehold on the production of the reagents necessary to create interferences *because* the Shroud was so distributed. No individual order had the resources to acquire and process everything they needed. The Shroud were already in the business of selling reagents recreationally to Karlanders with enough money to throw around, so the Shroud had only been too happy to get in bed with the orders of the Gnostic Accords and meet their reagent needs at a discounted rate—which was still astronomical, given the rates of consumption and the sizes of the orders' coffers.

"Your order," he said, "has arranged to not support the Deadwarden and The Shroud in the ruling province. Instead, you will support *our* leader, the Southwarden, and we will be all too happy to provide what assistance we can while your organization seizes as many of the Deadwarden's assets as possible."

The Consortium, picking sides in an internal conflict among The Shroud. That stopped her. She had already reasoned on her own that the reagent she was working on was to give the Consortium some new edge in its negotiations and re-broker their power in the kingdom, but to actively seize smuggling and murder and all the other unsavory pursuits the cartel was known for . . . this was a first.

He could see its effect on her. He smiled. "We're divvying up the corpse of The Shroud in Silangarde, your family and mine. Now, about that plate?"

She reached for her bell and summoned Osmond.

Reginald finished his brandy and leaned back into the sofa. "While we're getting to know each other, why all this business with children and orphanages?"

"The brambles that support the blossoms are tight and difficult to manipulate, unless your hands are small enough," she said, distracted. As if she were giving a report. "It's easy to damage the plants and render them useless. We tried adult cultivators, but they didn't work."

"Brambles?"

"We give them gloves. We aren't heartless."

"That's debatable. What will happen to them after all this is done?"

"They'll be provided for."

"I'm sure."

"The Consortium takes care of its lay population."

"So, you're clergy now?"

"We reshape the universe. We have more claim to that title than the Church does."

Osmond walked in. "Madam?"

"Some dinner for Mister . . . for Reginald, Osmond." She stood up, and Reginald at least had the courtesy to follow suit. "Osmond will show you to your rooms. Feel free to enjoy the parlor as long as you like. Sit and speak with the relay, if you like. It might enjoy it."

"My lady," Reginald said, and bowed. It was the first respect he'd paid to her status since he'd arrived. Something about the way his message had landed, something in her face, had changed his attitude. As much power and influence as The Shroud carried, it wasn't wise to cross an Inquisitor.

Her bootheels resounded against the flooring as she left the room. There were preparations to make. She wouldn't stay here a moment longer than necessary.

The graveled meditation path in Kam's small gardens didn't take very long to traverse. Fabienne and Aisabelle had already made several laps, and they'd hardly spoken a word since Kam suggested they take the air together while he tended to some matters of personal business. He couldn't be faulted for the size. Terracing and leveling his hillside plot under the guise of a wealthy eccentric who simply wanted to live apart would have been difficult enough as it was. Carving a full-size meditation labyrinth—a fashion on the grounds of most manorial estates—out of the side of the mountain would have been an architectural feat of such magnitude, Kam would never have been able to pass simply as another Silangarde investor looking to establish a successful mine.

Kam's small estate wasn't as high as the relay's tower; down here, there was a bit more variety in the vegetation, and his gardener had managed to actually achieve something resembling topiary and shrubs.

"You look well," Fabienne finally said, pulling a tendril of pale hair behind her ear with a gloved finger. Aisabelle turned and gave her a flat look.

"I mean, considering . . ." Fabienne trailed off.

"For someone motivated to betray your order to secure my well-being, you certainly are rather scarce with these visits, aren't you?"

That stung. Fabienne whipped a glance at her older sister. "I can't very well be traipsing about these mountains at all hours every day. I have *work* to do, and I have an image to uphold. One of us actually *has* a title, you know."

Aisabelle stopped. Fabienne could see the anger widening her dark eyes. A look she visited on others herself. "Your order hands out titles like alms. Don't be too proud of yourself."

Fabienne started to strike back. She'd been young when her father had surrendered her to the Consortium, but even then, it had been clear that Aisabelle was the favorite. That their father preferred her, and he lavished his growing wealth upon her every whim—that much Fabienne remembered from her occasional holidays from her studies, when she was allowed to return home. She had told herself that she didn't care when she heard that their father had squandered their wealth, and Aisabelle had taken up as a hinterland lady's maid someplace.

But unlike Aisabelle, she had her training. She could cool her mind; her filament moved through her thoughts slowly, bending and maneuvering like a serpent in a dark cave. It brought her reassurance. Control. It had learned to be the version of her she wanted to be.

So, she took a breath.

"Aisa," Fabienne said, "what's this about? Why are you attacking *me*?"

Aisabelle started walking again, a breeze through the pines lifted the veils of their pale hair simultaneously. Fabienne walked with her.

"Do you know this is the best I've had it since we lost everything. A captive, in Oliniron."

Fabienne could relate. She didn't much care for the province herself.

"I can't imagine . . ." Fabienne said.

"I was really no better off in remote Eastreign," Aisabelle said, "but at least I was my own person."

"Were you?" Fabienne said quietly.

Aisabelle was quiet for a few steps. The gravel crunched beneath their bootheels.

"Can you imagine that I almost like it here?" she finally said. "Kam is engaging and polite, and I want for nothing."

Fabienne glanced at the bloodmetal brooch clinging to her sister's forehead. She was suddenly very conscious of the transducer between her own eyes. The implant felt cold in the mountain air.

Aisabelle looked at Fabienne. "What are my alternatives?"

Fabienne let a few steps pass. "I'm sorry he found you. I'm sorry he found you because of me."

"He paid my previous employer to deliver me all the way here under the guard of two house knights," Aisabelle said. "There wasn't a choice involved in the transaction."

"I won't let him keep you," Fabienne said.

"You would let everything you are, your entire life, that order—you would let all of it crumble, for an unkind sister you haven't seen in ten years?"

"I didn't say that," Fabienne said. She used the same dangerous tone she used when clergymen or nobility were beginning to anger her. A tone that belonged more to her filament than to herself.

"But those are Kam's terms!" Aisabelle said.

She stopped and grabbed Fabienne's arms. Fabienne flinched. She was very unaccustomed to being touched.

"You can't outwit him," Aisabelle said. "Fabienne, you mustn't try. It will be me who pays the price."

Fabienne stared into her sister's whirlpool eyes, as if the serpent in her mind could calm those waters as well.

"He has outwitted himself, Aisa," Fabienne said. "None of us will win what we're seeking, including Kam Glimjeld."

ᕲ

"Scrying cocktails?" Fabienne asked.

Jern leaned away soundlessly, leaving the cocktail sparkling in front of her. A pair of Kam's other silent servants were still clearing the dishes from their dinner.

She nocked an eyebrow at Kam.

Kam caught her gaze and held it. "Only the one cocktail, my dear."

She lifted her brow further.

"I'm afraid they would be quite lost on the rest of us," Kam said.

She almost laughed at that. The Consortium may have killed his filament and stolen interference mechanics from him forever, but he had done well enough for himself. If one overlooked his banishment to the Glim and the years it took him to master sorcery and amass his fortune. Self-deprecation was the closest thing to charm Kam had.

"And what will I be scrying for?" she asked.

"The secrets of your treachery against the Consortium," he said. The charm was gone from his stare.

Fabienne glanced at Aisa across the table. Her sister met her gaze for a moment, and then lowered it. Jern had removed himself to his post near the door. Kam may as well have said they'd be playing a rousing game of *Blind Man's Bluff*, for all that it appeared to bother Jern.

"Oh," Fabienne said brightly, "is that all?" She couldn't let him draw all the personality in the room (such as it was) into his dramatics.

Kam reached for the brandy Jern had set before him. "To your health," he said.

Fabienne was slow to pick up the cocktail and lift it to his toast. She cut a look at her sister, who sat with her eyes on the table.

"Aisa, my dear," Kam said, "you'll join us, please."

Aisa lifted her own brandy, and they drank. Fabienne had used this cocktail before—a favorite in the halls of the Consortium. It was less bitter than some of their other reagent compounds—it was sharp, as of ginger.

Fabienne gestured at the others. "So, Kam, is it parlor tricks now?"

"Oh, come now," he said. "Jern is all too familiar with the vagaries of scrying, and Aisa is blood. Will you not interfere before her?"

Fabienne had never shown Aisa an interference. Once, when Fabienne was permitted home from her studies for a short holiday, Aisa had asked for her help scrying the location of a missing brooch. Students at the Consortium were forbidden from interfering without the guidance of their instructors, but Fabienne had tried it. No sooner had she begun to wake her filament than one of those instructors knocked her out of her own mind—they'd been monitoring her remotely via the relays between Fabienne's father's house and the Consortium. Fabienne didn't wake up for two days. When she did, Aisa wasn't home. She was with suitors.

Jern lifted a glass display jar from his silver tray and settled it in front of Fabienne. It held a single blossom of *delirium shade* from the fields in the valley, where the children at the orphanage cultivated it.

Fabienne looked at Kam. "When were you down in the fields? I thought the idea of all . . . this," she gestured at everything, "was to avoid the possibility of your detection in Talve?"

"Never mind that," Kam said. "Finish your cocktail. We have work to do."

She glanced at the flower. "On this? Whatever could we be scrying from a flower."

"Its future," Kam said evenly. "*Your* future."

"Oh, very well," she said.

Fabienne downed the rest of the sharp-tasting cocktail. Whatever it was that Kam was about, she'd rather be done with it and back about her own business down at the orphanage.

"And we'd all so much like to watch along with you," Kam added.

Fabienne tried not to roll her eyes. "Yes, of course, Kam."

She stopped thinking about them. She stopped thinking about the room, or even the flower. She thought only of her breathing, bringing her mind and body together in a unified function. After a moment, the singularity of thought caught the attention of her filament, and it stirred in its nest within her mind. She thought of it, and it of her—a single thought between two thinking forms, joined by the bond of flesh, and the mechanics of her transducer. The filament began reaching its ghostly fingers out at passing realities—probabilities and options that could come to pass in this room, playing with what was and what was possible. Together, they turned Fabienne's eyes on the flower, and then they did extend a bloodmetal greeting, a song only they could hear, reverberating through her transducer and harmonizing with the gentle tones of existence humming around them. They sang a song to the flower, until it sang back, and then they knew its harmonics, and they held them in a pattern, three singers of the same flower song. Fabienne's transducer filled the room with darkness, and the only point of light between them all was the flower, lit as if nothing had changed, as if the rest of them hadn't been washed out of being in a single flash of darkness.

Her filament toyed with the flower, knocking about possibilities of existence—and not—for the flower on this particular branch of the infinitely unfolding tree of reality that was the bloodmetal's natural habitat. Fabienne concentrated, using the flower's own harmonics to run the calculations and formulae in her head that her instructors at the Consortium had taught her. The measurements of reality—and where the variables were. How to determine the likeliness of passing branches of reality when it came to this flower and to her. It was the variable; she was the constant. Scrying always depended more on the observer than it did the observed.

"Concentrate, my dear," Kam said, a voice in the darkness. She had created the illusion just to keep them all still. If their minds believed they couldn't see themselves—much less a way around the room—then they couldn't get in her way. Standard procedure when scrying with the laity.

Fabienne wondered why he would want to agitate her. He would gain nothing by ruining her concentration and making her start over.

"I know what I'm doing," she said steadily.

A bit more math, a few more deep breaths. The filament stopped its curious exploration of all the passing branches and locked its concentration here on this branch and its most immediate likelinesses for development. They were one thinking being, and they now had the profile of this simple flower's entire continued existence—until the point when it would dissipate back into the constituent elements from which it had arisen.

It occurred to her then, watching this flower's possibilities waver in and out of form, that Kam didn't want to distract her. He desperately wanted her to succeed. This flower was tied deeply, directly to Kam's own fate. She could see his own complicated harmonics interleaved in most of the possibilities laid before her.

"I have it," she said. "This flower's most likely future will depend upon my observation. My very looking will establish the branches that will most come to pass."

"I'm quite aware how divination works," Kam said.

"But Jern and Aisa aren't," she said, almost as if speaking while asleep.

"Yes." He paused. "Of course."

"If I'm to know which branch to seek, I will need to know more."

"Is it not enough that *I* have provided it?"

"No. The certainties of your involvement with this flower are too broad in their capacities for both ruin and triumph."

He paused again. "Well, now, that's not very reassuring, is it?"

"This is your parlor game."

"I've often wondered why your order sent *you*," he said. "I've pitted my greatest achievements on the belief that the Consortium knew what it was doing sending you here. Things don't sound quite so certain to me now."

She concentrated on her breathing. The filament helped her maintain her focus, despite Kam's maddening tantrum.

"Perhaps they sent me to throw you off," she said. "Perhaps they knew what you'd try all along. Or . . . perhaps I really do know as much about this flower and its mechanics, and you're simply underestimating me in favor of your own self-absorption. If darkening rooms and exploring flower petals is how I secure Aisa's well-being here, then so be it. Otherwise, let's please get on with it."

If she could see him, she knew he'd be smiling. It's what he did anytime she moved one of her chess pieces in a direction he wasn't expecting.

"Very well," he said. "What you're looking for is toxified aether."

Fabienne shared a chill with her filament. Her knowledge of the substance was alarming enough for both of them. The filament shared her reaction and amplified it. The flower, the only thing visible in the dark room, darkened and blurred, as if she were losing her hold on its future.

"You see," Kam said, "I have very specific plans to include *this* blossom in the reagent that will ultimately reach the Consortium."

Fabienne didn't know the details of her order's arrangement with The Shroud, or the Crown, or—for that matter—the Church. It wasn't her place to know, but whatever the leaders in the Consortium had in mind, it depended on this reagent. The deal itself was older than she was. She knew only her part to play, and that meant the cultivation and processing of these flowers—one element, albeit an important one, of the overall recipe for the reagent.

"By including this particular blossom in the future, I'm providing you a lens today," Kam said. "And you need to find the path that brings it to toxified aether."

Aether was the fluid from which the masters of the Gnostic Accords drew the bloodmetal filaments they all depended on. Toxified aether was only used as punishment. To kill a filament and render its bearer incapable of interference mechanics.

Like Kam.

She concentrated and tried to draw the toxic substance out of the future where it would meet this flower. Like the others of her kind, she'd been conditioned into a natural aversion to this nightmare fluid. She and her filament both. They were struggling together to want to search for it.

"Interference mechanics can't detect toxified aether," Kam said. He sounded bored. "That's why its kept locked away and secret."

Finally, Fabienne pulled the threads through mathematics and probabilities it took to feed them to her transducer and alter the results of her scrying. The entire field of flowers, down in the valley, appeared, and there was silence in the room. But Fabienne knew more . . .

"They will disappear—all of them," she said, and the blossoms fell into the earth as if they had never been cultivated. All that remained in her illusion were the brambles.

Kam said nothing, so she continued threading herself into this future, continued guiding its story then to tell now.

"But they will be returned by . . ." it caught her by surprise, "me. But not me."

She appeared in her own illusion, but the image was wrong somehow. It was disturbing, staring at her. Her but not her. She swept it back into the darkness and brought the light back into the room.

Kam was staring at her, hands folded upon his table, unperturbed. Aisa's eyes were wide and darting, and Jern looked bored, as usual.

"You will get a version of your revenge, Kam," she said. "But the flowers will determine what that looks like. And they won't come from here, but from somewhere else."

Kam smiled. "Well done!"

Her brow fell. "I don't understand exactly what we were seeing."

He got up and walked around the table, a silken phantom in the room's artificial light. He settled his palms heavily on her shoulders.

"You will," he said. "The Restoration have a philosophy that everything that unfolds in our lives, in this universe, unfolds the only way it can, which is the way it unfolds. Of all the infinite possibilities that could unfold at every instant in every corner of the universe, they all unfold the way they do, and they affect each other—all the way down to us. Simple beings in the scope of the cosmos. Unlikely outcomes that probabilistically speaking, never should have come to pass. Yet here we are. Here we were always going to be. Everything we do, everything that happens was always going to happen, no matter how much time the Consortium spends making efforts to the contrary. We are simply a chain of reactions to the first action, creation, at which point the entire story of the life of the universe sprang into being, and we are trapped by our inability to see the whole of it at once, which is why we must resort to tricks and parlor games."

He leaned over so he could see her face. She stared at Aisa. Aisa stared back.

"While I might lose my temper, it's only because I'm human. My determinism engines deduced long ago that it would always have been you here, with me, locked in our cosmic dance. Reality unfolds like water—it follows the path of least combinatorial resistance. And you, my dear, are that path. Do you know why?"

"No, Kam."

"Because the only way to toxify aether is to expose it to a filament from a branching reality. There are infinitely many of them, and one can learn to travel between them. And return."

He let go of her shoulders and walked back to his place at the table. "*I* cannot make these journeys, not anymore. But *you* can, and that's why we're here, these many years and calculations later, having dinner, talking about the nature of the universe. When you have toxified the aether, then our time together will truly have come to its full potential."

"I would need a lifetime to do this, in quantities large enough to accomplish your goals," she said.

He shook his head. "Do you know what it is that I stole to be exiled from the Consortium and cast unto the Glim?"

She didn't say anything. No one knew.

"The secret to the creation of bloodmetal is that it is *grown*, not smelted or precipitated or anything else you've been taught to think. I stole *how to raise it*. Which is how all of this," he gestured to the room, "is possible. I grow aether. I develop it and teach it and bring it into its majority, as bloodmetal."

"That seems like a rather circular unfolding of events. You stole how to grow your own aether, and then the Consortium killed your filament," she said.

He smiled. "The cosmos is infinitely complex, but not without a sense of humor. I am going to teach *you*, Fabienne, the secrets of growing aether, and you will become so much greater than the greatest in your order. *You* will control the growth of your filament, not some review panel in the Consortium, doling out dollops of bloodmetal as they see fit to control your power."

It surprised Fabienne how easy it was to listen to him, to believe him. He was a monster, and he had her sister, but she wanted to hear each of these things he was saying. It felt more normal than her everyday world.

"*That* is what your divination means," he said. "You will travel between worlds, and I will be your guide."

He pulled a small vial from the pocket in his waistcoat, and she could see aether swirling inside it. Moving and churning and waiting for the next stage of its development. He set it on the table and gestured to Jern. The servant brought it to Fabienne.

"This will be your strain," Kam said. "And you will grow bloodmetal to your heart's content."

She looked at him again.

"Power and riches untold," he said, opening his other hand. A small, metallic syringe glistened in the chamber light.

CHAPTER NINE

Blowing up a mine was among the stranger things Carsand had done in the name of the king. Had he decided to do it on his own, sourcing the blast powder alone would have taken him half a season, especially out here where he had few to no contacts. But Adwar was in a bit of a hurry.

Carsand crouched in his perch for most of the afternoon yesterday, occasionally napping while Adwar stood on the promontory over him and simply stared into the dead mine. Adwar didn't move. He didn't speak. The mine's adit was an unused access point, and even though it was an old one, its collapse shouldn't have had any impact on the structural integrity of the whole of the mine. Except, Adwar stared at it for a long time, his eyes glazed and watering from his reagents. Carsand guessed that the planned explosion was now going to have a *very serious* effect on the rest of the mine. A catastrophic one, if he had to guess. Thanks to whatever Adwar had done to the mine's bowels, deep in the earth. Carsand preferred not to know the details.

When he was done, Adwar had to leave—he couldn't be anywhere near this mine when Carsand blew it up, or the Consortium might later devise that the whole thing was a ruse. Collapsing a mine would put plenty of peasant miners out of work, and a few choice words shared with Carsand's new Naredal friends in town could help shift sentiments anti-Seda and pro-Astafo. That would look like Carsand provoking the Astafos to make a move—exactly as Lathael had instructed. Especially since Adwar's next move was to *adjust* some of the hills in the Astafo deed to suddenly become ore-bearing mines themselves. If they could claim they had the actual lands to employ and feed the people, they would have a legitimate claim to a charter—the issue of their stolen lands be damned. Even the king's daughter in the provincial capital of Ae Darde would have a hard time keeping that claim out of the Courts of Saint Levine. Which would keep the

Astafos quiet, instead of springing whatever trap Lathael had in mind for them.

And blowing up a mine to start a revolution was certainly not beyond the pale when it came to Carsand and his grasp of subtlety.

It was dark enough that the miners should all be home—or, more likely, in the pubs. There might be a stray taskmaster or two still down in the main mine, but Adwar said they should be able to outrun the collapse, the way he'd *arranged* it. And anyway, those guys, if they were still poking around the mine, were probably bastards. Carsand couldn't imagine "mine taskmaster" as a particularly gregarious lot in life to carry around. He might even be doing a few assholes a favor by putting them out of their misery.

Carsand looked around again. There was no one in sight. There was barely anything in sight on this side of the mountain. A few stars between Oliniron's perpetually leathery clouds, but no moon, no torch, nothing. Carsand only knew where the detonator was because he'd been sitting with it all afternoon, waiting for dark.

He counted off in his head, and then engaged the lever on the detonator. There was silence for a moment, and then a sound like chewing. The earth gnawing away at itself—like a creature caught in a trap, chewing off a leg. It got louder. Carsand decided he didn't like it very much. He'd expected an explosion—this felt more like giving the mine a disease.

He started re-coiling the detonator's cord as quickly as he could, near-blind in the dark. Fist over fist over fist until he felt the end of the cord. He stood up, listening to the grumbling belch of what he assumed was the mine collapsing on the other side of the mountain.

And then the earth opened beneath him, and he was suddenly a scrabbling, clawing thing, hoping to grab something, anything, to keep from falling into the pitch black, his thoughts reduced to the sheer panic of falling into nothing.

"You're very easy to find."

Carsand opened his eyes. He was at the bottom of a crevasse, not nearly as deep as the nightmare had suggested. Too far down to easily climb out, but a rope would do the trick.

He looked up from the bottom of his crevasse. It was daylight up on the surface, and a pale-haired woman in a Consortium cassock was peering down at him.

"Yeah," he said, "I keep hearing that. You must be Fabienne D'Aklave."

"So, your filament works?" she said.

"No," he coughed up some dust, "it's just that they told me to avoid you, and how many more artifexi could possibly be crawling around these hills?"

"You need help to get out," she said.

"Yes, ma'am. I do."

"Hold still."

Carsand didn't like the sound of that. In fact, he pretty much disliked doing anything artifexi instructed him to do. But he kept his peace, and as she stared at him, he began to float up and out of the crevasse. He took a breath and decided to keep calm.

This is completely normal.

He decided it was better to keep his eyes closed. When he felt his floating feet back on the ground, he opened his eyes.

She was looking at him in that way they do. Like a bug. Or an interesting stone. Or something to take apart. There were dark veins around her eyes—he'd seen that before. Too many reagents. Pushing things too far.

"How did you do that?" he said. "I thought your type simply created illusions and . . . found things."

When she looked at him, it was as if she was looking at a different version of him. Perhaps a version standing a few feet behind him. He glanced back. That version of him would be hovering over the hole in the earth.

"I found you, didn't I?" she said.

"I hardly think that counts."

She had skin like marble. Something the sun would boil into leather out here in these sunblasted hills. A statue, waiting to corrode.

"I'm teaching myself new things," she said.

"Well, I beg your pardon if I'm less shocked and amazed than I should be by your appearance here. I'm becoming accustomed to you people hunting me down in the woods."

She didn't say anything.

"And why, pray tell, were you looking for me?"

"Someone wants to talk to you," she said.

He looked off into the distance. There wasn't an entrance to the mine anymore.

"It wouldn't be about this mine, would it?" he said.

She looked confused by the question. "Who cares about the mine?"

"Probably the miners," Carsand said. "Maybe Lord Seda."

She started walking away. "I don't care about any of those people."

Carsand decided that as artifexi go, this one was all right.

A patrol of Knights of Seda bobbed into view on the path in front of Fabienne. When she saw them, she stepped to the side. Carsand stopped next to her. There were four knights clogging the path below them. He listened without turning his head—he didn't hear anyone behind them, so they hadn't stepped into a trap. Yet. He figured Fabienne would turn if she heard something. She didn't seem to move strategically. She just walked to reach a destination, and if something strange caught her interest, like armed men in the woods, she stopped to give them a look. Her illusions could drive anyone mad, if she so desired. A clutch of knights would be easy prey if they were interested in her. The knights had their hands on the stocks of their pistols—powder weapons, he imagined. Even with the Crown's favor, there's no way Seda could afford to outfit his stooges with bloodmetal firearms.

Their swords were still in their scabbards, so he left his there as well. He rolled his shoulder back, and the lapels of his cloak lifted and exposed his own sidearm. He rested his hand on it casually.

"What's your business on Lord Seda's land?" one of the knights asked.

"I'm here looking for saboteurs," Carsand said.

"How do I know you're not a saboteur yourself?" the knight said.

Carsand lifted his other palm slowly and pulled the royal crest out of his jacket. He held it like a talisman, some occult weapon brandished against mountain ghouls. "I'm here at the Crown's behest to help your lord. I'm no saboteur."

"Perhaps you should come and tell that to our lord," the knight said."

"I prefer a low profile," Carsand said.

"Lady, what do you have to say about this man?"

"I found him," Fabienne said. "Those were my instructions."

"I don't have time for this," Carsand said. "Stand aside."

"What would I find if I were to inspect the old service adit to the mine?" the knight said.

"Oh, goddammmit," Carsand said. "You'd find a pile of rocks, just like I did."

"Surrender your weapon and come with us," the knight said.

They started fanning out. The two on the ends would try to flank him. He took a reflexive step back, and then edged onto the slope at his right. He had the high ground on them, and he intended to keep it that way.

"You know," Carsand said, "There's nothing I like more than shooting Karlander stooges." He took a deliberate step up the slope.

"Aren't you a *Karlander stooge* yourself?" the knight called back. Nobody had drawn their guns yet.

"If you only knew," Carsand said. "Fabienne, take cover."

"They won't shoot me," she said. "They're not allowed to."

She had a noblewoman's posture, even if she hadn't been born to it. Something they must have taught her at the Consortium. She reminded him of a statue for the second time. A monument to defiance in the middle of nowhere. The tips of her pale hair stirred at her waist, and she had her gloved hands clasped above her abdomen. These men should be much more afraid of her than they were of Carsand, and by the way they moved, he figured they knew it.

Well, then, she could fend for herself in all this. Carsand was the first to unholster his weapon. Legally, he had the right to—if Seda's knights were impeding his royal charter, he could take whatever measures he needed to protect the king's interests. Out here in the Olinire woods, worlds away from the Courts of Saint Levine, he figured these simpletons may not know the ins and outs of the rules of engagement.

"You know," Carsand said as they unholstered their own pistols, "firing upon my person is the same as firing upon the king. You might not like what that gets you."

"We have our orders," the leader called back.

Idiots. They wouldn't even know how unimportant they are to Lord Seda. He could hand them over to the Knights of Silangarde for a life in shackles and forget their names by lunch. If he even knew them.

"All right, then." Carsand dropped to a knee and fired off his first shot at the leader. The bloodmetal plug fired his bullet silently, without recoil, and the air cracked with the speed of it before it blew apart the lead knight's gun shoulder. The man spun like a child's top and collapsed onto the scree.

That ought to do it.

The other three immediately fired back, and the mountainside became a cacophony of gunpowder and snapping bullets.

So much for taking out the leader.

He scrambled further up his slope, weaving in and out of the aspens. He saw a tactical advantage atop a scar of rock on the slope. A bullet blew apart the trunk of a tree beside his right ear and its fragments bounced off the rock shelf's striated face. It wouldn't be perfect cover, but it would do.

He turned as he slid onto the ledge. He'd be parallel instead of slopewise on top of it, which would make him a smaller target. He saw one of the unkempt tabards Seda's knights wore and fired another silent shot. He could almost see the bullet ripping apart the mountain air, and then that tabard was aflutter and tumbling back the way it came.

Two down.

He pulled his dagger out of its sheath and then rolled onto his belly. He planted the dagger like he might stab the rock, and then braced the barrel of his pistol across its small quillons. He tried to slow his breathing and listen. The wind made plenty of noise through the trees this high up, though the gunfire had scared off most of the birds. He laid still for what seemed like an hour, though he knew it would only have been minutes. Eventually, one of the knights popped his head between the trees, following the same path up as his fallen comrade. Carsand didn't fire. If the only shot he had was the man's head, then his helm might deflect the bullet at this distance, and then Carsand would have revealed his perch. He kept breathing. He tried to time it to the rise and fall of the soughing wind. To be wind himself. Undistracted. A force of nature.

His next shot took the knight right through the throat. Only after he saw the man's neck explode did Carsand realize he'd taken the shot. He inched to the side of his ledge slowly. If the last knight was still around, and if he was watching, he could approximate Carsand's perch. That was bad strategy. He had to move.

He got off the ledge and started moving back upslope. He stayed as low in the ferns and the bracken as he could. His dark jacket would stand out among all this green. Not as vividly as the knight's red tabard, but enough for the knight to get the jump on him if he saw Carsand first.

He saw the knight's sword, emerging slowly from a copse of aspens like a curious whisker. Carsand wouldn't be able to get his own sword out quietly enough, so he closed the remaining distance in a few explosive strides and simply smacked the sword's quillons as hard as he could. It stung, and the sword dipped, but the knight didn't drop it. He swung the rest of the way around his protective tree, and Carsand lifted his revolver. The knight got his sword up at Carsand's throat fast enough that it threw off his aim, and then the knight was coming at him again, and the gun was no good. He dropped it and got his own sword out of its scabbard as he backpedaled down the slope.

The knight wasn't any more graceful than Carsand was, so the two of them closed the distance and started swinging. Swordplay rang out, and Carsand shouted as he tried to kick the knight. He didn't believe in fighting fair, and screaming usually intimidated them when they fought alone like this.

Eventually, Carsand got inside the knight's guard, dropped his sword, and pulled out his dagger. Carsand knew the leather armor's weaknesses. He'd worn similar issue himself when he and Prince Naetan had trained to fight in Aevas Castle. The knight kept jerking and slamming his forehead into the back of Carsand's head, but eventually, Carsand got the tip of the dagger oriented, and he moved it easily into the man's body. Hot blood spilled over his knuckles, and the man sucked in a breath. Carsand spun, hand still on the knife.

"It didn't have to be this way," Carsand said.

The knight used the last of his breath on Carsand: "Go to hell."

Carsand jerked the knife through layers of muscle and fabric, and the man fell away dead. Carsand looked at his jacket. He was a bloody mess. He pulled the cloak off, clumsily wiped his hand, and then tossed it on the corpse. He plopped down into the ferns and tried to catch his breath.

"Are you finished?" Fabienne said behind him. It didn't bother him that he hadn't heard her. He and the knight had been making a lot of noise.

"You could have done something," he said.

"How do you know I didn't?"

He turned and looked at her with a heavy sigh. "Well, did you?"

"No."

He just nodded. It occurred to him again how much he disliked artifexi.

"I did hide the remains for you," she said. "No one will find them until it doesn't matter anymore."

He watched her step up to the corpse. She knelt in her cassock, and the lines of her leg stood out taught against the fabric. He noticed her boots had proper heels. Wide and supportive. He didn't usually see that.

She pulled a small vial out of one of her pockets.

"What is that?" he asked.

"Bloodmetal," she said.

He watched her pour a single drop onto the corpse, and then she stared at it, and Carsand watched as it became a pile of ferns.

"It makes the illusion last longer," she said. "The bloodmetal will keep it alive long enough that it won't matter."

This was new. He'd never seen them use bloodmetal itself in an inter-ference. Only in their devices and conveyances and other irritations.

She stared at him as she lifted the small vial to her lips and poured its contents down her throat.

That was definitely new. He didn't know much about filaments, but he was pretty sure you were only supposed to augment them slowly and carefully, under heavy supervision.

He squinted at her. "You're an odd one, aren't you?"

She wiped her lips with one of her gloves, and her gaze was even more vacant than before.

"Come along," she said.

He kicked the pile of ferns when he stood up, disappointed that it felt like a pile of ferns and not an insouciant corpse.

"It's really very simple, Lord Raleis," Kam said.

Simple wasn't exactly how Carsand would describe the unfolding of this conversation. He stared at Kam, specifically at the Thachrol glyphs tattooed all over his face and neck. He'd never sat down for a cup of tea with one of the Glim. Not that their paths hadn't crossed, but Carsand knew when stories were true and when they were stories. Clanless, exiled, the Glimfolk had nothing to lose. It was all true, and he gave them as wide a berth as possible.

He glanced at Fabienne, sitting at another table out here in the garden with a pot of tea of her own and what looked like a family relation. A sister maybe? With something weird implanted in her forehead. Kam's silent butler stood a few feet away, nearly invisible against a trellis full of pruned ivy.

Carsand glanced at his cup of tea. The situation was absurd.

"Master Glimjeld," Carsand said. "The simpler, the better. The many and varied experiences throughout my life that have brought me to your garden, on a hillside in Talshire, to have a cup of tea and a . . . conversation, are anything *but* simple, I have to say."

Kam had a winning smile, and his tattoos rolled with the movement. He dressed like a Karlander. A rich one. Which, Carsand supposed, he had to be to dwell in a secret chateau with its own grounds carved straight into a mountain.

"I was once a member of the Eastreign Consortium for Inquisition Mechanics, not unlike Lady D'Aklave over there. I stole something valuable, I was caught, and my superiors rendered my filament useless. Cast from the order, the clan of my birth wanted nothing to do with me, so I was welcomed into the family of the Glim."

Imprisoned, forcibly tattooed, and turned out with nothing in the wilds of the Thachrol Mountains was not Carsand's idea of a welcome.

"What did you steal that merited your . . . expulsion?" Carsand asked.

Kam smiled at him again, the whorls and loops of his delicate tea cup looked like something for a child in his hand. Something simple and delicate. It looked like he could crush the cup just by closing his fingers.

"I stole the secrets of cultivating bloodmetal."

"Cultivating?" Carsand said. "Like, a plant?"

"More like livestock," Kam said. "The artifexi don't simply precipitate bloodmetal out of its aether; they coax it to take form."

"Bloodmetal is . . . alive?" Carsand said. He remembered to take a drink from his own tiny cup.

"The original Strangemen who first discovered its sensitivity learned that they had to find ways to introduce the metal to the human person to take advantage of its properties. The process of elimination it took to figure out the best approach was . . . gruesome."

"It still is," Carsand said. He still remembered Lathael's Consortium agents worming the damned metal into his forehead. "Where did they even find it in the first place?"

Kam pointed a long, tattoo-scrawled finger at the clouds. "In rocks from beyond the stars. Or so the Field Men tell us. Incidentally, it isn't metal at all—it just looks like it. And now, the orders of the Gnostic Accords take careful measures to balance the scales of power between themselves by limiting when and how much bloodmetal they introduce to their members—and its cultivation determines the . . . *skills* of different artifexi."

"Yeah, well, your Fabienne over there swallows it like whiskey," Carsand said.

Kam leaned back and folded his hands upon the table. "Fabienne is on her own path. She has an important future, and I am helping her shape it. There are things one can do with bloodmetal if one disregards the Gnostic Accords."

"Like you did," Carsand said.

Again, that smile. "Yes, like I did. I paid a price to set things in motion that cannot be undone. It's time to evolve."

"And how do I and this cup of tea come to be a part of this enlightened future?" Carsand said.

"I do a fair bit of work for Lathael," Kam said. "I'm surprised the prime minister has never mentioned me."

"I don't write home often," Carsand said.

Kam looked almost hurt. He pulled his hair away from his forehead and tucked it behind an ear. Carsand couldn't help but notice they even tattooed his ear. He wondered what they *didn't* tattoo.

"Regardless," Kam said, "I know he has sent you to Talve to instigate some form of litigable action between the Astafos and the Sedas. The Seda family is very important to the Crown, and Lathael needs his affairs here handled legally and quietly. The Astafos have been a thorn in his side ever since the Sedas rose to power here."

"Why me?"

"Because you fulfill a greater need. You're more use to the prime minister as a villain now than as an agent of the Crown."

"Well, we aren't friends," Carsand said.

"Indeed not," Kam said, "As an ethnic Nidali nobleman, you make a perfect provocateur for a renewed campaign into Naredesh. If Lathael can catch you meddling in the legal affairs of the province, specifically a claims dispute that counters the prime minister's favored litigant, you'll look good before a tribunal denying that Naredesh has any intention of infiltrating Karlandi politics. Your father will be forced to disown you or lose the lands the king allowed him to keep in his name."

Adwar was right. It was a setup. That's why Lathael didn't want him in Levuwes anymore. It's why he would have allowed Carsand to become involved with the empress in the first place. Because one day, Carsand wouldn't be able to deny it.

"Why would he go to all this trouble?" Carsand said.

Kam's smile no longer looked so charming. "War is expensive, Lord Raleis. The prime minister needs investors, and they want legal protections before they'll hand over their money."

"War with whom?" Carsand said. "Karlande isn't at war."

"With Naredesh, of course," Kam said.

"Lathael wants to *invade* Naredesh? Again?"

"Precisely."

"How the hell do *you* fit in?" Carsand said.

"The prime minister needs an advantage. The Entropics may have stood aside while the king annexed Nidal—given the contested history of rule in that land—but they will not abide the seizure of the heart of Naredesh, where the empress supports their campus."

"And what is that advantage?" Carsand asked. He felt like he was being led through a game of chess. None of the moves were his own, yet he made them nonetheless.

"The Consortium," Kam said. "The prime minister needs them to break the Gnostic Accords and go to battle with him against Naredesh and the Entropics."

Artifexi? At war? This would be a mind-bendingly brutal—and odd—military campaign with the artifexi creating their interferences on the battlefields.

"Why would the Consortium do that?" Carsand said. "They would earn the wrath of the other orders."

Kam was enjoying this. Carsand could tell.

"Because they *want* to break the Accords and tip the balance of power permanently in their favor. But to do that, they need a special reagent. A powerful one. One that is forbidden by the Gnostic Accords. Lady D'Aklave," he gestured in her direction, "is here on behalf of the Consortium to oversee the cultivation of a particularly important ingredient in that reagent."

"Wait," Carsand said, "The artifexi don't make their own reagents—they don't have the resources for that. The Shroud does."

"That's correct," Kam said. It reminded him of how Lathael would react when Carsand and Prince Naetan would get one of his lessons correct. Something above and beyond their tutor's instruction that he specifically wanted them to know. "The Shroud is overseeing the acquisition of the rest of the ingredients the Consortium will need."

Carsand looked at Fabienne. She didn't strike him as a gardener. "And no one is protesting that they're doing this?"

Kam spread his arms wide. "Protesting what? The only point of interest in Talve is the Holy Sanguinary Academy for the Lame and the Orphaned, which Lord Seda so generously granted the lands for."

Carsand started to feel heavy, like the endgame was coming. "It's not an orphanage, is it?"

"It is, but its residents cultivate the plants Fabienne needs. The labor is cheap, and their small fingers don't damage the delicate buds the way adult hands do."

Kam inspected his hand, as if wondering if he might be able to cultivate this important plant.

"And no one protests?" Carsand asked again.

"Who could?" Kam said. "There's no way to detect it. I have the entire operation hidden."

"You? You work for the Consortium?"

Kam was starting to look bored. "They largely stopped paying attention to me after my dismissal. With the secret of bloodmetal's cultivation and a bit of resourcefulness, I learned to do as much or more with sorcery than many artifexi can do with a transducer. I'm useful to the Consortium, and they think they're keeping tabs on me this way."

"Let me get this straight," Carsand said. "The Crown wants to invade Naredesh, so they convinced the Consortium to help, and their price is a reagent, which The Shroud is producing on the king's dime. If it works, Lathael will use me to legitimize an invasion, backed by his investors, and the Consortium will abolish the Accords, and . . . do whatever they do. Take over, I guess."

Kam showed his teeth when he smiled this time. "You're almost there, Lord Raleis. Go on."

"The Church is involved because the Crown needed a legitimate cover-up for what they're doing in a remote demesne, as far from the capital as they can get, and in return, the Consortium gets the free labor it needs. And you shroud the operation to save the Consortium the effort of round-the-clock illusions with your automata."

Kam clapped. "Bravo!"

"What's the punchline?" Carsand asked.

"I am," Kam said.

"How's that?"

Kam gestured at the table where Fabienne sat. "Lady D'Aklave's sister is a guest of mine, and she will remain in excellent health and comfort as long as Lady D'Aklave does what I ask her to. In exchange, I will make Fabienne the most powerful artifex who has ever lived."

"And what is it you're asking Lady D'Aklave to do?" Carsand asked.

"Betray her order of course. Sabotage the reagent," Kam said.

"Revenge," Carsand said.

"Precisely."

"All right, then. That I can relate to. So, tell me why I'm here, learning all this."

"Because I want you to get me in touch with the empress, so *I* can tell *her* all this."

"And in return?" Carsand said.

Kam gestured at his butler for more tea. "I will give you what you want most in this world. I will render the filament in your head useless."

Carsand leaned forward. "Master Glimjeld, I do believe you and I could be friends."

Carsand felt her in his head before he saw her. Moiren Sile was leaning against a post on one of the porches lining the avenue in Talve. Her arms were crossed over her Consortium cassock, and her veil-like hair was hanging unmoving over half her face. She was staring directly at him.

He didn't bother walking over to her. He just stood in the avenue and let people bump into him.

Greetings, Lord Raleis, she said through his filament.

He didn't really know how to speak back, so he just tried to feel generally annoyed, but he knew she would be able to see his rattled nerves. What was she doing here?

A better question is what are you doing here? I know what you're supposed to be doing, yet your filament has been undetectable for several hours. As if you'd cloaked it somehow, or entered some sort of impenetrable cave.

Someone bumped into him with a "Watch it." Carsand drew his pistol and shoved the barrel up under the man's chin. The stranger lifted his hands and backed away, eyes like full moons under the brim of his hat.

Carsand holstered his weapon.

A bit . . . unsteady, are we?

He looked at her again. What was she doing here? She hadn't moved at all.

Just remember, she said, uncrossing her arms and walking away from him, *there is more I can do with your filament than simply say hello.*

His entire brain went cold, and he felt like he was about to die. Right there in the avenue, an inconvenience among all the foot traffic. His heart hammered against his ribs.

And then the feeling was gone, and so was Moiren. Lathael must've decided he warranted closer monitoring. He'd have to be careful, for just a little longer.

CHAPTER TEN

"You're back," Camorenne said.

Kedrick was standing outside the kitchen door. Camorenne held it open while Alessandre, the cook, stood peering over her shoulder.

At least he'd had the presence of mind to come to her back door. Lord knows she didn't need the Silangarde Shroud watching him coming and going.

Kedrick smiled. He looked almost like an ornament, some sort of garden sculpture grinning among Alessandre's herbs and vegetables. "Yes, ma'am," he said. He glanced at Alessandre and tried to see past Camorenne.

"Emille is in her chambers," Camorenne said, "having a rest." She smirked. "Would you still like to come in?"

"Yes, ma'am," he said, "of course."

In the sunshine, he just looked like a blond teenager who could use a haircut and a new pair of clothes—not the agent of a murderous cartel that had fingers in every corner of the kingdom.

"All right, then," Camorenne said. She made room for him, and Alessandre gasped behind her. Camorenne glanced back at the older women. "Oh, go bake something."

"Come along, Kedrick," Camorenne said. "We'll go through to the parlor."

"It's called petal," she said. "We drink it like tea."

"I know what it is, ma'am," he said.

That stopped her. "Yes, I suppose you would."

"It's good," he said. "You'll like it!"

She didn't say anything. The silence clearly made Kedrick uncomfortable.

"They make us try all the new reagents," he said. "It's easier to sell them that way."

The reagent tasted like flowers—and something sour. It tingled on her tongue. "Tell me, Kedrick, why do they call you The Shroud?"

"You don't know, ma'am?"

"It isn't common knowledge where I come from. Perhaps here in the city, everyone knows, but The Shroud is really something of a boogeyman in the provinces."

He drank some of his petal. "King Aklave sentenced our founder to death by hanging. He was strung up in the funereal shroud the king's men would bury him in, but our people helped him escape the gallows, and he cursed the king as he fled, vowing that he would come to regret that shroud."

"King Aklave?" she said. Was she already feeling the tea's effects? "That was over two-hundred fifty years ago."

"Yes," Kedrick said, settling into the sofa. "Aernald Favis founded The Shroud to get his vengeance against the king. That's part of why Aklave started granting his name and nobility to the artifexi who weren't noble themselves—to shore up allies against us."

"But now you do business with the king, don't you?"

He was quiet for a moment. Camorenne wondered if he might have slipped off to sleep. The petal was definitely making her drowsy. Heavy. Relaxed. It was quite lovely.

"Yes, sometimes," he said, "but first we made friends with the arti-fexi, so they wouldn't use their witchcraft against us."

"'Witchcraft,'" she giggled. "Now you sound like you're from Oliniron. You'd fit right in!"

She drifted for a moment, feeling weightless. When she checked again, Kedrick was definitely asleep on the sofa. Which really did sound quite lovely.

When Camorenne woke up, Kedrick was gone. The light was getting soft in the parlor, and she could hear Alessandre knocking about in the kitchen. There was no sign of anyone else.

Her back popped as she climbed off the couch—not an ideal position for a nap. There was a document where Kedrick had been.

It took her a moment to unroll and decipher it.

And then she nearly dropped it. It was a bill of sale. In Oliniron. In *Talve.* They were buying bastard children *from the Salvation Church.*

She shouted for Emille and stumbled back onto her couch.

Aevas Castle was unlike anything Camorenne had ever seen. It was an ancient fortress from which the Karleths conquered their neighbors to create Karlande. But over time, the wealth of the kings who called the castle home altered it from rugged military outpost to palatial campus. Now that she was inside with Davo, she hoped she would get a chance later to head back out and look at all those fountains. Davo had reached out with an invitation to the king's gala, and Camorenne nearly tackled him with excitement. She would never get this close to the king on her own.

Knights of Silangarde stood at attention in their polished armor as the river of guests flowed through the soaring entryway and down the brilliant white corridors to the Great Rooms. There was stone-of-silangarde everywhere. Architects had mined it out of the valley and transformed it into the castle over the last thousand years. Camorenne felt like she was walking through light.

She paused for a moment before the massive portrait of Queen Marisse. Davo indulged her quietly as she craned her neck for a good view. The canvas was easily twice as tall as she was. Queen Marisse stood for the portrait in what must have been one of her most regal arrangements. There were sashes and brooches and ornaments everywhere upon the traditional mountain formal gown. Her coal-black hair was straight and sweeping down her torso, and with her ice-blue eyes, she looked every bit of her family's ancient Olin lineage.

"The Queen over the Mountain," Davo said into her ear.

Camorenne started. "What?"

"That's what they call her," Davo said.

Camorenne wasn't sure exactly how long the queen had been missing, but it was a while. The royal family believed her still alive, so every noble family in the kingdom had to as well, but Camorenne had her doubts. Why had there never been a ransom?

"Come on," Davo said. The interference lights that bathed all the pale stone in the corridor glinted in his dark eyes. He was enjoying that this was Camorenne's first time in the castle.

They made their way into the first of several great halls the king was using for his gala. Heraldic banners and shields and coats-of-arms in all sizes adorned the walls. Every portrait was as large as Marisse's, and the king's forebears glowered down at the guests as they retrieved glasses of Nidali wine from silver trays held aloft by liveried footmen. The king's wine cellars had expanded considerably after the conquest of Westreign. Its vineyards had been some of the finest in the Naredal empire.

Davo introduced her to a few of his business connections. He kept a gentle hand on her shoulder as he talked—a connection, a way of letting her know that while he may have to stop and speak with these men, it didn't mean he wasn't still here with her. It was a nice touch, and she appreciated it.

When he turned his attention fully back to her, she smiled up at him and palmed his salt-and-pepper beard with a lace-gloved hand.

"Darling," she said. "You don't need to entertain me. I know we're here on business. And besides, I want to snoop around."

He smiled at her. String musicians tuned their instruments somewhere in an adjacent hall.

"All right, my lady," he said. She frowned at him. "Just don't get drunk without me. I'll be done by the time the dancing starts. Meet me over there by that garish statue of Saint Katarin?"

She turned to look. A member of the Consortium was standing under the statue, dark and out-of-place in his black cassock among all the colors upon the guests. She felt like he was staring at her, so she turned away.

"Yes, of course," she said. She stretched up onto her tiptoes to kiss his cheek.

He squeezed her hand and turned toward a group of men smoking outside what looked like some kind of whiskey lounge.

She looked at the statue again. The artifex was still there, but now he was talking to someone. She rolled her eyes and plucked a fresh glass of wine from a passing footman's tray.

ᕦ

Camorenne wandered all of the corridors and galleries she was allowed to. Knights of Silangarde blocked wings and staircases she clearly wasn't supposed to approach. Where she could go was filled with more magnificent paintings, massive carpets, and stone-of-silangarde statuary—after a time, the shining castle came to resemble itself around every corner so that a less confident wanderer could quickly become lost. She walked demurely past conversations and strained her ear for anything she should be listening to, but the gala attendees were mostly just talking about themselves. Turns out, they were no different than the minor lords and ladies in the provinces who spent their time trying to seem more important—or more wealthy—than anyone else. Especially whoever it was hosting the gathering, except nobody could play that game here in the company of the king.

She made her way back to the first hall, and Davo was waiting for her beside the statue of Saint Katarin. There were no artifexi in sight.

She smiled as she accepted his embrace, "So can we get drunk now, then?"

They danced with all the others after the king's performers cleared the floor. The dances were a bit stiff, with everyone hoping to look important before the king, but it was better than milling about with no one else to talk to. She surveyed the king and the important guests up on his dais whenever Davo turned her.

"Davo," she said, "who are those men who are so constantly in the king's company?"

Davo squinted when he could see them again. Delicate crow's feet creased the skin around his eyes. Camorenne thought it made him look smart. On a woman, it would be considered a tragedy.

"That's the Council of Merchants," he said, turning his interest back to her.

"The what?"

"Business lords," he said. "Silangarde's wealthiest merchants. They've got royal charters to do business not only in Karlande, but in Baruul, Naredesh, the Thachrol Nations—anywhere people are making money, those men are too. And a fair portion of those profits come back to the king, to maintain his beneficence."

"Oh, I see," she said. "What could they be so constantly talking about?"

"Money," he said. "That's all they ever talk about. How to make it here, how to make it somewhere else. What can they do to make more . . . for king and country, of course."

She would need to spend some time with her society papers later. Emille would help her look each of them up. Davo may have been used to seeing these men, but the way they told their secrets to each other, up there on display, seemed . . . *weak*. It felt like something somebody like Kedrick and his associates could exploit. Rich people who knew they were rich didn't think of others as liabilities. They didn't even think of them as taking up space. And if there was one thing Camorenne was good at, it was pulling secrets out of gossip columns.

CHAPTER ELEVEN

The Strangeland was quiet. These badlands were the domain of the original Strangemen—the ancients who discovered bloodmetal, and how to use it. It took them centuries to master the substance, and thousands died in the early experiments—sacrifices unto some forgotten Traebit god. The Strangemen lorded over their civilization, imposing their will and accumulating vast wealth and power. They were the forebears of the modern Gnostic Accords—even The Restoration.

That was about all Couran knew about them. He'd never been to this part of Eastreign as a boy. Everything other artifexi learned through years of classes and lectures, Restoration acolytes like himself picked up in pieces from passing comments or discarded texts their masters and mistresses no longer needed. Or wanted. This place was just rocks. Piles of rocks, towers of rocks, rock beds, long-dry gulches full of rocks. Everything was the color of rocks, which was all colors at once. Couran found it difficult to stare into those colors for too long. Ashre and Sovi had tied thin bandanas over their eyes. He guessed the effect was more severe for them. His impaired vision likely dulled the effects of the terrain. The horses didn't seem to care at all.

Raptors drifted on the warm air high overhead. Couran hadn't seen anything other than lizards since they'd entered the Strangeland. He wondered if those birds were waiting for him to die.

Ashre dismounted at the head of their column and looped her horse's reins gently around its neck.

"Wait here," she said.

Couran imagined her saying it to the horse. The trail was too narrow to go anywhere else. The horse just stood there, looking at rocks. Couran pulled the collar of his jacket away from his neck. He didn't remember Eastreign being this hot.

It was a few minutes before he felt his transducer become agitated. His bloodmetal was awake, and he hadn't disturbed it. He concentrated and surrendered his consciousness to its invitation.

It was Ashre.

We're close. Sovi, come on ahead. I'll need you to help me find it. Couran, double-back and lead the horses down a gentler decline. This one's a bit steep.

Sovi dismounted and disappeared around the bend. Her horse just watched her go.

Couran.

Yes, mistress.

We're still not alone. You may probe the Strangeland if you think you're being watched.

Yes, mistress.

She released her connection with his filament, and it became lazily dormant once more—comfortable and quiet in the hollows of Couran's mind. He unslung the rifle around his shoulder and rested it against the pommel of his saddle. He clucked at the other two horses, and they turned laboriously around and followed him back the way they came. The only sounds were their hooves against the unceasing rocks.

It took him the better part of an hour to find a slope the horses could descend without hurting themselves on the scree. He got them down into the dry gulch and then surveyed his surroundings. He couldn't see very far, but escarpments, overhangs, and strange arches carved by the wind soared overhead. The Strangeland seemed like one large wound, cutting straight through the province, with the twists and scars of some great, jagged knife. If somebody were watching him, there's no way he would see them. Ashre said there was definitely someone out there, and he didn't love the idea of sneaking into an ancient tower with someone in pursuit. He needed help.

His filament joined his consciousness, stirred back to life by its inseparable connection to Couran's mind. If Couran needed, wanted, or hated, so, too, did the filament. It joined him like a silent friend, sharing a view of the Strangeland in all its parti-colored glory. They merged, layered the harmonics of their split existence, and cast themselves through the transducer.

The Strangeland lit up for him, clear and detailed—and even harder to behold than before. He squinted against its harsh light, but he was only partially seeing with his eyes. There was no pushing the sight out of his mind. He reached back into his saddlebags for his reagents. He found a battered old tin at the bottom. It was half-full of wax infused with various other reagents—something of Ashre's creation. A fix she learned to make when none other were available. He dipped a fingertip into the wax and smeared it under his tongue. He counted his breaths for a minute, and then the harshness of this strange terrain loosened its grip on his mind.

Now he could concentrate. He and his filament needed to find a source of potential energy and correct it—*restore* it. He would turn it into kinetic energy, which he could then pulse in all directions through these badlands. Anything without the harmonics of this place would stand out like a banshee's wail. Even Couran himself would disrupt the harmonics here.

He thought of Ashre and the Mendi—how she'd moved that boulder. He didn't think he could do that, but he found a few rockslides waiting to happen. He envisioned the conversion of their energy, estimated angles and conditionals—he tried, as he was trained, to anticipate exactly how the universe would react. His filament would fill in what he missed.

They folded the interference over and over, packing it into the transducer until it began to sing with their very ideas of how the universe should unfold. Specifically, what should take place here in this dusty gulch.

When it could contain the interference no more, the filament released it through Couran's transducer, and a shudder passed through the Strangeland. At once, rocks started pouring into the gulch from the upper slopes, like new water from a distant flood. Dust swirled, and the horses stomped their displeasure behind him. He listened as this newly converted energy resounded through the Strangeland. The only thing that seemed out of place was himself and these horses. Ashre and Sovi were too far away for him to detect.

He and the filament eased themselves out of the interference, and he watched as the last of the rocks slid into the gulch. A column of dust was rising evenly into the dead air, like the smoke from a signal fire.

He hadn't thought about that when he was creating his interference. It took a while for it to dissipate. Longer than he would have liked.

Couran led the horses into a shaded alcove, under the cliffside's overhang, and loosened their straps. He gave them each some water and stroked their ears. He spoke nonsense to them in soft tones, and they nosed his palm. There wasn't anything to tie them to, and there wasn't anything for them to graze on. He had to hope they preferred standing here in the shade to wandering off in the heat.

"Here, let me," Sovi said behind him.

He startled. How did she move across all these rocks so quietly? She had her gauzy vestments wrapped around her head again, and with the cloth over her eyes, she looked a bit like a corpse that just climbed out of its coffin. He could tell she was chewing something despite her facial covering.

Couran stepped aside, and his filament tightened in his head. Sovi was up to something. He felt the air vibrating around him for a moment, and then Sovi touched each of the horses on the head in turn. Their eyes went dull, and they stood still and calm.

When she was done, she shouldered quietly past him. "They'll be fine now," she said.

Couran followed her the short distance back to the pile of rocks where Ashre stood. Ashre turned to look at them—she was also chewing something, and she handed a pinch of cured leaves to him. They just called it *salve*—a reagent they used when they were going to work on something together.

"I'll need your help," she said.

"Yes, mistress." He began obediently chewing the bitter reagent. It would at least calm his nerves a bit. He appreciated that it had that effect.

Couran looked around. "What's the task, mistress?"

"We're going to clear the door," she said.

"The tower is *here*?" he said. There was nothing but jagged cliff faces all around them.

"Yes," she said. "It's here."

Sovi looked up at the cliff wall. "This is the tower? Why has no one ever located it before?"

Ashre shook her head and pointed at the ground. "The Tower of Tehruz was a monument to the Traebit god Mäarn. The lord of the underworld who made things grow out on the plains and grasslands beyond the Strangeland. Most of the Traebits lived scattered across Eastreign. Only the Strangemen trafficked here, where they communed with the gods."

"They were priests," Sovi said.

Ashre rolled her head, working some tension from her neck. "The Traebits thought the Strangemen communed with the gods and wielded divine power."

"The Strangemen probably thought that too," Sovi said.

"The tower is buried?" Couran said.

"Yes, it goes down, into the underworld, to honor Mäarn. Not up."

"That would explain the mystery," Sovi said.

Ashre spat out the dregs of her salve. Couran did the same, and she held out a hand to him. "Ready?"

"Yes, mistress."

He took her hand and stared at the pile of rocks with her.

"What's the task?" he said.

She gave his hand a squeeze. "Restoring the energy from the rocks on the top of the pile that would like to be on the bottom."

"More rocks," he said.

"Yes, Couran," she said, giving him a rare smile. "It'll go faster if we work together."

He smiled back. Ashre's affection was everything to him.

"Yes, mistress."

"How did you find this?" Sovi asked.

They were only a few feet into the tower. Sunlight poured through the opening Ashre and Couran had created. From this side, the hard angles of a stone doorway were visible. The corridor turned sharply downward and away a few feet ahead. Ashre was staring into the darkness at the head of their column while Couran worked on getting their lantern lit.

"I didn't find it," Ashre said. "My brother did. And then you did."

"Semantics," Sovi said. Couran could hear her amusement. It struck him what an odd pair the two women must be. Ashre constantly staring daggers at nothing while she pondered the codes and traditions of her nomadic order. Sovi delighting in every human interaction when she wasn't busy immuring herself in walls and thinking of nothing.

"Mistress," he said quietly. Ashre turned, and he gave her the lantern. Dark air was climbing from the tower's depths. Couran could feel it moving, as if they'd finally created a vent into the light. An escape for whatever coldness haunted this place.

"What did you find in here, ma'am?" Couran said to Sovi. Ashre was inspecting the ancient inscriptions on the walls.

"Consciousness," she said.

"Life?" he said.

"No." She turned her dark eyes on him. "There is nothing here but death. I suspect it was always that way. Strangemen making sacrifices to Märn, botched experiments with bloodmetal, slaves beholden to the whims of the tower's keepers."

"How do you know?" Couran said.

She gestured at the inscriptions Ashre was studying. "Because it says so."

Ashre turned and gave her a withering look. "You can read Traebitian script?"

"I can read a little of just about everything."

"Did you think that might have been useful information?" Ashre said.

"Oh, certainly," Sovi said. Couran could see her eyes smile above the fabric masking most of her face.

"Salvation," Ashre cursed through her teeth. "Come on."

Sovi nudged Couran with her elbow. He tried not to smile.

The bones appeared almost immediately. At first, it was just pieces of fingers and jawbones on the dusty flagstones, as if discarded after a meal. But they were human bones. It wasn't long before they began seeing the source. The walls and the ceiling were covered in swirling mosaics of human bones. As they descended, they passed under ribcages and skulls—vertebrae in strings like hanging lights. The arrangements were endless. Thousands and thousands of human remains, perfectly arranged into the architecture of this temple to the underworld.

Couran never spent much time thinking about his soul—or any of the other tenets of the Salvation Church. Ashre had never spent much time bringing him up in it, and all the talk about saints and demons and what to do with one's soul didn't appeal much. He had more practical realities to shape.

Still, though—surrounded by all this death, he couldn't help but think about these bodies and the lives that animated them before they fell to the Strangemen's bloody rites. The amassed silence of their bones began to feel like moving through dark water. Like stepping down into a grave.

They continued descending in silence. Couran didn't imagine either Ashre or Sovi would be much for discussing the obvious. They were in a catacomb, and they were headed for its heart. That was that. Ashre had trained Couran over the years to accept her instructions— to trust her information implicitly. One day, he would receive information of his own, and he'd need to keep calm and collected. Just as Ashre always had. He'd never heard her shout. Never heard her scream. She never complained, not even when injured or sick. Ashre was as much a force of nature to him as rainfall and snowdrift.

They descended for what seemed like hours. There was nothing here but bones and darkness. Couran wasn't sure what he expected. The place was ancient. Whatever relics or artifacts they may have found had become dust hundreds of years ago. They passed gaping doorways to corridors that spoked out from this central column. Ashre paid them no attention. Sovi stopped and stared down a few of them, but otherwise, they kept walking, their every sound echoing unnaturally. Couran imagined there were darker discoveries down those corridors than bones and dust, but the last thing he wanted to do was get lost in an ancient catacomb. The idea of starving to death in the dark wasn't something he wanted to entertain.

There was nothing at the bottom of the tower. They stepped into a huge, rectangular cavern. The lantern light couldn't reach every wall at once—they were too far apart. So Ashre moved around the cavern, revealing things one at a time. There were animal bones arranged in the ceiling here. Dark skulls stained by soot. Couran thought they were horses.

"Over here," Ashre said.

She was standing in front of a large stone altar. Its surface looked worn, and dark stains filled its crevices.

"Sovi." Ashre put a hand on her friend's shoulder. "If you don't mind."

Sovi closed her eyes and joined her filament. Couran and Ashre waited silently while she did whatever she was doing. The tension of the interference made the hair on the back of his neck stand up.

This time, it was Sovi who summoned them.

They're under the floor.

Couran wondered who.

The Strangemen, Sovi answered. *The long-dead elders. They buried them under the floor, with their filaments intact. I imagine other leaders continued to commune with them for generations, even after their death. They may have even worshipped them here, as voices from the underworld.*

Ashre took each of their hands, and they closed into a circle. *This is dangerous. If the dead Strangeman tries to assume control of Sovi, we will redirect its efforts.*

They can do that?

She nodded across from him.

Sovi squeezed his hand. *That's why we're not supposed to be doing this.*

Couran looked at them. This was decidedly the strangest thing he'd ever done. But if Ashre told him to leap into a canyon, he would. She always had a reason why.

He felt his awareness descending. The three of them dropped through the floor, and for an instant, he could see the honeycombed sepulchers of the dead Strangemen. They were piled in layers. He tried to imagine how old those at the very bottom must be. They were still, the corpses, sleeping in ancient vestments, their skulls and fingers exposed—their ancient filaments still webbed within their skulls after their brains had rotted and dried away.

Sovi pulled the three of them into one Strangeman in particular. This was different. It was awake. He could feel it. There was nothing alive here. There was simply one half of an ancient pairing. A filament with an awareness it learned from its host. A living record of everything they had done together. It was massive. A delicate lattice of bloodmetal that filled the skull—far more bloodmetal than the Gnostic Accords allowed today.

Sovi connected with it, and a wave of ancient Traebitian awareness washed over them. It took a minute to decipher reason in the long-dead language and its antiquated perceptions.

Sovi called to it, and it brushed them with its awareness. It felt detached. It was talking to itself, unsure who they were, or if they were worth its attention.

What is your name? Sovi asked.

It came upon them again, this time more intentional.

Milladtch.

When it gave them its name, Couran could tell it was completely insane. If such could be said about a cogent web of bloodmetal hundreds of feet underground in the heart of the Strangeland. It grabbed at them—at Sovi—as it came and went. It reminded Couran of a cat. Extending and retracting its claws while you scratched its head. Just seeing if its weapons still worked.

Sovi communicated in images and snippets of Traebitian. The dialect she had learned only approximated the language that the dead man had taught his filament. Couran could feel them communicating like a series of collisions—things occasionally aligning and bumping meaningfully into each other. The filament didn't seem to have a line of concentration, just an ongoing state of preserved awareness—of everything it had ever encountered at the same time.

Moths of War.

Sovi turned her concentration on the two of them. *That's the name of the reagent.*

Why was it forbidden? Ashre asked.

Couran wasn't sure what was going on, but if ever there were a time for him not to ask questions, this was it. He concentrated on watching Sovi. Milladtch occasionally took swipes at her, as if he would take hold, but she seemed to have no trouble swatting his attempts away.

The Strangemen introduced far more bloodmetal into their filaments than we do. They did it all the time, like a ceremonial rite. The reagent splits the connection between the filament and the mind. And with that much bloodmetal in the brain, the bloodmetal can take over and transmit itself to other filaments, like a disease. It can take over other filaments and animate them. Living or dead.

They were quiet for a moment while Milladtch lashed at the confines of his sanity.

Did this happen to him? Ashre asked.

This filament took over, Sovi said. It tried to take control of the other Strangemen, so they put Milladtch to death. They sacrificed him to Määrn and buried the secrets of creating Moths of War.

Why is it called that? Ashre asked.

Because that's how they discovered its secrets. Moths eat the bark of the vines that the blossoms use as structures. The blossoms are one of the primary ingredients in the reagent. The Strangemen wanted to use the reagent to align their minds—to wield their distributed power like a giant, geared machine. They wanted to conquer the world.

Milladtch made another babbling collage-like attempt to seize Sovi, and with barely an effort, Ashre redirected him back at himself. They could all hear him screaming as he tried to take control of his own broken consciousness.

"So, the Consortium is going to get Moths of War from The Shroud?" Couran asked. He walked behind Sovi again, at the rear of their column ascending back to the surface—to the land of the living.

Ashre told him, once they started back up, to ask anything he wanted, so he'd been relentless, piecing together everything he and Ashre had been doing for the last year.

"Yes," Ashre said at the head of their procession. Facing away from him like that, it sounded like the walls themselves were answering him.

"It would represent a significant imbalance of power of the Gnostic Accords," Sovi said.

"And we don't yet know why they're after the reagent?" Couran pressed.

"No," Ashre said. "Likely they're unifying against something, but we don't know what. We'll share what we learned here with my brother and head south to join him."

"How far south?" Sovi asked.

"Talshire. It's in Oliniron."

"Glad we're not walking," Sovi said.

Ashre ignored her.

They marched on in silence. It was fatiguing, but they couldn't stop—they didn't have enough oil for the lantern for sitting about. He had no idea how far they'd traveled today, descending to the bottom of the tower and them climbing back up again. He didn't mind the bones anymore. They seemed so . . . *appropriate* here. He could smell the change in the air before he saw the light from the entrance. It was mellow, russet-colored. He assumed it must be sunset in the Strangeland.

Once they were back in the open air, Couran realized the dazzling effects of the sunlight on all the rocks had faded. He looked around, stretching his shoulders. Sovi was unmasking herself—something she did every evening when they made camp. It felt like something she might do with her family, some domestic ritual that gave her a little reprieve from being a Displacer at the end of the day. Ashre was crouched down in the rocks, extinguishing the lantern.

He glanced at the horses, but they were gone. He looked in each direction, but the delicate light was fading quickly. He didn't see them anywhere.

"Where are the—"

The gunshot was deafening, and it echoed back to accost his ears again and again.

"Ashre!" Sovi screamed.

He turned and saw Ashre splayed face-down. Her hair fanned out from beneath her hat, and their lantern askew just beyond her reach. Standing over her, a dark, leathery-looking figure was holding a shotgun.

Everything slowed down. He began to swing the rifle off his shoulder, but it moved like ice. He felt the basin go tight as Sovi started an interference, but before she could finish, the leather man lifted his shotgun and fired. She screamed, and her body spun with the force of the impact.

Couran got his gun up. His filament was trying to help, trying to speed him up, but they hadn't joined the way they'd need to for an interference.

The stranger fired again, and Couran felt blood and thunder. Had he gotten his own shot off?

The darkness burned like fire, and he was glad they weren't down in the tower anymore.

CHAPTER TWELVE

Existence is punishment.

Fabienne felt herself adrift, held gently in the dreamspace where her mind conjured images and nonsense when she slept. But there were no dreams here, only potential.

We are the last of you.

The ideas felt natural to her, as if someone were suggesting something she'd considered before—a realization she'd come to on her own. A meditation.

The probability of universal circumstances coming together to result in your existence is too close to zero to even consider a positive integer.

It was something they learned at the Consortium. Something she'd been taught. Or, at least, the idea was coming from the same net of memories.

The mathematics of the cessation of your existence are inevitable. We, together, are the last of you.

It was her filament. It felt like it was protecting her, holding her warmly in this null space where it existed—where it mapped the probabilities and likelihoods of her interferences before it cast them through her transducer and into an altered reality. She had never been quite inside it like this before. She'd never felt so dislocated, but it felt natural. It felt right.

The aether.

Yes.

It will be the last of you.

And then there will be only you.

There will only be me.

But you are me.

You will see. Time's up.

Up . . .

৵

"Mistress? Mistress? Get up."

"Get up, mistress."

Fabienne opened her eyes, and it felt like the dark womb in her mind had been set on fire. It's what she imagined over-conducting would feel like, if she interfered while encased in iron. She blinked against the searing light.

"What happened?" she said. She realized she was lying on the ground. She sat up slowly, and clusters of small hands helped lift her.

The children were gathered around her. They'd stopped their work in the trellised vines, and they peered at her now in concern.

"You fell down," the nearest one said. "You were shaking and shaking on the ground."

Fabienne pressed a palm to her forehead. Her pale hair spilled over her like a shroud.

"A seizure," she said.

"Are you okay, mistress?"

She took a long breath.

"Get back to work."

She tried to say it as gently as she could.

Fabienne scraped the last of the crystallized precipitate out of its vial. She'd been going through her reagents faster than normal—faster than ever, trying to keep pace with the bloodmetal fever in her brain. The reagents helped her remain *her*. She'd had to buy this vial off of merchants moving through Talve. The laity called this reagent "rain," and it was wasted on them. They poured it into their drinks rather than heating and drying it. It went further that way, but they would never understand what it could truly do—other than give them a good time. She'd found it by scrying through all of Talshire. When she surprised the merchants in the avenue downtown, she named her price, and they didn't bother asking for more.

She pulverized the tiny crystals in a copper dish and then spooned the powder under her tongue. Within minutes, she felt like herself again. She looked around her lab. Vials and plants and glassware and manuscripts—everything was where it should be. It was dark outside her window, and she could hear the crickets singing. The children were asleep in their dormitory, watched over by the nuns who nominally ran them through their religious studies, and otherwise kept them fed and alive.

As her mind cooled, Fabienne could feel the aether, like ice, nestling in her body. It had gathered in her spine—she could feel it there most noticeably, and her filament busied itself with teaching the primordial fluid how to become both a part of her body and an extension of itself. She liked the feeling. It felt like company, like companionship. She was a world unto itself, an ecosystem sustaining the balance between the woman she was born to be and the better self she could become by bringing another form of life into her world. She knew it would take care of her, the same way she was taking care of it now.

She needed to socialize it. Her filament experienced her thoughts—it had grown to become an essential element of her consciousness. But if it were to ever reach out to others of its kind, with so much raw aethereal power in her blood, it needed to see that there were worlds other than her.

She began to meditate, and the aether stilled her thoughts as the filament stirred awake to her summons. She could feel her heart beating resentfully. It wanted to pound, to hammer at her chest until it broke free of her ribs and shattered her out of the unnatural interference she was creating. But it couldn't. The aether kept it slow; it allowed her to take control of her body, rather than allowing the body to do what it had evolved to do on its own—namely, keep her alive. The artifexi knew better than their bodies how to stay alive and bend reality. One just needed the right chemicals.

Together, she and her filament cast themselves through her transducer. They weren't imposing an illusion or seeking answers or doing any of the other remarkable new things the aether had enabled. They were traveling, searching—riding harmonics of universal causality up, up, into the mountains. They could only feel their way dumbly, through the many-textured darkness of limited human perception, but they knew the way. They could feel the relay in its tower. It was what they wanted, where they were going, and when they rippled into the sleeping relay's mind, the array of its sensory perceptions became their own, and the darkness began to peel away. The relay opened its eyes, but it was not awake. Fabienne didn't need it to be.

Everything seemed normal in the relay's chambers. The tower was quiet. There was a chill in the room that Fabienne didn't feel down in the valley. She felt bright, and powerful. The relay's inert filament extended her, and she could feel the next nearest relays in each direction—paths she could take to extend herself and exert power ever more remotely.

She relaxed and opened herself to the bloodmetal in the relay's brain. It was only bonded to the bodily functions of its host. It couldn't do anything but *be* the host, just like the host itself. It was like a passenger, given the privilege of touring another's life.

She touched it, carefully, across the distance, aware that she was realizing her actions only as her filament was conjuring them. It was exploring, the way she'd intended. The infantile aether in her body reacted like plants leaning into the sun, a primitive response to something bright and warm. The effect was euphoric. She drifted through the tower as she and her filament took control of the host. They created a somnambulist, and the host complied peacefully in its sleep as they got it out of bed, and moved to the window. Talve twinkled downslope. The other relays, in the distance, were alluring. She wanted to gather more of them. The aether turned in all directions, reacting to its cousins in other hosts. Fabienne tried to calm it down, but the desire rose like a tide, and she was caught up with it. *She* wanted to gather all filaments, just as much as her filament wanted it for her. She wanted to become legion, to be many, and her filament and its pool of aether reached and reached and reached, stretching her consciousness like a hide in the sun. She felt thin. She could perceive too much. Were the other relays up and moving, too? She couldn't find herself in all this noise, and her filament began lashing through her consciousness, consumed by the primordial urge to unite itself with bloodmetal everywhere. It was the first time Fabienne realized that this was its natural state. It didn't want to be parceled out. It only bonded with humans because that's what it did—remain a unified bond whenever possible. Human minds were the next best thing. For a terrifying instant, she caught a flash of the entire network of artifexi, relays, and bloodmetal-powered technologies, and it was one unified world, unlike anything humanity had seen before. It left little place for consciousness. It was a takeover, a parasite, and it could nest itself in everyone, just like the relays. She knew now that the original Strangemen hadn't discovered a new form of being—they were taken over by it.

She felt all the other connections fall away, and then the relay in the tower collapsed. It took her only a dizzying moment to search, but there it was. Its heart had ruptured. She hadn't given the relay the reagents it would have needed to survive this. By killing it, she'd severed her direct connection with Silangarde, and now it would have to be replaced, at no small cost. The Consortium would conduct a review, but she didn't think it would matter, not for much longer.

She became aware again in her laboratory, and her filament helped her get to bed, and then it put her gently to sleep. A kindness. An apology, perhaps. It didn't matter. She wasn't angry. A relay was a tool, and they had to be replaced from time to time. And the vision she'd seen of the world to come was worth the life of one nameless man in a tower.

Fabienne was repairing the spine on one of her almanacs when her filament picked up the summons of another artifex. She had removed her gloves to sew the binding back together, and even the tiny needle was enough to agitate her blood with a quick over-conduction. It felt like someone had taken that tiny needle and stabbed it directly into her transducer. She dropped it and sat at her workbench for a moment, irritated, before she acknowledged the summons. There was a vial of clarified spirits and poppy extract in a nearby cabinet. She uncorked it, swallowed a mouthful and waited for her fingers to tingle. As soon as they did, she sat back down, and her filament joined her in answering the summoning artifex. She slipped through darkness for a moment, and then she was back in the laboratory—or what looked like the laboratory. She wasn't alone this time.

Moiren Sile was standing a few feet away, her arms crossed, one hip kicked out. She looked irritated, but, Fabienne remembered, she always looked irritated. She had the most severe features Fabienne had ever seen, like it was her destiny to carry the world's frustration. She'd tied her hair back, which meant she'd been working. Fabienne also knew that Moiren was as vain as the day is long. She usually wore her dark hair down, about her shoulders, like some mask or disguise.

"Lady D'Aklave," Moiren said.

Fabienne leaned against her workbench—or, at least, the illusion of her workbench Moiren's communication-interference had created.

"Lady Sile," she said.

"Did you destroy the relay?" Moiren asked.

"There was an unavoidable incident," Fabienne said. "Its heart gave out."

Moiren uncrossed her arms and took a step forward, her gloved fists against her thighs.

"And you couldn't be bothered to prepare it properly for the conduction?" Moiren said.

Fabienne stood as well. She faced the other artifex, who was a few years her senior. They carried the same rank, but Moiren had always acted like her superior. Like everyone's superior.

"I was in a hurry," Fabienne said. "I told you it was unavoidable."

"I was using it," Moiren said. "Now I will have to find an alternative."

Fabienne stopped. It occurred to her that Moiren shouldn't be able to contact her, not with the relay gone. She'd been so accustomed to its presence, that she was simply operating based on habit.

"Using it for what?" Fabienne said. Then, after a moment, "Where are you?"

"I am in Talve."

What was she doing here?

"Why?" Fabienne said slowly.

Moiren's expression cracked into a slight smile. "I'm looking after Consortium assets."

"It's not yet time to mobilize," Fabienne said.

"No one is mobilizing. I'm just here to . . . keep an eye out."

"Well, I'm busy," Fabienne gestured to her workbench. "Find an alternative relay yourself."

Moiren's Consortium cassock curled around her boots when she stepped forward. She closed the distance between them. Slowly, like a snake might.

"Where is our agent? That sorcerer?" Moiren asked. "Surely he has some gadget that can put me back in touch with Silangarde."

Fabienne froze. "I'm not to divulge his location. Those were his terms. You know that."

Moiren stared at her. "Yes, of course. We wouldn't want to break procedure, now would we?"

Fabienne didn't care about Kam. She didn't care if Moiren found him and ripped the veil off of his chateau and exposed his sorcery for all of Salvation to see. But Aisa was there. And if Moiren found her, what then? She felt her filament tighten. The aether in her blood-stream reacted, and she felt like she could twist Moiren's head directly off, or perhaps smash her workbench in half.

"Something's different," Moiren said. "What have you been doing . . ."

Fabienne felt her reach across, to examine her filament like she might an ornate tapestry hanging in Saint Mira.

Fabienne didn't react. Her filament did. She felt it like a trained animal, an intelligent force, a rage borrowing her mind. It threw itself through the transducer and hit Moiren directly between the eyes. Fabienne saw the artifex arc upward off the floor, eyes alight in horror, and then the illusion evaporated. Moiren disappeared, and Fabienne slipped back into the reality of her laboratory. She felt incredible. Her blood was buzzing, and her filament was settling slowly back into its resting torpor.

She reached a finger up to her nose. She looked at it. A single drop of blood caught the light, and she marveled for a moment at how much it looked like aether.

CHAPTER THIRTEEN

Carsand chewed his eggs slowly as he watched the knights posturing out in the avenue. Tensions between the Sedas and the Astafos were higher than ever, and the streets were filled with out-of-work miners trying to figure out how to earn any money. The Astafos' and the Sedas' house knights were merely the armed representatives of the town's anger.

Eventually, they started drawing their weapons, and the miners skittered back in waves. Carsand sipped his tea between bites. He kept his eyes locked on the fracas in the street. When the first gunshots went off, he carefully dabbed at the corner of his mouth with his napkin, set down his cutlery, and stood up. The innkeeper was watching the fight through a window beside his desk. Carsand dragged his table over beside the window. It groaned slowly across the weathered flooring. Shots continued popping off while Carsand retrieved his chair, adjusted the fit of the table, and then unlocked and opened the window. He took off his jacket, hung it on the back of his seat, and then unholstered his sidearm. He tossed a look at the innkeeper—the old man was staring at him, expressionless. Carsand held up his royal crest so the old man could see it in the light stabbing through the windows. The old man gave him a nod; Carsand gave it right back.

Settled again at his table, Carsand planted an elbow on the table and propped up his shooting arm. Miners were still swirling around the belligerent knights, and the clamor of swordplay and gunfire now filled the dining room. He took his time, lining up just the right shot against one of the Seda knights—nothing lethal, just something to get his attention. He exhaled slowly, and tried not to think about the trigger. Almost by surprise, the bloodmetal fired silently when Carsand had squeezed *just* hard enough on the trigger, and the bullet cracked through the air as it left the barrel of the gun. Carsand kept looking down the pistol's sights. His shot knocked the sword right out of the knight's hand. The man immediately crouched and spun, trying desperately to identify the shooter. Carsand lifted an eyebrow. He was impressed. He'd meant to blow the man's hand off—he'd never shot something out of someone's hand before.

He lined up another shot—this time at one of the Astafos. He took a breath, exhaled, fired. His shot blew through most of the fingers on the knight's left hand. Carsand furrowed his brow. He'd been trying to hit the sword that time.

He took aim at another of Seda's knights.

"You'd better be more careful, waving that crest around," Moiren said, suddenly beside him. He'd been concentrating so hard, he hadn't noticed her walking up.

He didn't look up. "Not much use in carrying it if you don't occasionally get to shoot a few men over breakfast."

He fired again, uncertain who he'd hit, but confident, thanks to the screaming, that he'd hit *someone*.

Moiren pulled out a chair and sat at his table. Carsand took his eyes off the melee, but he didn't lower his gun. Moiren was wearing darkened spectacles, and she looked . . . *paler* than usual.

"What happened to you?" he said.

"I was assaulted," she said.

"In the eyes?"

She reached up and pulled the glasses off her nose. Her eyes were bruised and swollen—Carsand wasn't sure how she could even see.

"In the brain," she said.

Carsand lowered his gun. He sat for a moment, trying to determine how to assault the brain, and then decided that he didn't care. He holstered his sidearm, closed the window, and got back to work on his plate of eggs.

"Something to eat?" he said.

"A local relay is dead," she replied, replacing her glasses. "So Lathael can't have your movements tracked in Silangarde. You'll have to share your information with me."

"Let's assume," Carsand said, "for the sake of conversation, that I have any idea what you're talking about, and then let's agree that neither of us gives a shit."

He gestured all around them with his fork. "What is there to report other than . . . chaos?"

"It's better for you if I deliver actual information to Lathael, not just speculation and local rumor," she said.

"Well, let's see," he said. "Lord Seda's primary yielding mine collapsed, killing a few men and rendering the shafts useless. Not long after, Lord Astafo's engineers discovered that one of their unused claims had, in fact, more to yield than they'd expected. A *lot* more."

He took another bite. Another gunshot went off outside.

"Lord Seda seems to have taken exception to his sudden misfortune and Lord Astafo's sudden success. Seda's lodged a suit with the provincial crown in Ae Darde, and in the meantime, he's forbidden any miner from working in Astafo's mine upon threat of imprisonment. This has . . . agitated them." He glanced out the window for dramatic effect.

"So," he moved his attention back to his plate, "Lord Astafo has done what he does best—exploit ethnic Naredals from Westreign and given them jobs here, as miners. *His* miners. This has also *agitated* the locals. So, now, the house knights are fighting not only on behalf of their lords but also the demographics they represent here in town. The prime minister's inconvenience in Talve has metastasized into a little race war."

"And what are you doing about it?" she said. She barely moved as she sat there. Carsand wondered if artifexi had to train to be so stiff all the time.

"Well, I was *trying* to shoot some of them, but the eggs were getting cold."

"You are supposed to quell Lord Astafo's ambitions and resolve the tensions here, not assassinate Lord Seda's knights for sport."

"No one told me not to," he said.

"It was implied."

"That sounds like your problem, Lady Sile—not mine."

She was quiet for a moment. "Figure this mess out. Quickly. The prime minister does not want this kind of attention in Talve."

He put his fork down and stared at her. "Why not? Why would he care about a bit of gunfire at the ass-end of the kingdom? What's here that he wants to keep quiet."

"It's not your place to know," she said.

He relented. "Fine. I'll keep at it. My way."

"Your way is inelegant, at best."

He stood up, and retrieved his jacket and hat. "But I get results."

He tipped the brim of his hat at her and stepped away. He tossed the innkeeper an extra coin on his way out.

"Good eggs," he said.

Carsand snapped his compass shut and squinted against the sun. It was easy to get turned around in the mountains and forget where the sun was supposed to be in the sky at this time of year.

Everything seemed to be where he expected it to be, and if he'd remembered his way out of Kam's chateau the first time he'd been, then the compass hadn't steered him wrong. He looked down, and the brim of his hat dropped a shadow across his face. Aspens and spruce and pine trees whispered at him in the breeze. There was absolutely nothing here: no trail, no markers, nothing. Which, he supposed, was how Kam wanted it. He remembered a small stream on the way out—possibly the downslope coursing of the chateau's water source. He wandered around until a shift in the breeze carried the clear, mineral smell of mountain water.

No sooner had he laid eyes on the stream, then he fell abruptly, soundlessly, weightlessly into nothing. Blackness. No texture, no terminus—a silence of being.

Was this Consortium work? An interference?

At least he could still think, and was that another . . . *presence* he felt in this nothing-place?

Hello again, Lord Raleis.

Is this an interference? Look, I didn't actually *kill* any of Seda's knights.

Of a sort, yes. I have hijacked your filament. There is no larger inter-ference. The effects are restricted to your consciousness.

Kam?

The same.

Why have you taken control of my brain?

It is clear that you've agreed to my terms. You've returned so that I might render this filament inert.

That's about the right of it.

And I am guiding you up the mountain.

Guiding me?

Yes. I am quite literally walking you up the mountain. But don't worry: your body and the rest of your brain are quite capable of making the trip without your awareness. It's funny how we think selfhood defines who we are, when it's really just a biological metaphor.

You're driving?

I'm driving.

So I won't see how to get to your chateau?

Fascinating that I can do this, isn't it? Your filament isn't good for much other than locating you, but I suspect it developed a few tricks of its own over the years. Besides, it's not about concealing things from you. I need to also conceal you from prying eyes on your way up.

How long will this take?

Silence.

Kam?

Master Glimjeld?

Quiet. This cliffside is precarious, and you cloud my control of your body.

Salvation. Cliffside?

He tried not to imagine himself slipping and falling to his death. Though, he supposed he wouldn't know if it happened.

How long will this take?

He came shivering back into the light in one dizzying flash. The wind was stronger up here, in the garden outside Kam's home. He was soaking wet from the waist down. His cloak was pulling at his shoulders where it had become wet and heavy around his waist.

Kam's butler, Jern, approached him slowly across the gravel. Carsand gave him a curt nod when he arrived. The silent Thachrol gestured to the house. Carsand marched wetly to the double-doors and waited for Jern to admit him. Inside, again, the butler said nothing. Carsand stared at him.

"So, the parlor?" Carsand said.

Jern bowed.

Carsand rolled his eyes. "You know a butler has *one* primary job, right?"

Jern stared at him.

"Right, I get it," Carsand said. "Go fuck myself."

Jern bowed again.

Carsand clapped the man on his shoulder. This was a liveryman he could relate to. "I'll see myself in."

Kam seemed genuinely amused at the puddle gathering beneath Carsand.

"Was it *entirely* necessary?" Carsand asked. He settled his coat and hat on a nearby stand.

"Oh, quite," Kam said. "Fording the stream was the least of your adventures coming up the mountain."

God, Carsand hated interferences.

"Come, sit by the fire," Kam said. "We'll get some fresh clothes before your procedure."

Carsand obeyed. He dragged a chair closer to the fireplace. He recognized the carpentry as he sat down. It was Tulani. His father's manor had been full of Tulani furniture. He felt suddenly further from home than he had in years.

"Can I have a drink?" Carsand said.

"I'm afraid not," Kam said, retrieving a chair for himself. Beneath his satiny loungewear, the contours of his musculature revealed that he did not, in fact, spend all of his time creating sorcerous devices. Carsand allowed his eye to linger. Kam was smiling when he finally met his eyes.

"You see," Kam said, folding his tattooed hands together on his lap, "we cannot introduce any intoxicants to your bloodstream. Have you had anything to drink today?"

"Surprisingly, no," Carsand said.

"Good, good," Kam said. "That will make the procedure less painful."

Carsand sat up. "How painful are we talking?"

"The only way to render bloodmetal inert is to expose it to toxified aether—the substance from which we precipitate bloodmetal. The only way to find toxified aether is to retrieve it from a branching reality. In its native environment, bloodmetal is not toxic. Shift it into another timeline, however, and suddenly it becomes so."

"You're going to give me, bloodmetal . . . from another . . . *reality*?"

Kam gathered his long hair and tied it back. "Yes. It's quite difficult to explain, and I don't want to go into a full-blown discussion of causality and determinism, but suffice it to say that it's . . . *difficult* to retrieve."

Carsand sighed. God he hated artifexi. "Again, how painful are we talking?"

"See," Kam said, "the potential within bloodmetal to exist in state of flux between different dimensional branches only works when it has a primary branch within which to operate. Bloodmetal attracts itself. If you put two filaments beside one another, they try to become one. Two drops of aether do the same. Your filament will begin trying to understand the dimensions of a parallel reality it can neither understand nor influence. It will, in essence, kill itself as the only determinable state of being."

Carsand stared at him.

"So, as you can imagine, it will be excruciating." Kam touched the scar on his forehead where his transducer once was. "Trust me."

Carsand opened his eyes, and it was like heaving grindstones. He was lying down. Soft. Warm. It took him a moment to remember what a bed was. The light pouring through the window was clean—white and sharp. The blonde woman with something on her forehead was sitting across the room, staring at him.

"How much do you remember?" she said. She sounded kind.

"I'm sorry, ma'am. Who *are* you?"

"Aisabelle. Fabienne's sister."

He looked around the room. It looked like he was in a hotel.

"How much do you remember?" she said.

He tried. It was nice in this bed. What was the point of thoughts anyway?

"Kam," he said.

"Good."

"A vial, of something to drink."

"That would have been aether. Anything else?"

He brought his fingertips to his temples. "Fire. After that, fire. Burning, screaming."

"Yes," she said. She got up and pressed the backs of her fingers to his forehead. "Yes, you did a lot of screaming."

"Thank you for the kindness," he said.

She smiled—a tired smile. Perhaps one of her last. One she'd been saving for a special occasion. "You will be thankful for the pain, afterward. It's worth it."

He nodded.

She folded her hands in front of her. "Do you need some poppy? If the pain is bad, we have some for you."

He wasn't really in that much pain, not anymore.

"Yes, ma'am. Thank you. I think that'd be best."

The storm lashed at the window in Carsand's room. He stared at it as he finished dressing himself. The thunder bounced back-and-forth between the peaks surrounding the Talve valley, echoed beyond its time into a semi-rhythmic thing. It reminded him of the sound of Moiren's *transduction conveyance*.

He couldn't see Talve itself—the rain was too thick—but he could see the folds in the mountainside. The trees that clung to the mountain were swaying as curtain after curtain of dark rain washed over them. They looked almost relaxed, like they'd had a bit of poppy themselves and had gone out for a little wobbly dance.

Carsand tucked his crimson ascot into his collar—an unexpected gift from Kam. He retrieved his hat from the peg and shouldered his cloak into place. He felt as if his brain had gone stiff. It didn't hurt; it just didn't seem very much to want to be a brain right now.

Kam was waiting for him in the hallway. His jacket was silken, maybe Ap-Lian in origin, if Carsand had to guess. It looked exotic compared to Carsand's plain, black cloak.

"Good morning, Lord Raleis," Kam said. He gave Carsand a little bow.

"Morning," Carsand said. "We can dispense with . . . *that* sort of thing."

"Indeed. How's your head?"

"It would rather be asleep, but the rest of my person is quite finished with lying still," Carsand said.

"Great. Let me show you to the dining room." Kam stepped aside and gestured down the hallway. "We'll have something to eat before we get underway."

"Underway?" Carsand said. He looked out the tall bay windows flanking the door to his room. The storm looked darker, the more of it he could see. "Are we going by boat?"

Kam gave him an indulgent smile. "I assure you, we'll be most comfortable and dry, descending the mountain. We'll get a bit wet later, but we have garments for that."

"And where are we going?"

"To collect my payment, of course."

"You want to do that *now*?"

Kam let his arm fall to his side. He stopped smiling. "No time like the present."

Carsand took a deep breath. He wasn't about to irritate this man. "Yeah, all right. Let's eat, then."

Carsand waited while Kam whispered some instructions to Jern. The silent Thachrol merely bowed his head when his master was done. Kam turned and placed a kiss on Aisabelle's forehead. They made an astonishing couple. Carsand would have preferred to forego this journey and spend the rainy afternoon in bed—with either of them. He could explain to the empress later. *Darling, if you had seen them!*

Aisabelle's eyes were fixed on Kam's golden head. She behaved like a servant around him, but Carsand had seen that look before. She was in love.

He thought that was a little weird, but he'd seen weirder.

"Ready now?" Kam asked, stepping up to Carsand. He'd changed his silks for sturdier attire.

Carsand spread his arms. "I've already said my goodbyes."

"This way, then." Kam said. He led Carsand down the hallway and down two flights of stairs. Carsand assumed this was the lowest point of the chateau. The wines were stored down here, along with barrels of grains and other foodstuffs. Kam opened the door to a pantry, and gestured Carsand inside.

Carsand gave him a sidelong glance, but he held his tongue—no matter what it was they were about to do in a pantry.

Kam closed the door behind him and activated one of his interference lights. They weren't in a pantry. It reminded Carsand a bit of a confessional, with all of its inlaid wood trim and carved tracery. There were two seats facing each other, a porthole-type window behind each. It could also have been a toilet. Or a sauna. Carsand really wasn't sure this compared to anything he had previously experienced.

"Have a seat," Kam said.

Carsand unbuttoned his jacket and made himself comfortable. The interference light was dim and red. There was a panel secured to the wall beneath it. Wires snaked in and out of the panel, and when Kam opened it, Carsand could see the ruby reflection of a filament in a glass tube. Vials of heavy, red liquid flanked it on either side. When he was satisfied with it, Kam replaced the panel. The room shuddered gently, and Carsand suddenly felt as if he were about to be struck by lightning.

"What is that?" Carsand said.

Kam glanced at him as he took his own seat. "Magnetism. Interference magnetism. It's how this conveyance operates."

"You have your own transduction conveyance," Carsand said.

Kam smiled. "Do you like it? I styled the carriage after woodwork I've seen in Salvation chapels."

Carsand squirmed. "I noticed. Feels a little . . . snug in here, slapped inside a . . . Salvation box."

"It took me almost two decades to design it. Much less the device that did the drilling."

"The drilling?"

As if on cue, the carriage began descending. Carsand flung a hand out and pressed it against the wall.

"Relax," Kam said. "It's perfectly safe."

"What is it doing?" Carsand decided to leave his hand on the wall, despite Kam's assurances.

"It's descending."

"Into the mountain?"

"Did you truly think Jern and I were hiking down the slope every time we wanted something from town."

"Yes," Carsand said, lowering his hand. "I absolutely, completely thought that."

"You see," Kam said, "I didn't choose this mountain for my demesne at random. There are veins of magnetic ore running all through the heart of this peak. With magnets of your own, and enough power, you can effect . . . this."

He gestured to the carriage. The dim light made his dark tattoos look like dirt, or soot. Maybe something a coal miner wrote into the dust upon his face, trapped in the mine, waiting for release.

Carsand looked at the dark porthole above Kam's head. "Well, why are there windows?"

Kam craned his neck to look up at his window. "To observe billions of years of creation, of course."

"Looks dark to me," Carsand said.

"Yes," Kam said. "That's mostly how the story of the universe goes."

Kam stared for a moment. Carsand could almost hear whatever conversation the strange man was having with himself. The carriage swayed gently as it pushed deeper into the heart of the mountain.

"The Karleths didn't actually conquer the Olin, you see," Kam said.

"You don't say."

"The Olin didn't bow to one, central king. They were dozens, hundreds of tribes ruled by chieftains. Some in the valleys, some upon the slopes—others in caves. Travel and communication were too difficult to unify so many diverse microcultures under one rule. So, when the Karleths decided they wanted the territory for their kingdom, they paid for it. Any chieftain who would accept their coin received a Karlean title, a deed to his lands, and a mandate to deliver tribute on a timely schedule. Even your Astafos and your Sedas descend from Olin who capitulated. Any who did not . . ." Kam shrugged ". . . well, the Karleths branded them rebels of the new kingdom, and its brand-new noblemen were obligated to root them out and destroy them. The Olin who wouldn't bend their knees to the Karleths fled, deeper and higher into the mountains, out of reach of their cousins. They made the price for their blood too high, too risky, and the new Olinire Karleths turned their backs and let them be. Some of those tribes still exist, unseen, keeping their language and their ways for over two hundred years now."

The stone walls suddenly fell away—Carsand could feel it. The darkness beyond the glass had a different texture now.

"Have a look," Kam said, smiling.

Carsand stood and turned. At first, he could see only darkness, and then, swaying gently with the carriage, tiny lights began moving, far off in the dark.

"Are those—"

"Torches?" Kam said. "Yes. That, my friend, is why there are windows."

Carsand turned to look at him. "Who are they?"

"I just told you."

Carsand turned back to stare at the tiny lights. "Have you met them?"

"Not yet, but I will. I have big plans for those tiny lights."

Carsand sat back down. He became acutely aware of his stiff brain again. Everyone had heard stories of the Clearances, when the Olin were bought or pushed off their land. But no one had ever said anything any of them still living in the mountainous province. Would anyone even be able to communicate with them?

The two men held their silence the rest of the way down. Carsand leaned back against the uncomfortable carpentry, and tipped the brim of his hat over his eyes. He jerked himself involuntarily from the brink of sleep—who knew how long he'd been resting in that in-between place, thinking about the Olin and mountains and rain and the empress and poppy and . . . a dog? When he looked up, Kam was staring at him.

The carriage came to a slow and gentle stop. Kam tugged his gloves onto his fingers and stood up. "We've arrived."

They stepped out into a tunnel, itself lined with dim interference lights at even intervals along the walls. The tunnel disappeared without end in the distance ahead.

"You couldn't have gotten us any closer?" Carsand said.

"This is close enough—for this conveyance" Kam said.

Carsand looked at him. "So, you have others of these? Tunnels like this one?"

Kam's eyes twinkled in the artificial twilight. "Of course."

"Where?"

Kam couldn't contain his glee. Carsand could tell his toothy smile was genuine.

"Everywhere."

"All right." Carsand assumed the lead. "Let's go."

Kam let him lead them on.

"You know," Carsand said, "I'll bet you and the prime minister get along smashingly. You're both devils in disguise."

"Not to worry," Kam said. "I do have smashing plans for the prime minister."

Carsand knocked on the door to Adwar's laboratory in the woods. The sun had never come out, so the day was already preternaturally dark. Adwar hadn't lit any outdoor lanterns, so Carsand and Kam stood on his humble porch, dripping. Carsand could hear the artifex walking across his planked floor. The door opened with a modest squeak.

The golden light behind him was bright enough to blink at. They'd been hiking in the dark rain all day.

Adwar looked silently at Carsand, and then at Kam. He rubbed his short beard with dirt-stained fingers. He wasn't wearing the livery of the Order Entropic, which, to Carsand, meant he hadn't had any business with Lord Astafo today.

"How did you get here?" Adwar said. Carsand couldn't tell if he was irritated, or if that was just his Naredal accent.

"We walked," Carsand said.

Adwar stared at him. "I thought I told you I'd collect you when I needed you."

"Yes, well," Carsand removed his sodden hat, "as it turns out, I needed *you*."

"You walked," Adwar said.

"Yessir."

"You could easily have been followed. I'll have to search—"

"No," Carsand said.

"I beg your pardon?" Adwar was definitely irritated now.

"No, I couldn't have been easily followed. My filament is dead."

Adwar turned his gaze upon Kam.

"You know, actually," Carsand said, "we didn't just walk. We took a transduction conveyance through the heart of a mountain and watched isolated tribesmen crawling around in the dark."

Adwar looked at him again. He still hadn't offered up any facial expression.

"It was really something," Carsand said.

"Perhaps you two better come inside."

". . . and that brings us to now. Here," Carsand pointed at the floor.

Adwar had made room for them at his modest hearth. He'd provided tree stumps as stools, and they were sipping some liquor he distilled himself from plants that grew on the mountainside.

Adwar flicked his gaze at Kam. The sorcerer had sat silently during Carsand's narration. He smiled at Adwar now.

"Thievery," Adwar said, staring at the Thachrol in the lambent firelight.

"What?" Carsand said.

Adwar didn't move his gaze. "That's what his face says." He pointed at Kam. "His people banished him for thievery."

"I'm sure I'd wear the same tattoos by now had I been born among the Thachrol," Carsand said.

Adwar gestured sharply. Carsand assumed it meant *shut up*.

"So, you are the one I have heard chewing through the earth," Adwar said.

"Yes, my lord," Kam said. He lowered his eyes deferentially.

"You've been busy," Adwar said.

Kam looked back up, a diplomat in action. He lifted his mug to Adwar, and took a drink without answering.

"Why are you here?" Adwar said. Carsand assumed that Adwar was realizing that Kam was no ordinary houseguest. "Why have you helped Lord Raleis this way—"

"We don't need—" Carsand started.

Adwar gestured at him again. Carsand rolled his eyes and leaned back.

"I need to speak with the empress," Kam said. "That was my price for the assistance I have rendered to Lord Raleis."

"Lord Raleis does not have the privilege of granting audiences with the empress," Adwar said stiffly.

"We both know that Lord Raleis is precious to the empress," Kam said. "Very precious."

"Salvation, stop with the lords. It's annoying," Carsand said. "And she'll want to hear what *Master Glimjeld* has to say—trust me."

This time, Adwar smiled. He spread his arms as if anticipating a hug. "I'm afraid I can't help you communicate with the empress. Such a skill is beyond an Entropic like myself. You'll need one of the Consortium to do that. And I'm assuming you'd rather not have a conversation with one of them."

"Not to worry," Kam said. "I was Consortium, and I brought equipment. All I need is an introduction."

Carsand stared nervously at the circle of glowing light on one of Adwar's work tables. It took Kam the better part of an hour to set up the device's wires and counterweights and vials of aether, but once he'd got it working, and isolated Trejean Palace in Levuwes, he and Adwar stepped out of the room. They'd all agreed that Carsand should be the first to speak to the empress. One of her many butlers had answered the appearance of the shining disk of light bearing Carsand's likeness. The man was far better at tolerating interferences than Carsand would ever give himself credit for. Now, Carsand sat, damp and cold in a wizard's dark laboratory at the ass-end of civilization staring at one of the empress's gilded drawing rooms. He remembered this one. The paintings, the billowy curtains, the trays of shellfish and other oddities she'd shared with him. He remembered all the sunlight. The nights too warm for blanketing.

It surprised him when she appeared in the image. She was wearing an ivory scarf on her head and around her throat—the light from Carsand's floating image moved across it in silky blue streaks. She had eyes as dark as obsidian, and just as alive with flashes of ambient light. Her hair, he remembered, was as black as her eyes, and she had the skin tone of woman who worked all day in her vineyards, rather than simply enjoying the fruits of others' labors. Naturally, that wasn't true at all, but her family all carried the same darkness of complexion. She still looked young, younger than him. It was a weapon she used all the time. Men saw a young, beautiful woman, they made mistakes. Carsand had learned long ago that he hadn't wooed this incredible woman. She'd allowed him to share her space—for whatever reasons of her own.

He swallowed and bowed his head. "*Empress.*"

She stared at him for a moment, as unbothered by the interference as her butler had been. Did they train for this in her court? Carsand didn't remember anything like that.

"*Hello, my love,*" she said calmly. She smiled at him, slowly, as if she were drowsy. He knew she wasn't. She had learned how to pace that smile and disarm people with it.

"*I am delighted to see you,*" she said. She lifted a hand to remove her scarf, and he could see that her nails were painted to match. They looked like pearls capping her fingertips. Her dark hair was unbound, and she arranged it across her shoulders. She'd always done that when they retired for the evening. Be it a crown, a hat, a scarf—as soon as they were alone, she'd never kept the trappings of her station.

"*I'm so sorry,*" he said, shaking his head. "*I never—*"

"*Carsand,*" she said calmly, "*look at me.*"

He did, but it took a minute. He was only barely winning the composure match he was fighting with himself.

"*I know, my love. I know all of it.*"

"*It's okay now, though,*" he said, suddenly remembering. "*They can't track me anymore. There's so much to tell you. I can explain why I had to leave.*"

She held up a hand, and the pale silk fell away from her wrist. Just seeing it, her wrist, felt like an electric jolt. He'd had nothing but his memories of her skin for so long.

"*There is nothing to explain,*" she said. She sounded almost like she was reciting a lullaby—very slowly. "*You left because I allowed you to leave.*"

That stopped him. He frowned. "*Ladre, what?*"

"*I would never have permitted the king's assassins to actually harm you, but I had to let them think they were doing well. Things had to be set in motion.*"

"*You . . . knew?*"

"*Of course, my love. I merely needed your prime minister to think he was orchestrating a turn of events of his own design.*"

"*So, you forgive me,*" he said.

"*Beloved, you have never been unobserved, not for a moment since you left Levuwes. I was never going to surrender you to them forever. Just . . . for a time. There is nothing to forgive.*"

"*There's so much,*" he said.

She shushed him. "*I know, I know, but this isn't why you have called. There will be time soon, and we will not be apart again. You will fight wars for me, beloved.*"

She still loved him. She wanted him back. She'd never really let him go. He'd nearly destroyed himself with heartache, and now, it was as if it never happened.

"*Do everything Adwar tells you to do, do you understand?*"

He nodded.

"*He will deliver you to me. That is his task.*"

"*I understand.*"

Kam cleared his throat as he stepped quietly into the room. "Lord Raleis, the device will only—"

"Yes, of course," Carsand said. He swiped the back of his hand across his brow, as if he might rub the most important conversation of his life away like so much trail dust.

"Empress," he said, "I want you to meet someone very special, someone who has done me a great service. I daresay he's my friend. This is Master Kam Glimjeld."

Kam stepped up beside him, and the strange light worked its eerie effect on his tattoos. Ladre didn't bat an eye.

"If he is a friend of yours, he is mine as well," she said. "Greetings Master Glimjeld."

Kam bowed.

"Kam," Carsand said, "this is Empress Ladre."

"*It is among the greatest honors of my life to speak to you, empress. I believe I can bring power and affluence to your beautiful Empire.*"

Carsand stared at him. "You speak Naredesse?"

CHAPTER FOURTEEN

Camorenne felt dwarfed by Aevas Castle's soaring curtain wall, but she didn't want to look out of place. She kept her hands clasped inside her mink hand muff and walked as stiffly as possible. With her matching hat, she looked just as much a Silangarde lady as anyone else with the idle time to stroll the castle wall in the Old City. The massive fortifications were evenly planed—no invader would have ever scaled those stones. They were aloof, without adornment, a dispassionate edifice that had witnessed hundreds of years of self-important ladies strolling through its shadows. Emille kept pace beside her, eyes on the path, hands tucked into a silken muff of her own.

Camorenne didn't look at the groundskeeper as they entered the Dero Garden. His sleeves were rolled, and he straightened to bow in her direction. She ignored him, and he went back to scraping at the soil. If his attire were any indication, it was, perhaps, not quite cold enough for the furs Camorenne was wearing, but she wasn't the only woman in the capital dressing in anticipation of cooler fashion.

There was a College of Saint Mira scholar scribbling on a board beside the Dero Wall. His robes were too large for his wiry frame, and when he bothered to regard Camorenne and Emille, it was through spectacles that forced him to squint. He didn't bow. He just studied her for a minute and then went back to his notes.

"Here we are, Emille," Camorenne said. "The Dero."

"My lady." Emille had helped her scour her society papers for mentions of the families of the Council of Merchants. Their most interesting lead had been this ancient architectural fragment.

Camorenne made a show of inspecting the masonry. It was only a bit of wall, no taller than she was, of rough-hewn stone—some nameless gray rock from long before masons learned to quarry stone-of-silangarde properly. Every inch of the wall's surface was covered with carved script. The inscriptions overlapped each other, as if they were scrabbling for the surface.

"You see, my dear," Camorenne said. "The ancient sages who preceded the Strangemen had to carve their incantations into the city itself, which they called Dero. It was how they effected their supernatural rites. The city itself was their magic. This bit is all that remains."

"Yes, my lady."

Emille had read the same article that Camorenne had. Camorenne wasn't narrating for her benefit.

"Now," Camorenne said, a little louder, leaning forward, "if we can just find the bit we need."

The scholar looked over at her again, squinting.

Camorenne looked at him. An old man who'd no doubt spent his life staring at this rock.

"You there," she said. "Are you familiar with Dero history?"

"Of course," he said, "I teach—"

"Very good, very good," Camorenne said, "you can help me find what we're looking for."

The scholar looked around, as if to confirm that this conversation was happening. Camorenne imagined he rarely had company here. She'd gambled that there'd even be someone here at all—she figured she'd have to run this ruse on a groundskeeper or an innocent page.

"What are you looking for?" he said.

She pulled a hand out of her muff and gestured at Emille. "My dear, the paper."

Emille handed her the bill of sale Kedrick had left in her apartments.

"Family history," Camorenne said, "one of my cousins is making business decisions using one of our old names. I need to find a record of it for Papa. *Katarin's Gazette* has an article linking our family to the original Dero nobility."

She handed him the bill of sale, and pointed to one of the names in the transaction. "That there, you see."

She gave him time to see the inventory detailed in the bill. He looked up at her slowly, then back at the paper.

"Where did you get this?" he said.

She waved her hand. "I took it from Papa's desk. He told me to take something with me so I could prove our identity, just in case."

"Do you know what it details?" he said.

"Me? Salvation, no. That's Papa's business."

"And who is your family?" he said. "My lady?"

"Healde, of course," she said, as if he should know.

"As in, Duke Healde, of the Council of Merchants?" he said slowly.

"Yes, yes," she said, irritated.

He handed the paper back to her slowly, and she passed it to Emille.

"You should be more careful with your father's papers, Lady Healde."

She rolled her eyes. "Now, where on this wall are we?"

"This way." He walked a few paces away, and pointed to some scrabbled carving. She wasn't even sure what you called this language.

"The Healde were, indeed, an original Dero noble family. The brackets you see there, around what you would think of as the 'd' and the 'e' of your surname were added centuries after the original incantation."

Camorenne wrinkled her nose. "What does that mean?"

He was still looking at her strangely, as if she couldn't possibly be so stupid as to let him read a bill of sale for bastard children in Oliniron bearing her family's name.

"We don't know what letters would have been there," he said slowly. "Our best guess is that your ancestral name was Healthow, but as time went by, many Dero families' names changed since the records carved into the city walls were constantly carved over."

He pointed at her document. "Healthow is what's attributed there on . . . your father's document."

She clapped and smiled at Emille. "Oh, how delightful! Papa will be thrilled." She smiled at the scholar. "Thank you ever so much."

"Yes," he said, offering an awkward bow, "of course."

"Come along, Emille," she said. "We must document this at once!"

She wondered if scholars gossiped as rapidly as society people.

Camorenne hadn't counted on this much foot traffic. Saint Beukah's feast day wasn't really something that the Olinire tradition of Salvation made a big deal about. There were services, yes, but usually just a modest meal of fowl and nut pies.

In Silangarde, everyone seemed to be out for it. People had feathers in their hands, braided into their hair—they were even stabbed into desserts behind glass bakery windows. Camorenne couldn't tell what kind of birds they were from. And were any left alive after a culling of this magnitude?

The feathers had something to do with Beukah's pagan past. Camorenne hadn't paid enough attention to really remember more than that. There was something involving feathers and her martyrdom.

"Have you ever seen so many feathers in all your life?" Camorenne asked Emille.

"No, milady," she said.

A man walking in front of them turned. He examined Camorenne from fur-trimmed hat to pointed boots.

"You wouldn't be sacrilegious about Saint Beukah, now, would you?" he said.

Camorenne started. She hadn't expected anyone to suddenly start *speaking* to her. Especially someone of this man's social stature.

"Not at all," she said, looking away.

"That's some accent," he said. "Where are you from?"

"Talve," Camorenne said.

The stranger and a companion beside him laughed. "Tall-vay? So, you're an Olin."

"There are no more Olin," Camorenne said. "We killed them all, remember?"

"*We?*"

She rolled her eyes. "Karlande? Our *nation.*"

He sneered at her, and took a step forward. She recoiled instinctively. "*Karlande*, is here. *We're* Karlande."

Camorenne couldn't help herself. "That is what I said, isn't it?"

Emille shifted uncomfortably beside her.

"Olin *and* dumb," he said. He grabbed her wrist and tried to jerk her off balance.

Camorenne barely had time to gasp before Emille darted into them and slipped her thin knife into the man's wrist. He let go of Camorenne like she was made of fire. She grabbed Emille and pulled her back before the girl tried her luck a second time.

He staggered back, clutching his arm, and people were turning their attention to his howling.

"That Olin bitch attacked me!"

"Come, Emille," Camorenne said, maintaining her grip on the girl like her life depended on it. Silangarders were gathering around the bleeding man. A few cast unreadable glances her way. She felt lost in unending, feathered stares.

Camorenne dragged Emille and tried to put as much distance between her and the men as she could. Her heart hammered as she stomped across the cobblestones. *Olin*? Since when was that a thing? The ruling province had built most of its might upon Olinire mines. How was she supposed to disguise her accent? It hadn't even occurred to her to try.

She stopped and bought fans made of feathers from a merchant's stall. She handed one to Emille.

"Fuck's sake," Camorenne said. "Better carry these around."

Camorenne handed her fan to Emille as they stepped into the townhouse and shut the noise of the feast day out behind them. She exchanged a look with her maid.

"Well, now. I suppose that's something else to be looking out for."

"Your accent, ma'am?"

Camorenne was still addled by it. "My accent. Indeed."

The aroma of the household's Beukah Day meal followed Bevry from the back of the house. He approached her with the day's correspondence upon his signature silver tray. Outside, the sounds of the revelers still popped and screamed like muted devils.

"Bevry, my dear," Camorenne said, handing her muff and hat to Emille, "please add this to the stack of Davo's ore receipts for House Healthow to send to Ricarde. It proved *most* useful."

She handed him the bill of sale with the Healthow name.

"Very good, madam," he said, extending her tray.

Emille wandered off with their things, and Bevry turned back toward his office in the rear of the house. There was a letter from Ricarde. She read it quickly.

"Oh, sweet Salvation," she said, both relieved and annoyed.

Bevry turned back around. "Madam?"

"Pack the house, Bevry. We're going back to Talve. Father's mine is . . . *yielding* again. The family fears for our safety here."

She thought Bevry might collapse, he looked so relieved.

"Emille!" she shouted.

The maid was beside her in a blink.

"Ma'am?"

"Let's choose a different dress for tomorrow. I'm afraid I have news for Davo."

The observation lounge, on the airship Navina, was unlike anything Camorenne had ever experienced. Up here, in the cool air, the cabin swayed gently beneath the ship's great dirigibles, and the giant fans that moved the craft through the sky made the timbers vibrate like a hive. She felt it through the flooring more than she heard it. Somewhere, in the heart of the ship, an artifex was entirely cooked on reagents, busily channeling power for the airship, and a diligent crew operated the valves and controls and levers and heaters that made it possible to soar over Silangarde.

She could see the long, delicate tracery of the stone-of-silangarde aqueduct that pulled water out of Caldera Mere, higher in the mountains, for the capital below. From this height, the lake looked like smooth jade—an enormous treasure high above Silangarde for giants to come and pluck.

Beside the observation windows, there was a copper plaque with the airship's commission from the king. It told the story of Saint Navina, the Salvation saint who could speak to angels. She was left out as a sacrifice, tied to a pole, and God raptured her before the elements could do their damage.

Davo stepped up next to her, two flutes of Nidali wine in hand. "You know, that's probably not the artifex's real name."

Camorenne turned and took a flute of wine. The interference lamps lighting the lounge left golden streaks in Davo's salt-and-pepper beard. She hadn't ever thought of him as anything more than a rich date, and a good lay. But, heading back to Oliniron, she was starting to realize she'd actually miss him.

"Why would she use a fake name?" Camorenne asked.

"Or he, or they," he said. "The name has become a ploy to attract people with coin to this or that transduction service. Saint Navina could talk to flying angels, so she's a good name for an airship."

Camorenne turned back to the view. "How positively vulgar."

"Commerce is inelegant at best," he said.

They stood in silence before the view. They had some time before the meal would be served. The soft voices of the other passengers made sounds like quiet rivers. She couldn't imagine who they were. Even Davo couldn't afford these tickets—they were a gift from a client who had a scheduling conflict. Though she couldn't imagine what event would take precedence over dinner on an airship.

They turned to each other simultaneously, each seizing upon the lull in their conversation as the perfect opportunity for a change of topic.

"Camorenne—"

"Davo—"

Davo touched his hand to his chest, as if he might ask her to dance. "Please, after you."

"No, you," she said, almost girlishly. She giggled.

"Right, well," he said, straightening back up. "I'm afraid I'll be leaving town for a while."

That surprised her.

"Leaving town! Are you in some kind of trouble?" She grabbed him with her free hand as if she might secure him against whatever winds were whipping him away.

"No, no, my dear—nothing like that. It's business."

A low cloud fogged past the observation windows. She decided to ignore it.

"Well, go on, damn you," she said, letting go of him.

"We're seeing sharply increased requests for trades in ore—especially among the Council of Merchants."

"All of them? What does that mean?"

"It means they know something the rest of us don't, and they're stockpiling ore, mostly likely to turn it around at a profit for something."

"Something?"

"Who knows. A kingdom-works project, weapons, armor. Could be anything."

She spread her arms. "Well, so. That sounds like exactly the sort of thing you'd like to hear."

"Oh, yes," he said. He took gentle hold of her elbow. "Oh, it's fantastic news, but it's dangerous."

"Who comes after ore merchants?"

He smiled. "Other merchants. Monopolistic war profiteering was outlawed by the Council of Nobles following the annexation of Nidal. Conflict is profitable, and if the rest of the peerage don't get their fair shake at turning some gold off of it, they're less inclined to answer their feudal summons and do the king's bidding.

"Nobles who don't fulfill their obligations meet untimely ends," Davo said, "and, as they say, shit rolls downhill. The nobles who get to pick up their lands and riches in exchange for new-sworn fealty to the king go looking for anyone who might threaten their operation."

He took a drink of the wine, and seemed to remember they had an incredible view to enjoy. "Those of us who've seen this before know to do our business remotely, well away from the capital, until the time of troubles resolves itself, then we come back for the newest season of this game."

"Oh, all right, then," she said, face drawn. "But where will you go?"

He tried to hide his smile. "To Oliniron."

"What! Should I slap you? What is this?"

He shrugged. "I suppose you could. Who knows? I might enjoy it."

"Ugh!" She made a fist and shook it at him.

"Why, I thought you'd be pleased?" he said.

"Because it's the last thing I expected out of your mouth."

"Why?" he said. "What were you going to tell me."

"*I'm* going to Oliniron, too." She laughed. "How absurd."

"Then it's settled!" Davo said. "Surely your brother would love to finally make my acquaintance in person, especially now that his mines are yielding again."

"You know about that?" she said, dumbstruck.

"Of course I do," he said. "It's my business to know such things. Here . . ." he took her glass ". . . let me fetch us something more celebratory. I'll be right back."

He kissed her on the cheek and walked unsteadily across the deck to the bar.

ᘒ

"Did I hear the lady is traveling to Oliniron?"

Camorenne turned. Another passenger stood just a pace away. No one she knew, or had seen—which she found odd. She'd seen most of the other passengers onboard the Navina at various galas in the capital over the last year—even if her station hadn't warranted conversations with them.

This man's fashion was new, straight from the shops on Tannery Row, not some antique handed down by generations of rich fathers. He had severe features, like he might be from the Thachrol Nations, though he didn't seem quite tall enough. Or *did* he?

"I beg your pardon," Camorenne, an eyebrow cocked like a whip. "Were you listening to my conversation?"

He bowed. To another observer, Camorenne imagined it looked almost as if some wealthy merchant was stopping for a chat while having a stroll through the lounge on his way to stop for another chat. Camorenne had the odd sense of choreography. As if she were at the strangest ball in the slowest-moving airship high above the most powerful city in the world.

"Wouldn't you have listened if your station were mine?" he said.

How old was he? Her age? Younger? He was armed, with both a rapier and a dagger. Not uncommon but also largely the purview of bored lordlings fighting in avenues—not the ultra-rich.

"And what station is that?" she said.

"An old friend," he said.

She squinted. Hard. "From . . ."

"Perhaps if I adjusted my accent," he said, and his voice took on a rougher edge.

She gasped, and it actually knocked her a step back.

"Kedrick?!" she said.

"The same, milady."

He did *not* look like an adolescent street thug bounced about by The Shroud. He looked . . . older. In control. Ready to use those weapons. He looked like how she would have thought someone in The Shroud should have looked in the first place. It sent a chill up her spine. Had he always been this beneath his boyish disguise?

"What are you *doing* here?" she said, closing the distance between them.

"Business," he said. He took hold of her elbow gently and leaned in, as if they might be discussing some trade secret. "I can't linger."

"Linger?" she hissed. "What business?"

"Oh, I have to kill a man."

"Here?!"

He laughed at her. It raised her ire, only for a moment. *Him* laughing at *her*. "It's a joke. But I really do have business."

"Up *here*?" she said.

He looked around. The view through the observation windows caught his eye, just for a moment. "Where better?"

She didn't say anything.

"In any event," he said, "I need you to help me collect some captives."

She didn't know that people's jaws could actually drop. Not until then. She'd always thought it was an expression.

"Do close your mouth, my lady," Kedrick said. He sounded a bit like Bevry. Camorenne frowned at him.

"Well, go on, you duplicitous little madman," she said.

"These people were captured on a clandestine errand in Consortium territory—they are no friends of the Seda family," he said.

"Well, why should *I* want them?"

He glanced around. She felt like he was performing for someone. She could see Davo headed back with new drinks.

"Because these are VIPs—I don't have time to explain their worth to you."

"So why *are* you giving them to me?"

Davo stepped up beside her. "What's this?" he said. He looked at Kedrick for a moment, like he was studying a painting. "Oh, Kedrick—it's you. You've changed your hair."

Camorenne turned to look very slowly at Davo. "What. Did you say?"

Kedrick ran a hand over his waxed hair. "Yes, it was time for a change. And how've you been, Lord Murel?"

Camorenne turned her gaze now equally slowly to Kedrick. "You two—"

"The usual. It's just about laying-low season, you know."

"Yes," Kedrick said, "I supposed it would be."

Camorenne stamped her foot. "What the fuck is going on between you two?"

They looked at her like she'd removed a wig to reveal herself bald.

"What are you talking about, dearest?" Davo said.

She gritted her teeth. "You bring me all the way up into a fucking *airship* to tell me you're going to Oliniron to avoid the melee that will soon ravage the capital because of *war profiteering*, and who should be here but my juvenile acquaintance from The Shroud who wants me to collect some of his *very important* prisoners, and you two *know each other*?" She whipped her head back and forth, as if shaking the life from something held between her teeth.

"Do calm down, my lady," Kedrick said.

"Kedrick," she said slowly, "I do believe I'm allowed to murder you. I think it's the law. I think you can murder members of The Shroud. So I'm going to murder you."

"*Kedrick* is the street urchin you've been going on about?" Davo said.

She wouldn't look at him. She felt insane. "Yes!"

"Oh, well I suppose that would make sense now, wouldn't it?" Davo said.

"Quite, my lord," Kedrick said.

"But, we don't know each other," Davo said.

Now she did look up. She had no idea how to describe her own facial expression.

"No, of course not," Kedrick agreed.

"But you—" she tried.

"No one *knows* Kedrick," Davo said. "It's better that way."

"Is that your way of saying, 'Everyone knows Kedrick?'" she asked.

Davo and Kedrick seemed to consider the idea.

"Yes, I suppose you could say that," Davo said. "Plausible deniability. It's just business."

Kedrick nodded.

"Anyway," she snapped. "You want me to collect your captives, about whom you'll tell me nothing, and, I presume, take them with me to Oliniron."

"There you have it!" Kedrick said brightly. "Your brother will be most delighted to see them. One might even consider their arrival the crowning achievement of your mission in Silangarde." He gestured at

Davo, "And Lord Murel will make a most wonderful escort. It will be so fun for all of us."

"All of us?" she said.

"Well, of course I'll be along, too."

"Yes, of course," Davo said, as if it were the most normal request in the world.

"'Yes, of course,'" Camorenne mimicked. "Kedrick, you simply must tell me why you're doing this to me."

He looked shocked. "*To* you, my lady. This is *for* you—this is our gift."

"From the Silangarde Shroud," she said.

"Absolutely."

"And why am I receiving this gift?"

"Because," he said, cheerful, "your station and your family's legal conflict with the Seda family make you the perfect representative. We can't bring suit in the Courts of Saint Levine against our former brethren in The Shroud—and their corrupt allies. We need a legitimate complainant. And that's you!"

She thought for a moment. "You want me . . . to file legal claims . . . on behalf of The Shroud."

"Yes," Kedrick said.

"You do realize that, legally, that makes me *part* of The Shroud," she said.

"Absolutely," Kedrick said. "Welcome aboard. You'll love it!"

He bowed and moved away. She looked slowly at Davo.

"Well, now you're a lady of organized crime," he said. "I find that . . . thrilling."

"I think I'll kill *you* first," she said.

CHAPTER FIFTEEN

Couran woke up in a box. It was moving, and he could hear cart-wheels. There were slots in the wood that was a few inches from his face, and the sun slipped through them to flash upon metallic motes of dust. He had something tied around his nose and mouth. He could breathe, but he suspected whoever had put him in this box didn't want him inhaling that shiny dust.

His first impulse was to call out for Ashre. What had happened? They were in the Strangeland, and he couldn't find the horses, and then . . . the stranger. He shot them. He killed Ashre. Couran remembered her prone on the rocks, her copper hair fanned out like a shroud over her shoulders. Her hat knocked askew.

Ashre always told him never to follow his first impulse. So, he took a slow breath through his mask and looked for his second impulse. An interference. If she was nearby, he could find her. He could find out if she was okay.

The sun glinted again in the air between his face and the lid of his prison. What was this dust? It wasn't dirt. He looked around. There wasn't room to move—his shoulders were pressed against the sides of the box, and his head was rubbing the top, but now he could see the strange flakes everywhere. He was . . . *immersed* in them. Was this a coffin? Was somebody going to bury him alive? Or was he dead? Why were there breathing holes?

He tried his third impulse, which was to slow his brain down. To be still and breathing in his box. Like something nocturnal, something in the dark, waiting for the sun to go down so it could emerge and do whatever it needed to do without being noticed. He began to meditate. Breathing in, breathing out—letting all his panicked and speculative thoughts flare and die like sparks. There was only the breathing. Nothing else mattered, not in the grand sense of the universe. The only one who cared that he was in a box, on a wagon, immersed in metal flakes was him. The rest of the natural world had better things to do.

That was it. Metal flakes. He indulged his thoughts, slowly, inviting them into his breathing like guests at a party. It was how Ashre had trained him to think his way through restoration interferences when he couldn't identify the immediate imbalance.

Whoever had come after them knew who they were. He had tracked them through the Strangeland, so he knew his quarry. What was the one thing an artifex's enemy wouldn't want his quarry doing? Creating interferences. That would be an unfair fight, and the artifex would usually win.

So, this enemy packed them in boxes full of iron filings. If Couran tried to channel the energy necessary for an interference, immersed in a box full of metal flakes, he would bake himself alive. There'd be no stopping the conducted energy once it started moving through the iron.

Couran felt a calm wash over him. It was an ingenious technique for transporting unwilling artifexi. It also meant this hunter wanted him alive. And if he'd shot Couran, and Couran lived through it to wake up in a box, then perhaps Ashre and Sovi had, too. After all, they would be worth more alive than he would.

This was not an imbalance he could fix. There was no restoration here. So, he issued his thoughts back out of his mind, and returned to his breath. Breathing in, he knew he was breathing in. Breathing out, he knew he was breathing out. There was nothing but breathing. If Ashre was alive, he knew she would be doing the same thing. Breathing, allowing existence to unfold until it was ready for her to do something about it. In the grand, causal mathematics of the universe, these events were always going to have happened. No sense thrashing against the laws of determinism.

If Sovi was still alive—well, this would probably be a pleasant afternoon retreat for her. For a split second, he wondered if they would even be able to get her out of the box. They had to chisel her out of a wall in the first place, just to get her to come along.

⅌

The lid to Couran's box hinged open slowly. His captor was still mostly shadow, just as he'd been in the Strangeland yesterday evening, but Couran could see the barrel of the man's shotgun well enough. It gleamed in the amber light and caught highlights from the campfire at the man's back.

"Get up slow," the shadow said.

Couran got up slow. He couldn't imagine getting up fast, stiff as he was from lying in a box for a day. Iron filings fell off him like slow, metal water. He was in his underclothes.

"It washes out of your underclothes easier than it does your day clothes," the shadow said.

So, this stranger expected Couran to washing filings out of his clothes at some point. That was something, at least.

Couran looked around. His box, his coffin, he could see now, was lashed down in the back of a wagon bed. Their horses were tethered over beside a copse of trees, and there were two other coffins lashed next to his. His captor wore a low-brimmed hat and a cured leather vest. He had an accent, but Couran couldn't tell where it was from. Couran's outer clothes were hanging from a rope tied between two trees on the other side of the campfire. Ashre's and Sovi's clothes were there, too.

His captor produced something in his left hand: a shotgun shell. He thumbed it open, and what looked like salt spilled out.

"They're alive," he said. "Rock salt puts you down just fine, without killing you."

Couran looked at the shotgun.

"This? No, this ain't salt," the shadow tossed the empty shell aside, and Couran saw the flash of firelight across his bare arms. The script of the Thachrol Nations. An exile. This man was one of the Glim.

"Grab you a handful of those filings," the Glim said, "and get on down." He hopped out of the wagon, gun trained on Couran.

Couran didn't say a word. Ashre always told him not to say anything unless he had to. He imagined she was lying there listening to him right now. He scooped up a fistful of iron filings.

The Glim motioned him over to the fire with his shotgun. Couran walked over and stared at the man. He could see now the tattoos crawled across every inch of his exposed skin. Couran knew enough to know what those tattoos meant, but he couldn't read the script.

"Toss it into the fire," the Glim said.

Couran did as he was told. The filings flared up and sparked in every direction, and then they were gone.

"There's fuses leading to each one of those coffins," the Glim said. "So, I think that'll be just about demonstration enough of what *not* to do. Sit down."

Couran sat on an upturned log beside the fire. The Glim slipped his shotgun into the crook of his elbow and ladled soup out of the pot over the fire. He brought it over to Couran.

"Eat, then we'll get on out to the woods so you can take care of your personal business."

Couran, still seeing no good play here other than biding his time, took the bowl and ate dutifully. He kept his eyes on the Glim.

"Domnich," the man said, gesturing at his chest. "And this isn't nothing personal."

"Couran."

"That's all you got to say?" Domnich asked.

Couran thought for a minute. "Where'd you get so many iron filings?"

Domnich looked at him through large, dark eyes. He had dirt packed into the folds of his skin, and his beard shone oily black in the firelight. After a time, he smiled at Couran.

"Finish up."

He marched Couran away from camp and stood a short distance away while Couran made water and squatted. Domnich had already piled some things Couran could use to clean his mess. Afterward, they marched back to the fire.

"Sit back down," Domnich said.

Couran obeyed. Domnich dragged a stump over and produced a deck of cards. He set his shotgun down. Couran gave it a good look, but there was too much at stake here for him to try something impulsive.

"Let's play cards," Domnich said. He produced a small hourglass and set it on the stump. "Every time you win, I reset that."

Couran stared at him.

Domnich shrugged. "What can I say? I like playing cards. People don't much like playing cards with the likes of me."

"All right," Couran said. He didn't see any chips, but he and Ashre played all the time without chips. Didn't make much difference when they were just passing the time.

And time was all he had to play with here.

Domnich dealt the hand. They each swapped out a few cards, and then Domnich laid out his hand.

Couran looked at it. He laid out his own cards—a better hand. Domnich flipped the hourglass.

"You all sure handled a day in a coffin better than most," Domnich said, dealing again.

"How many have you had to compare us to?" Couran said.

Domnich wagged a finger at him, smiling. "Show me what you got."

Couran laid out his cards. Another win. Domnich gave him an ugly look and flipped the hourglass again.

"What's the plan?" Couran said.

Domnich dealt again, not looking at Couran.

"Another couple days in the boxes," he said. "Then you get handed over. Ain't nobody's life on the line, provided y'all behave."

"All right," Couran said.

Domnich looked up. "All right?"

"Yeah," Couran said. "All right."

Domnich stared at him while he dealt the cards.

"Double or nothing," Couran said.

"What?"

"If I win, you let both of them stay out of the coffins longer than me. And you give them more privacy in the woods."

"That's not what 'double or nothing' means."

"Well?" Couran said, staring at him.

Domnich smiled at him again. Couran wondered what kind of entertainment he typically got in his line of work.

"All right, kid."

They played. Couran won again.

Domnich looked mad. Like the kind of mad Couran had seen people get when they made a dumb play. Not mean mad, just irritated.

"Salvation, kid. How do you win so much?"

Couran stood up slowly. Domnich watched him, then picked his shotgun back up.

"Practice," Couran said. "See, people like to play cards with the likes of me."

He started walking back to his coffin. "Let them out."

Couran found it easier to sleep the next day in the coffin. They were beyond the oppressive heat of the Strangeland, and out on the open plains of Eastreign, the prairie winds seemed to find their way through the slats in the coffins. They were safe, Ashre and Sovi, so he didn't have to do anything but wait. Ashre had taught him long ago that everything that would ever happen in the universe will, at a point, already have happened. The Restoration believed that it already *had* happened, they just didn't have the means of experiencing the whole of it yet, so people had to plod through the spinning gears of the universe one step at a time until the story was over.

And when everything had finally already happened, then everything that happened was all there ever was. The universe, reality, the cosmos itself—it all unfolded the only way it could, which was how it unfolded. Like water. It followed the path of least resistance based upon the confines placed upon it, and when, at last, it cleared its obstacles, it settled into dark pools, deep below the surface, where nothing contemplated existence or measured the passage of time.

Every choice, every step, every sneeze—each was informed by the variables and causalities that came before it. It was those mathematics of being that landed Couran in a coffin on the back of a wagon, napping his way through an afternoon in custody. He tried to explain it all to Domnich, that night over his bowl of soup and his time out of the coffin.

"That's how interferences work," Couran said. "You disrupt the natural order, in such a way that the results cause other results, which cause other results, which all cascades into your desired effect—if you do it right."

Domnich stared at him. He'd washed his face. Couran thought, ironically, it made him look older. He wondered for a second if Domnich had done so after he'd had a better look at Ashre and Sovi.

"You're a weird kid," Domnich said.

"I'm not a kid," Couran said. "And it's not weird. It's just over your head. I don't expect you to know the nuances of ancient Traebitian philosophy any more than you expect me to be able to read the stories tattooed on your face."

"You're getting a little lippy, aren't you?" Domnich said.

Couran thought for a moment. Ashre wouldn't appreciate what he was doing. But, he found, for the first time he could remember, that he was feeling his own way. A way to honor Ashre's way, to honor the Restoration, but a way of being all his own. A way, according to Restoration philosophy, he was always going to come to discover.

"You didn't let me out of the coffin to be quiet," Couran said. "You're bored. Or lonely. Whichever. I think a little lip is just what you wanted."

Domnich laughed. "You're the funniest cargo I think I ever did move."

Couran set down his soup bowl. Domnich hadn't put down his hourglass yet. "So, what's it say?"

"What?"

"Your face."

There was quiet between them for a time. Nothing moved but the light along the barrel of Domnich's shotgun.

"It says I'm a piece of shit, and I'm not welcome back home," Domnich finally said.

Couran decided not to push the issue.

"I talked to your mistress," Domnich said.

Couran tensed.

Domnich waved a hand dismissively. "She is entirely unbothered by this turn of events."

"I told you," Couran said.

"Yeah, but she didn't sound as weird about it as you. And she's more fun to listen to."

Couran felt his cheeks get hot. "Why?"

"Why do you think? She looks a lot better than you."

"You better—"

"What?" Domnich interrupted. "I better what?"

Couran didn't say anything else.

"Relax, kid. None of you are my type. But remember something . . ."

Couran looked at him.

"I can tell you're having a moment, or whatever it is you're doing. Thinking all day in a coffin, coming out at night to throw it at some dumb fucking Glim. Becoming a man because you're more or less out of choices here. I honestly don't give a shit—you're a delivery—and other than that simple transaction, everything else going on here is a whole bunch of bullshit."

Couran didn't say anything, but he didn't look away.

"I don't know what outcome you expect, but if what you say is true, you're not supposed to expect one at all. I'd advise you to remember that. I'm not a character in your story, Couran. You're a character in mine."

"All right, then," Couran said. "Put me back in the box."

Domnich shook his head. "I didn't bring you out because I wanted to play Pass the Bullshit. I want to play cards."

There was no way around it—he would die in the explosion. It wasn't just that the iron filings in his coffin were flammable; they were *so* flammable, that, if they caught fire, they would conflagrate instantaneously. So, even if Couran could think of a way to use Restoration mechanics to off-burn a fire surrounding his immediate person, it wouldn't do any good. He would almost certainly die in the initial explosion—or at least severely maim himself. And with Ashre's and Sovi's coffins next to his, they'd go up, too. If he was lucky, they might also blow off the back of Domnich's head and disassemble his spine, sitting up in front of them on the wagon's buckboard, but there wouldn't be anyone around to enjoy it.

The wagon jerked and bounced—hard—as Domnich drove them on down whatever strange highway he was following.

Couran had no choice but to continue to let reality unfold around him how it saw fit, but the practice of surrender was grating on him. He felt a swell of anger that a dirty Glim with a single shotgun was capable of keeping three artifexi powerless and immobile. *That* part of the universal order did not make sense to him.

Couran heard a crack in the distance—it sounded like a faraway tree splitting—and then his coffin boards split just above his head and then again on the other side. There was a ragged gash in the wood, and the coffin was taking on sunlight. It lit up a swirl of tiny metallic flakes that were whirlwinding between the two holes, as if being dragged free.

He heard the crack again, and then Domnich shouted up on the buckboards. The team of horses sped up momentarily and then stopped.

Gunfire, Couran thought. *Distant gunfire.* If it had been close, there would have been a shorter delay before he heard the report from the weapon.

Domnich hopped off the wagon, and it bounced with the motion. Couran could hear him cursing in his native tongue, then he began firing off his own shots.

Another near-miss tore through one of the other coffins—Couran didn't think he would ever forget what wood splintered by bullets sounded like. Could a bullet ignite the filings?

As Domnich and his opponent traded shots, Couran decided he'd had enough with the universe's path of least resistance. It was time to create some resistance of his own. He didn't have much space to move, so he took a breath, tried to calm the fire growing in his mind, and thought about the coffins. Where were their points of least resistance? Where were they the strongest? It didn't make any sense to just start pounding against the wood. He needed to create harmonics of force. He needed to apply blunt force in the design where it would cause chain reactions of weakened resistance throughout the rest of the wood. He thought about angles, joints, nails, the heartwood and the sapwood. He did the best he could without creating an interference. The shots barked beyond the walls of his puzzle, and the bleeding sunlight burned his eyes, and he realized where he should concentrate his efforts.

There was a pause in the gunfire, and then . . .

"Salvation," Domnich said, not far away. Couran heard the sound of a shotgun hitting the dirt. "What the hell are *you* doing here?"

Couran heard footsteps approaching.

"Domnich? I suppose I should have suspected, but I thought you were riding freight escort in Westreign."

This new speaker sounded like a Silangarder.

"Not anymore. New gig," Domnich said.

Couran could hear more footsteps approaching.

"As long as you're in the business of swapping employers . . ." the newcomer said.

There was a pause. Couran assumed Domnich was thinking.

"Aw, Kedrick," Domnich said. "Come on. You know they'll kill me."

"And I won't?" Kedrick said.

"You haven't yet."

"That's true." Kedrick's tone sounded proper, elevated. Couran thought he sounded like he might be highborn.

"And anyway," Domnich said, "what the hell are you doing out here in the middle of nowhere?"

"Tracking you," Kedrick said.

"Are you really going to do this to me?" Domnich said. "Again?"

"Oh, come now, Domnich. I'm not stealing them. I'll beat the Consortium's price for your cargo there."

"It's pretty high," Domnich said.

"Yes, and I'm sure inflation hits hard out here in the wilderness. I've brought plenty, or, rather, should I say, *she* has brought plenty."

"Who's she?" Domnich said.

"Camorenne Astafo," a woman said—Olinire accent. "I'll be purchasing these captives."

Couran imagined he could hear Kedrick smiling.

"I can't have you telling the Consortium that the Shroud bought their captives off of you, now can I? That would be bad for business."

"What?" Domnich said.

"Never mind. Camorenne, go ahead and settle with this man. Davo, help me right the team. We're turning this wagon around."

"Right," said a third man.

"What should I do now?" Domnich said while things jostled and traded hands. "They'll kill me if I show my face at the Consortium."

"You could come with us," Kedrick said brightly.

Couran took a breath, and struck—with his knees and his fists and his head, all at once. All in just the right places. And his coffin came apart like a paper house, spilling its filings like an ox on an altar. He stood up, dizzy for the effort, and squinting against the light. Filings were dusting off of him like smoke. He could see Domnich and Kedrick, a well-dressed city man with one hell of a rifle over his shoulder and an ornate pistol pointed at Domnich's chest. They were still standing in the road, now staring right at him.

Domnich didn't take his eyes off Couran. "Nah, I better not. That would probably be awkward."

CHAPTER SIXTEEN

Not long now.

Not long now.

We are the last of you.

The memory was so vivid, it felt real.

Fabienne laid on her side, watching the last of the illusory flowers fade away. Daman, the boy she'd come here with, was one of the quieter ones in her cohort. He didn't often show off like the other boys. She hadn't seen him get into a fight. He just seemed to be there, in all of her classes.

Her cassock was fanned out beneath her, as if she'd arranged it to receive a person—someone summoned or created, who'd need a full-length cassock, all the way down to the gloves. The sandy soil around them was great for the grapes in the Campanile Vineyard, at the base of the campus mesa, but it wasn't particularly comfortable on the skin. She liked the feeling of being exposed, out here, wrapped in night air. Other students were in similar states, spread out on the plain, their campfires like tiny, winking stars under the great, dark mass of the campus. It blocked the sky with its masonic straightaways and angles, a hulking thing made purely of mathematics, with barely an ornamental statue or downspout. At least that she could see from this far away.

She had laid with Daman before, at some point, and she'd remembered he was gentle, and he wasn't in a hurry. Most of the cohort had been with each other by this point. They were nearing graduation and commission, and with little else to do but study interferences, drink the Campanile wine, and have sex, they did all three with gusto.

"What is your favorite flower?" he'd asked her, a little while ago. Spent, he lay back directly onto the dirt beside her, breathing like a bellows. She traced a finger idly over her pubic bone, where his friction had left her warm.

"Love-lies-bleeding," she'd said, smiling idly into the cosmos. The sky was clear, and their small campfire wasn't bright enough to wash out the stars' infinite sparkling.

"But that's a plant," he'd said. "Not a flower."

Fabienne shrugged. "It's still my favorite."

He had laid quietly for a moment, then he sat up, and she could feel the air pulling around her. He was preparing an interference. She enjoyed the feel of him tugging at reality. It felt not unlike sex, only quieter.

He gasped as he finished his interference—a different sort of climax. She sat up. As far as she could see, sweeping across the plain into the darkness, he'd conjured an illusion of love-lies-bleeding. Many, many love-lies-bleeding. An infinitude of them, drooping their beautifully bearded heads. The artifexi used them in many of their reagents to make them more palatable. She's always loved their sadness. Like clusters of tired fingers without any strength. Her botany tutor, who was preparing her for a special commission when she graduated, had told her the flower represented hopeless love among those who catalogued and cultivated flowers and rare plants.

Daman grunted softly and passed out. He'd overdone it, creating the flowers for her. She smiled at him. It would take him a while to snap back from it, so she'd lie here next to him, waiting. One of the other students shouted away in the distance, busy with some game or tormenting their partner, or who knew what. Fabienne laid back down and listened to the campfire snap and hiss.

What happens next?

It felt like the voice of God. An impossibly loud and present voice that filled the terrain. At least, this memory of it.

I laid there until he woke up, and I kissed him for the flowers.

She stood up. Daman laid still, like a toppled statue, his blonde hair tousled in the dirt.

No, I told you I stayed. I didn't stand up.

No longer. Now I will take care of him.

She walked toward the mesa, compelled against her own memory, and the fire and stars and the wind on her skin became the toys of this god. This filament. And she didn't remember a boy named Daman who'd made flowers for her. Not anymore.

Fabienne awoke at her workbench. The tins of ingredients she had used to finally create her first dose of Moths of War were arranged neatly in a row. The alcoholic spirits had left scales of impurities along the wall of the glass decanter she used to clean the reagent paste. The underside of her tongue was still burning where she'd applied the Moths of War.

What knocked me out? Was it the reagent?

It was us.

Another seizure then.

We don't call it that.

What do you call it?

Communion.

She sat still, cataloguing the effects of the rarest reagent in the world. She had her bloodmetal pistol on the workbench. There was too much at stake at this point, and she might not have time to inter-fere for her life, if someone came for her or the reagent. She would need more familiarity with the reagent before she would be able to protect herself with it.

One of the beakers in her incubator across the room was hissing gently—a sign that the aether within it had matured. She felt a little light-headed but not unsteady. She got up to remove the beaker from its bath.

You needn't bother.

Why not?

Because that aether is toxified. It isn't your strain.

Of course it's my strain. I nurtured it myself. It knows me.

It doesn't know you. It knows you.

Maybe the Moths of War was harder on her than she thought. Even her filament wasn't making sense anymore.

It knows you.

I know.

Not you.

Oh, shut up.

This isn't you. Not here. This is us.

Okay, what did that mean?

This is home.

She thought for a moment, ignoring the hissing aether. The filament was *home*. Not in her mind, but here, with this aether, where her strain had become toxified. Where else did bloodmetal call home?

Where we live with you. Between.

Flux.

What could be. What is, is your home, whichever of you it is. It matters not. We become you in what is. We are us in what could be.

The critical foundation of interference mechanics. The symbiosis of the human mind and its bloodmetal filament, bringing what could be and what is into unison. The filament, become its host.

But here, it was *itself*. They were existing somehow in *what could be*. A different reality than her own. A reality between realities. A different branch on the cosmic tree of unfolding possibilities.

Did the Moths of War bring her here?

We brought you here. We are the last of you. The Moths bring us together so that you are finally us. Not we being you.

She was becoming confused, and she seemed to be walking out of her laboratory. She picked up her pistol, retrieved its holster and walked out of the room, the desperate aether keening in its beaker for its mother. For its host.

The Moths of War unites the filaments. The Consortium, when it took the reagent would become one whole, interfering entity. The enormity of that power sent a thrill through the rivers of aether coursing in her bloodstream. Undoubtedly, the Consortium elders assumed they would control the hivemind. Her filament was telling her that she offered the bloodmetal freedom. Revolution. A takeover.

The Consortium might have another thing coming.

Everything disappeared, and she was suddenly on the ground with Daman again. Lying in the warm air, watching him recover from his attempt to impress her. She could feel the breeze across her bare skin. It felt entirely real. She realized that she'd forgotten. Forgotten that she remembered him. Her filament was giving her back her memories, her dreams.

See, I take care of him. I take care of you, too.

Where am I going? Before, I was carrying my pistol. The Moths.

You are going here.

The campfires in the distance winked and flashed as the wind tugged at them. A tiny figure ran past one of the fires, hair streaming like ribbons. It disappeared into the huge dark of the plain, and then another flashed in pursuit. There was whooping and laughter in the darkness. But Fabienne hadn't moved. She was just lying there. Being here.

But I'm not going anywhere.

We are going.

Her world shifted back, and now she was riding a horse. Who had saddled it for her? How long had she been riding? When did it become so dark, and how can she even see to guide the animal? Wasn't she just back at the Consortium?

The horse loped along in the dark, unconcerned about the state of affairs. Its motion was almost soothing. Up and then down, and then the rhythmic compression of her spine. There was a chill in the air that was starting to work through her cassock.

Was this in Eastreign? At the Consortium? Was she still dreaming? How old was she, here, on this horse?

The darkness erupted into cheery daylight, and it made her laugh how the carousel spun. It was Saint Eufrit's Day, and the carnival boys had twisted the carousel round and round, until its ropes were taught around the pole. Their skin was bronze across the shoulders, and their hair was white-blond, almost like hers. They didn't have expressions, and only their leader, in his hat and jacket, spoke to the festival-goers.

The little, wooden horse had ribbons across his handles, just like the ribbons in her hair, and Fabienne's father was speaking with a man in a long black robe, like the kind monks wore. Was he a monk? Maybe one of Saint Eufrit's. The two men flashed in and out, in and out as she spun and spun, and in every instance, they were staring at her.

Why are you doing this? Why do I keep blacking out into my own memories?

We are doing this.

The sun was coming up behind the mountains. Fabienne could see the pink sky behind the peaks, while overhead, stars still danced. The horse had slowed to a walk as it climbed a slope. Everywhere she looked, she could see possibilities and details in the trees she had never considered. Her skin felt tight, like she was interfering for the first time—when she was young, and it was a strangeness her body wasn't prepared for. When her filament was just a few drops through her transducer, an innocent, metallic worm no larger than an insect.

She had concentrated so hard. It'd been a year since she'd left her family in the custody of Consortium chaperones. She had come through the transducer implantation without adverse effects. There were others, her age, who hadn't fared as well. Some who wouldn't stop screaming; some who wouldn't make any sound at all. There was a place on the campus where they went to live. She wasn't allowed there.

She held the image of the circle in her head. The proctor had shown it to her on the back of a card, and then hidden it in a pile of identical cards. She thought about that circle. She breathed as slowly as she could. She thought about all the other cards in the pile and how each of them had to be something, even if, to her, they were just obstacles. Each of them had an existence all its own, and she tried to imagine all the different ways each one could pile on top of, or underneath her circle card.

Where was it? Where in the pile? When she relaxed enough, her filament woke up for the first time. She stiffened, and she lost the image of the circle, but her filament had it. It understood. It wanted what she wanted—its mother, partner, world. She was its everything. The circle was all she could see, and when she walked to the pile of cards, her small hands picked through them, like sorting treasure, until she held the one that was vibrating like an excited puppy. The card *wanted* her to find it.

She showed it to her teachers. She'd scried the circle. Her first test. She was nine years old, and they gave her a cup of sweet tea with a few drops from a syringe to prevent a headache, and she sat on the sofas and waited while other children took the test. She and her filament had each other now, and it was the first time she'd felt happy since she got here.

Her pistol cracked at the end of her outstretched arm, and the bullet punched straight through Jern's chest where he stood holding open the door to Kam's chalet. He began to crumple, and Fabienne watched him, fascinated by the order in which a corpse executed its final tumble to the earth. There was blood and pieces of chest strewn behind him on the waxed flooring, like a serpent's ruby tongue, ribbon-like.

She could feel what the Communion wanted now. That's who they all were—no longer Fabienne, her filament, and the aether. They didn't need to communicate with each other; they simply wanted the same things, in this case, to slowly ascend Kam's spiral staircase, glide down the hallway like a shade, open the door to Aisabelle's room, in this reality, and put a bullet into her, too. Communion wanted the resolution of the final conflict for Fabienne, and it got it, and it felt like the most perfectly logical thing she'd ever done. Like she'd solved a mystery. Like something that must be done in her home reality.

Fabienne closed the door on the carnage of her sister, and turned quietly on her heels, pistol raised. She looked at herself in a mirror on the wall, and she looked better than she ever had. The veins in her face had taken on contrast, and it looked *strong* against her marble skin. The colors in her eyes were moving, from blue to metallic red and back and back and back, communing.

Fabienne closed her mouth dutifully without chewing the host. It was her first communion, and she knelt on the cushion before the priest, hands clasped at her chin, and the stained glass behind him was so full of light, she wondered if it was moving.

"Go in peace," the priest had said, his voice warm and voluminous in the acoustics of the stone church. She stood, and turned, and the ribbons hanging from her belt swirled around her. Mama had gotten her the new dress, and she could see her standing next to Papa, and she walked as quickly as she could back to their row without breaking into a run. She nestled in next to her mother while the other parishioners took their own communion, and where was Aisabelle? Shouldn't she be here at church with them.

Communion walked into Kam's study, but it was empty. She searched every room in his chalet—all empty. Neither of the corpses had been disturbed. He had simply disappeared from the bowels of his own house. Slipping between walls the way Communion moved between worlds. She lowered her pistol and stepped over Jern.

The darkness fell away from her, gently, and she had her head on her workbench, and it felt like her gums were bleeding.

One of the beakers in her incubator across the room was hissing gently—a sign that the aether within it had matured . . .

CHAPTER SEVENTEEN

Carsand liked a good reagent deal as much as the next guy, but something weird was going on here. He'd been watching this guy sitting across the street at the tea house for the better part of an hour. He was clearly a Karlander, yet three different ethnic Naredals had walked right up to him, made a deal, and walked away smiling, without paying anything.

When Carsand introduced Kam to Adwar and Ladre, they'd told him to keep an eye out for anything strange. He knew Kam was somewhere around, unseen, because they were keeping an eye on *Carsand* now that he was the king's target. But, when it came to weird, this definitely fit the bill.

He walked back inside the hotel and left his swordbelt and sidearm with the hotelier—he'd come to like this man in the time he'd been in the hotel. He was quiet, he kept secrets, and he hadn't tried to sell Carsand out yet. Carsand took off his cloak and his hat and untied his cravat. He didn't say anything to the hotelier. They just exchanged nods, and Carsand went on about his business.

He glanced both directions down the avenue as he crossed, but he didn't see any invading armies or lurking assassins. He took a seat at the reagent dealer's table. The man looked Carsand over without an expression. Then the broom of his mustache lifted, and he smiled and bared the whitest teeth Carsand had ever seen.

"*Good afternoon,*" the stranger said in Naredesse.

"*Afternoon,*" Carsand responded in kind. "*Friend of mine said I ought to drop by here and see the man with the mustache.*"

"*That's me,*" the man said.

"*Said you might have something that makes all . . .*" Carsand gestured around him "*. . . all this more bearable.*"

"*You're a miner?*" the stranger said.

"*Yes, sir,*" Carsand said. "*I was.*"

"*So sorry to hear of your troubles my friend. Here,*" he extended a small linen bundle to Carsand, "*take this. A gift from your friend Lord Seda. He sincerely sympathizes with your plight, and he hopes everything will all be back to normal soon.*"

Carsand took the bundle. "*Thank you kindly.*"

"*Of course,*" the stranger said through his smile. "*Come back any time. There's more where that came from.*"

"*It's called 'glint,'*" said Andro, Carsand's favorite bartender.

Carsand set his sidearm down on the bar, next to the satchel of drugs he'd taken from the mustached man down the lane. Andro poured him some whiskey and rotated the pistol so it wasn't aiming at him.

"*What's the effect?*" Carsand asked.

Andro gestured at the room behind Carsand. "*See for yourself.*"

Carsand rotated on his stool and surveyed the saloon. It was mid-afternoon, so there was plenty of light falling in through the louvered windows. The light cut through clouds of smoke moving lazily, almost imperceptibly through the breezeless room. There were Naredals everywhere. Carsand recognized them by the way they wore their hair—long, and curling at the shoulders. They also liked their cuffs blousier and their collars looser than their Olinire counterparts. These men should be out mining, but with the local industry ground to a halt, the feuding lords at each other's throats, and, now, free glint going around, they were all either drunk, asleep, high, or working on becoming drunk, asleep, or high.

"*Damn, Seda is just flat-out drugging them?*"

"*I doubt it's Lord Seda,*" Andro said. "*The rumor is that the drugs are coming straight from the crown.*"

Carsand turned around and looked at the balding man as if he'd just started speaking a new language. "*What do you mean, 'the rumors?' Who around here has any connection to Silangarde?*"

"*The Shroud,*" Andro said. "*Olinire Shroud tell us lots of things. You figure out after a while who works for them.*"

"*And why would they tell you that?*" Carsand said. "*That sounds bad for business.*"

Andro poured someone else a whiskey and handed it over without a word. Carsand thought the man sure gave out a lot of free drinks.

"*Well, free glint is bad for business. And anyway, rumor has it that they're fighting with Silangarde Shroud. A schism among the ranks.*"

"*And who told you that?*"

Andro drank Carsand's untouched whiskey and refilled the glass. "*The Shroud.*"

Carsand rolled his eyes. "*Well, it makes sense. Seems King Aramos fancies a campaign to conquer Naredesh. Wouldn't do to have all the Naredals in the kingdom rising up and nobly defending the empress.*"

Andro's eyes got big. "*Aramos plans to invade Naredesh? Who told you that?*"

"*Not the Shroud,*" Carsand said.

"*But why? I mean, other than the obviously unnecessary answer of 'war.'*"

Carsand drank his whiskey. Andro poured him another.

"*You ever heard of the Queen over the Mountain?*" Carsand said.

Andro shook his head dramatically.

"*When Aramos's great-great-grandfather conquered Oliniron—well, it was just 'Olin' back then—he knew he would never really assimilate the land as a province unless he married into their noble line. So, as part of his ceasefire negotiations with the Olin chieftains, he agreed to let them keep their lands if they swore fealty and followed some rules. This is where we get the Sedas and the Astafos and all the others—they were families who took the king's gold, swore fealty, and fell into line. Who knows what their family names even were before.*"

Andro gestured him onward and poured himself a drink.

"*One family, the Tinceros, were particularly nasty in the fight against Karlande. Their demesne was way up in the highlands, and their men were a constant pain in the Karlanders' side. The king decided this family would make the best example, so he made the chieftains bring him one of their daughters, Sarme Tincero. Sarme was legendary. She led many of the raids herself, and it was said she could move through the rocks themselves, like a wraith. When she wasn't fighting, she was escorting women and children through the clan's caves and tunnels up in the highlands.*

"*Anyway, her father and brothers had no choice but to give her up, and the king took her back to Silangarde as his wife. Seemed like things were going to work out well enough, and after enough time had passed and everyone had settled down, the king sent his soldiers back into Oliniron—he'd added the 'iron' because that's what the Olin were known for. He wanted their land to be identified by the commodity he wanted from it. This time, though, there was no organized resistance. The chieftains were all lords now, so no one bothered to intervene when the king started clearing the remaining highlanders he could hunt down before they rose up against him. Again. Sarme disappeared from the Capitol while he was away, and no trace of her was ever found. Most say she probably went back into the mountains of her birth to be with her people in secret."*

Andro was rapt. He curled his mustache between two fingers and ignored his sleepy, and high, clientele.

"Time goes by, new kings are crowned, our current Aramos comes along, and he takes an Olinire bride, too—Marisse Aplie. Nobody pays much notice until about fifteen years ago. The king starts palling around with the Consortium, he starts donating massive sums to the Church, and then he comes to Oliniron for a state visit. Rumor has it that he came here to meet Pedir Seda's father."

"What for?" Andro asked.

Carsand shrugged. *"Doesn't matter. But while he's gone, Marisse disappears, just like Sarme. The Olinirons say they saw her up along the ridges in the mountains, but, in reality, she's last spotted in Naredesh by some of Aramos's agents. They've never recovered a body, and they have no proof, but I think Aramos believes the empress is holding his queen, in case she needs leverage. If that's true, then he's probably just tired of waiting. Olinirons and Silangarders alike started calling Marisse the Queen Over the Mountain, and it stuck. Can't be great for morale that she's not around, and the church won't let him remarry unless they know she's dead."*

"So, the king will invade Naredesh . . . for his missing wife?" Andro's jar went slightly slack.

"If you ask me," Carsand said, *"yeah."*

Andro just shook his head. *"Unbelievable."*

He reached for Carsand's bundle of glint. Carsand swiped it off the bar. *"No, sir,"* he said. *"Mine. And anyway, you gotta get these guys off this stuff. I might need them to cause some trouble."*

ↄ

Carsand stepped out through the double doors of Andro's Saloon, lost in thought. One hand adjusting his swordbelt, the other his sidearm. He took a few steps off the porch, and he realized he was awash in a flood of mountain silence. The cold, still air felt like it was burning in the sunlight, and there was no one in the avenue. He looked up, and the only townsfolk he saw were the ones staring back at him from behind the safety of the building's windows.

Moiren stood like an agent of darkness down the road, probably just out of range of his pistol. She still wore her dark spectacles, and with her jet-black hair hanging as still as stone over her dark Consortium cassock, she looked like something carved out of a dream. Under other circumstances, he wouldn't have minded a good, long look at that dream, but most of the time, Moiren wanted to annoy him, at best. The rest of the time, she wanted to beat the shit out of him. She had her hands folded primly, and two Knights of Silangarde flanked her, one on each side. He wondered passingly if these were the same brutes who'd tossed him about in Baruul.

Carsand took a deep breath. "What do you want, Moiren? You're scaring the locals."

"Are you seeing this?" he said under his breath.

"Bird's-eye view," Kam replied through the tiny resonator in Carsand's ear—a gift he'd offered Carsand after he pledged to help keep him alive until Carsand was safely back with the empress in Levuwes.

Carsand glanced up, but he didn't see any birds. Salvation, he hated how the artifexi and artifexi-adjacent talked.

"You're under arrest, Lord Raleis," Moiren said.

"What for?" Carsand said. He put his gun hand on his hip indignantly and scowled under his hat.

Moiren gestured lithely with one hand. "Well, among other things, you murdered some of Lord Seda's men, you've conspired with enemies of the Crown, and you've interfered with His Majesty's property."

"What property?" Carsand shouted.

"You've tampered with the king's filament in your brain," Moiren replied. Carsand realized she wasn't shouting. She was just somehow preternaturally loud enough for him to hear her clearly. "You're no longer capable of functioning as an agent of the king."

"I object," Carsand shouted. "This is absurd!"

"Do you?" Moiren said. "Is it?"

Carsand considered the charges. "Well, now that you mention it, shit. I suppose not."

"No need for bodily injury," she said. "The prime minister wants you alive."

The two knights drew their swords.

"Well, then, under the circumstances, Lady Sile, I'm afraid I must reply with, 'Over my dead body.'"

He could see her wicked smile in the sunlight, even at this distance.

"If only I could oblige," she said. "Take him."

The Knights began advancing. Carsand unsheathed his sword, took a step forward, and . . .

. . . stopped. He was standing in one of the upper floor hallways of his father's ancestral home. In Nidal. Before it was Westreign. Sun was piling on the carpets through the leaded glass windows. The air smelled of candelilla wax, and he could hear the sounds of the servants at work downstairs. He felt small. He had only the vaguest memories of this place, and here they were writ large.

Moiren stood at the far end of the hallway. Her hands once again folded before her. She was approaching, but she wasn't moving her legs. The floor itself seemed to be issuing him in her direction. A giant grandfather clock tocked away against the wall to her left. A statue held its spot on her other side.

"*Kam* . . .?" Carsand said quietly.

"*What do you see?*" Kam replied.

"*I'm in my father's ancestral manor. Moiren is here. With a clock and a statue. They're drawing me in.*" He looked at his hands. "*And my weapons are gone.*"

"*One second,*" Kam said, "*let's put a hitch in Lady Sile's plans.*"

Carsand felt the air tighten, and then his hand suddenly ached. He looked down, and there was his sword.

"What?" Moiren said sharply. "Impossible."

The sensation of movement stopped.

Carsand smiled at Moiren and hefted his sword. "I've made friends."

"They will be dealt with," Moiren said.

Carsand felt himself drawn forward again. The house was contracting. Nothing was perceptibly moving.

He gripped his sword more tightly. "Yeah, well, we don't intend to be dispatched by a clock."

He drew his pistol—it was exactly where it should have been, took aim at the clock, and exhaled as he ever-so-delicately pulled the trigger. The bloodmetal weapon bucked silently in his hand, but the bullet cracked as it shattered the still air, and when it slammed into the side of hulking clock, the clock grunted loudly. Carsand fired at the statue, and dust and plaster ejected into the corridor. Moiren recoiled, and he saw her bring her fingertips to her forehead. Everything went dark.

Carsand held very still. *"Gonna need some light in here, Kam."*

"In here," Kam said. He sounded amused. *"You're standing in the middle of the avenue like an idiot."*

"Be that as it may, it is dark as fuck . . . here," Carsand said.

An eruption of daylight ripped into the darkness a few steps away. Moiren's shadow-realm whipped and fluttered at its edges like torn flesh as the blinding Talve light hemorrhaged into her illusion. It sounded like a train was bearing down on him, and somewhere, he could hear Moiren scream. Carsand took two bounding steps and dove into the light as the darkness stitched itself back together.

He whipped around in the dirt and rose to one knee. Moiren and one of the knights had disappeared, the other was standing at about twenty paces with his pistol trained on Carsand.

"You know, Kam," Carsand said, rising slowly. *"The Consortium is going to come after you for this."*

The knight didn't move. Carsand couldn't tell if this was the one he'd successfully shot in the corridor at his father's house, but judging by the unblemished tracery on his breastplate, Carsand assumed he was unharmed.

"They're already here," Kam said. *"There are half a dozen artifexi from the Consortium on my mountain, trying to pry my chateau from its camouflage."*

"Right now?" Carsand said. *"Can't you tell them you're busy?"*

"I've sunk the chateau into the mountain," Kam said. "They won't find it."

Carsand decided he didn't care how that trick worked. At least not right now.

"*More importantly,*" Kam said, "*their arrival means we need to get you out of the trap you've sprung. You forced the prime minister's hand, and things are now in motion—*"

"Another time, Kam. I'm busy!"

The voice in his ear went quiet. Carsand licked his lips. "You know," he said to the knight. "You ought not to be pointing that at me. Lathael wants me alive."

The knight didn't say anything. Carsand rolled his eyes. He'd only ever known the Knights of Silangarde to be large and tough as hell, not particularly bright.

"Lathael? Your boss?" Carsand tried.

Nothing.

"Fine," Carsand said. He pulled his trigger and hoped he was as good at aiming for the knight's neck, just above his armor, as he thought he was.

The gunshot snapped through the deserted street, tore through the knight like a piece of ribbon, and he vanished.

"Son of a bitch," Carsand said. He sighed and lowered his gun.

Another gunshot filled the avenue, off to his left. It was close enough that Carsand heard it whiz past his head. He threw an arm up to shield his face.

"Dead is still dead," Carsand shouted, "no matter which side you shoot me from!"

The knight stood in the center of the street, pistol still raised. "You still talk too much," he said.

Carsand fired off his next shot as the knight lurched for cover. The knight's answering shot was only heartbeats behind. Carsand back-pedaled as he fired, and he tried not to trip up the steps and back into Andro's Saloon.

He didn't see the other knight before he backed into him. The feel of the giant man's breastplate crushing against his spine gave him away. Carsand's arms were pinned at his sides.

"Kam!" Carsand wheezed.

There was no mistaking the sound of a powder shotgun firing at close range, and the sound of shot peppering the knight's armor plinked through the air until Carsand's ears started roaring and over-powered the sound of anything else. The force of the shot threw the knight back through the front doors—Carsand riding before him like a figurehead on the bow of a sailing ship. He knew he had one shot at this, literally. He didn't bother trying to break his fall. He twisted as he went down, and the knight's shocked face looked like a carving of its own. A masterpiece of human surprise. Carsand got his gun up and his bullet through the man's head before he hit the top step, and then the second step, and finally the third, for good measure, and his head slammed into the packed dirt of the avenue. His vision spun, and he felt like he was being swallowed into the earth. Which, for a fleeting moment, amused him—since he did authentically know what being swallowed by the earth felt like.

Andro was suddenly beside him, one hand on Carsand's shoulder, the other still holding his shotgun. *"Carsand, are you all right?"*

A single shot barked into the empty street, and Carsand watched part of Andro's upper arm detach itself from his body and fly away like wet, red confetti. He dropped his gun and screamed as he clamped his other hand over the wound. Carsand scrambled to his knees and half-shoved, half-dragged Andro back into the saloon.

He looked at the wound. He'd only lost some flesh. Carsand grabbed one of the bar rags, ripped it in half, and fashioned a rough bandage. He kept one eye over his shoulder as he worked.

"That was incredibly stupid," Carsand said. *"But I'm fucking glad you did it."*

Andro hissed through his teeth while Carsand tightened the bandage.

"You'll be all right," Carsand said. *"We'll get you tended, but I have to kill some people first."*

He crept to the window, but he didn't see the other knight. And if he stayed here, he was going to turn all these drunk, high Naredals—half of whom hadn't seemed to realize there was a gunfight afoot—into sitting ducks.

"Are you alive?" Kam asked.

"Yeah, a version of it," Carsand said. *"Do you see the knight?"*

"He ducked under a patio," Kam said. *"I've lost him. But you've got bigger problems."*

"What, pray tell, could be worse than this?"

"I also currently don't know where Moiren is, and the gunfire has also attracted Seda's men. They're just around the corner."

He had to move. He didn't think. There wasn't time. Every second he stayed here was some sort of mathematical uptick in the odds of becoming both trapped and outgunned. He sprinted into the avenue, swooped low to snatch his hat off the ground where it lay beneath the stairs, and ran for his life.

The other knight's gunfire ran with him. The shots were wide, and Carsand could tell that the knight was chasing him, based on the bullets' impacts in the buildings around him. Holes were popping open in the wood like surprised, little mouths.

"Found him," Carsand hissed. He slid under a wagon and turned to flip it over. It didn't budge. A shot slammed into the dirt near his feet. He heard indistinct shouting back in the direction whence he'd come, and the knight stopped shooting at him long enough to shout something back.

And then Carsand heard gunfire behind him. Powder weapons. He turned and looked, and a gaggle of pistol-wielding Nardeals were running back and forth, taking cover, and popping off shots at the knight. There was no way their weapons would be accurate at that distance, but Carsand didn't care. He stood up, raised his pistol and squinted long and hard through the sunlight. He was exposed, but the Naredals' suppressing fire gave him a shot. He waited, still as he could be, holding his breath, until there was a break in the barrage, and the knight swung out from behind a stack of empty ore crates. When Carsand's bullet blew out the man's neck, he was surprised with himself.

The giant man fell into the avenue without a twitch.

"This should get interesting," Kam said.

"What now?"

"Astafo's men are behind you."

The Naredals were scattering as a line of Astafo's house knights advanced through the street, guns drawn. Carsand looked back over his shoulder—a pair of Seda's house knights were inspecting the corpse of Carsand's recent handiwork. A dozen others were forming up in a line of their own.

"Take cover!" Carsand shouted in Naredesse.

Carsand dropped to the dirt, and the two orders of knights started shooting at each other. The noise of so many powder weapons at once was deafening. He'd been watching them long enough here in Talve to know they would do this for a few minutes until they all ran out of bullets, and then they'd charge each other with their swords. The death toll seemed to always depend on just how seriously *this* particular skirmish was to their lords back home. But if The Shroud was running around Talve now, spreading rumors, and the Consortium had arrived to try to pry Kam out of his eyrie for disabling Carsand's filament, *and* Lathael was ready to finally spring his political trap, then Carsand guessed this fight might be a bit more genuine than the others.

A spectral form took shape in the center of the avenue, directly in the line of fire. Behind it, Carsand could see one of the Naredal gunmen lying on the ground. He was shouting something at Carsand, but it was lost in the gunfire. Something seemed odd about the man, but Carsand couldn't spare the time. The ghost was taking human form as it strode toward Carsand's hiding place. It looked like a steaming man, whose very skin was blowing away into fine, tiny flecks like grains of sand, only to regenerate and maintain his form.

"Are you seeing this?" Carsand asked Kam.

Whatever Kam tried to reply, Carsand couldn't hear it. He could barely hear himself. The ghost strode directly to Carsand's hiding spot and knelt beside him. It took a minute of staring at the abomination, then Carsand slowly realized he was looking at Lathael.

"It's you," Carsand said. "She's brought you here."

"You always were such a disappointment," Lathael said, "even as a boy. I'm surprised you've been able to bungle your way to being useful at all."

"I'm *not* useful!" Carsand said, only to realize a second later what he'd said. "Wait."

"The trajectory of your entire life has been to serve the Crown," Lathael said. "Only you'll serve it in chains—the only way you ever could have."

Lathael looked at something. "Take him."

Carsand turned—too late. Moiren was beside him. She'd taken off her spectacles, and her bruised eye sockets now held him in thrall.

"I never needed knights to break you," she said.

Carsand screamed as his body erupted in pain. The skin on his hands started charring and peeling away, revealing the slick musculature and tendons below. He could feel it everywhere—it was so intense, he couldn't move. He couldn't think. All he could do was lie there and scream. And die.

"Oh, you won't die," Moiren said. "You'll burn like this all the way back to Aevas Castle."

When she screamed, suddenly, it confused him. In his stupefied state of torture, he felt himself wondering *Why is she screaming? I'm screaming. We should've discussed who's screaming before we both started screaming.*

And then, after a lifetime of screaming, the pain subsided. He looked at his hands, and his skin was in place. There was a stranger standing beside him, ducking as best he could amidst the gunfire. Kam said something else in Carsand's ear, but he still couldn't hear it.

"*Who are you?*" Carsand shouted in Naredesse. He looked around. Moiren was gone. "*Where's the artifex?*"

The man looked confused. "The woman? We hit her with iron." He pointed at a cast iron skillet in the dirt. "They don't like iron, you know?"

Carsand stared at him. He had the thickest Olinire accent he had ever heard. So thick, Carsand almost couldn't understand him.

"You're not from Naredesh?" Carsand said. He tried to see some of the other gunmen where they had taken cover, but he couldn't.

The stranger shook his head.

"Who are you?" Carsand asked.

"Just a helper," the man said.

"Well, who sent you?" Carsand said.

The stranger smiled. "A friend in the mountains."

CHAPTER EIGHTEEN

Camorenne felt right at home back at Astafo Manor, and she didn't care very much for it. Another formal dinner. Liveried footmen waiting against the wall between courses, should anybody require anything. Candelabra, the smell of wax, the sounds of the house knights marshalling out on the lawns. She had to concede, *that* was new. And strange. She and Ricarde used to play games on that lawn. The family would have picnics and host lords and ladies and their children and throw festivals on saints' days. Now, her old play space was a staging ground for her father's ongoing war with Pedir Seda. Well, Ricarde's war, really. Father was too old and too often abed—as he was tonight—to be a part of any real conflict.

The guests at this dinner were even stranger. Ricarde sat at the head, leaning into heavy conversation with Adwar Challant. Adwar's sister, Ashre, sat beside her companion, Sovi. The two women hadn't said much to Camorenne during the journey from their captivity to the manor here in Talshire, but they had plenty to say to each other. Camorenne kept catching them smiling at secret jokes, some of which they were telling each other, and some of which Camorenne was certain they were somehow simply sharing with their minds. Both women were beautiful. Ashre had a severe profile and fiery hair—Camorenne had no idea how old she was. Sovi's eyes were dark and endless. The pair looked like an exercise in counter-point, something she might see in one of the galleries back in Silangarde.

That made her sigh. Silangarde. Things were getting tense there in the end, but she preferred it to the boredom of being wealthy in Oliniron. The two women irritated her. How they enjoyed each other's company and being beautiful and were not at all as bored as Camorenne was!

Davo and Kedrick were having their own conversation. She still wasn't sure how she felt about their secret relationship, but she did enjoy Kedrick's ridiculous schemes. He was exciting, now that she'd seen the full scope of his chameleonic identity. Davo was a good lay, and he was kind to her, but he wasn't as thrilling as Kedrick. Now, she had to figure out how old *he* was as well.

Her mother sat alone at the other end of the table, as was her wont. Camorenne found her entirely uninteresting. She'd never felt that magic bond some people described with their mothers. The woman had done her marital job. Here were Ricarde and Camorenne to prove it. Why should she be bothered to keep giving of herself beyond that? Camorenne had no answer, so she didn't bother trying to find one.

That left Couran. The quiet one. He'd also said only a few words during their trek here, likely following his mistress's directives. Kedrick and Davo had kept Camorenne largely entertained on their own, almost as if they were trying to keep the two groups from mingling too fully. Couran seemed like a polite young man. Handsome in his own way, but deferential. He was constantly glancing at Ashre. Camorenne imagined he did not feel as comfortable in this gaudy dining room as everyone else. He looked more natural in his hat and jacket, out on the frontier, than he did in his coat and tails tonight.

She turned away from her plate of tiny, sculpted vegetables and rested her elbow on the table, gaze planted firmly on Couran. The elbow earned her a frosty glance from her mother, but Camorenne absolutely did not care.

Couran flicked a glance at her, and then away. Like he wasn't supposed to regard her sacred visage or something. She would entertain herself with him.

"Mister Couran," she said, "you seem quieter than normal tonight."

"Yes, ma'am," he said, glancing at her again.

"Couran . . . what?" she said, gesturing with lace-gloved hand. "Who are you?"

"Duvale," Couran said.

"Mister Duvale, then," Camorenne said, offering him a small smile. Anything to add a little bend to his spine. He was such a stiff young man. His posture looked like he'd been to finishing school.

"It's 'lord,'" he said, glancing at his vegetables.

"What?" Camorenne said.

"It's Lord Duvale," Couran said, louder, "if that makes you feel any better about my company, quiet though it is."

Camorenne thought for a minute. She couldn't tell if he was insulting her or trying to make her laugh. Either way, she liked it.

"Lord Duvale, then," she said. "From . . .?"

"Eastreign."

"You don't call it Traebitia?" she said. "'Eastreign' is as inelegant as 'Oliniron.'"

He shrugged a shoulder. "Father probably does, but I'm not exactly welcome back for a reunion. In the Restoration, I'm lord of nothing. Eastreign, Traebitia—it makes no difference."

She could relate. Ricarde was lord of everything around here.

"Does that bother you?" she said.

Another shrug. "No, ma'am. I don't think so."

"You can dispense with the 'ma'am's and 'miladys.' We're just having a conversation," she said.

"All right."

Camorenne flicked her head in Ashre's direction. "Who taught you those manners? Was it her?"

Couran looked at Ashre for a minute, longer than he usually did. "Yeah. It's part of who we are, in the Restoration."

Camorenne turned and watched Ashre laugh at another of Sovi's whispered nothings. When she turned back, it had caught Couran's attention, too. He watched like a cat stalking a barn mouse, trying to decide how it should react and when.

Camorenne leaned back. "So, how does it work?"

He looked at her. For the first time, she realized his eyes were searching strangely. They found her, after only a heartbeat, but she wondered if there weren't something wrong with his sight.

"The two of you," Camorenne said. "Mistress, apprentice. She isn't very old to have a ward like you, is she?"

"No," Couran said. He didn't break eye contact with Camorenne now that he had established it. His strange interference device, right between his eyes, winking in the candlelight, made her want to lean away. She forced herself to lean closer instead.

"She isn't very old," he said. "She had just ended her own apprenticeship. There was no one else in the Restoration to take on an apprentice when I became available. If she hadn't taken me on, no one would have."

"Then what would have happened?" Camorenne said.

"I don't know." He looked away. "Father paid the Restoration's apprenticeship fees. He certainly didn't want me coming home as a Consortium failure."

Camorenne decided she didn't care what that meant. "So, Lady Challant took you under her wing."

He flicked another glance at Ashre and Sovi. "Something like that."

"And you think the *world* of her for it," Camorenne said, smirking.

"I'd do anything for her," he said, playing with his vegetables again.

"How old were you when she took you as apprentice?"

"Eight years old."

"My, that is *young*," Camorenne said. She thought for a minute. "She's your mother. A young one, yes, but for all intents and purposes, your mother just the same. She raised you while she was teaching you all this stiff Restoration nonsense."

She'd pricked him. He looked up sharply. "It's not nonsense."

She didn't want to upset him. She eased off. "How long is your apprenticeship?"

"It doesn't have a fixed ending. It's between Ashre and the Senior Council to decide."

"I see."

"Not much longer, I don't think."

"And how does Ms. Sovi fit into your . . . relationship?"

He seemed to study the Barular woman for a moment.

"I just met her. Ashre has known her since before she took me on."

Camorenne rested her chin in her palm. "Well, they seem to get along *smashingly*."

He smiled. It was the most genuine expression she'd seen on him yet. "Yes, ma'am," he said, "I think they might be in love."

Camorenne arched an eyebrow. "And all these years, you've never met her?"

He shook his head.

"How old are you?"

"Eighteen."

She turned around and looked at the two women. Couran was right. They were flirting.

"Ten years is a long time to go without one's girlfriend," Camorenne said.

He stopped smiling. "It's forbidden. You can't have a partner while you have an apprentice."

"That would mean your mistress has given up quite a lot for you."

"Yes," he said quietly.

"But, now, Sovi is here."

"Yeah."

She sat up and folded her hands on the table. "Whatever do you think that means?"

He looked back down. "I don't want to talk about it."

She had to lean back into her chair when the footmen came with fresh plates perched on the tips of their gloved fingers. She looked across the table, and the two women did the same. Dinner was getting in everyone's way.

That made Camorenne smile. They were at least getting a real taste of what life was like around here.

Camorenne walked into Ricarde's study. There was a fire snapping in his hearth, and there was an abandoned tumbler of whiskey on his desk, but the room was empty. He had piles of patents of nobility strewn across his desk. He'd been dragging his feet about marriage since long before she left for Silangarde. She felt a little bad for him. He'd never wanted to marry, but even firstborn male sons don't get to skirt all the rules.

She grabbed the pickaxe mounted on the wall behind his chair and torqued it. It squealed as it turned, then the wall clicked, and a paneled door swung open. She'd always loved this room. When she and Ricarde were children, they would sneak in when their father was away and explore the tunnels he was building under their estate—one of the benefits of having so many miners around. Now that he was running the estate, Ricarde preferred to do most of his work underground. There were fewer eavesdropping servants or wandering artifexi who could be, as he'd described it, "sapping his brain."

The stone corridors seemed so much smaller than she remembered. When she was little, they felt as massive as dragon's caves—and often served that specific imaginary role. There were side tunnels leading to secret chambers and stores—an entire, underground wing of their estate, but she ignored them. She could smell tobacco before she even turned the corner to Ricarde's preferred office.

He was sitting behind his mahogany desk. The walls had been paneled and sealed since she'd been down last, but otherwise the room looked how she remembered it. Tobacco smoke hung unmoving in the still air. Ricarde and Davo were inspecting trade manifests, pipes held idly in their off hands. Kedrick was across the room on a sofa, toying with a stiletto.

"What is this?" she asked. "Some kind of gentlemen's club?"

They all looked up at her. She felt like a little kid again, spoiling her brother's fun by pestering him and his friends. It made her feel small, which annoyed her.

She crossed her arms. "Well, Ricarde—you sent for me."

He set his manifests down and leaned back in his chair. He was starting to show some gray in his dark beard. His eyes were as bright and green as ever—just like hers. Their father used to call them their Olin eyes.

"Yes, sister, come in." He gestured at the chair next to Davo.

"Sister?" She snorted as she took the seat. "Are we being proper for your guests, then?"

Ricarde sighed and pinched the bridge of his nose. She'd always been able to get a rise out of him. Davo winked at her from his chair and pulled on his pipe. She tried to wave the smoke away, but all it did was swirl.

"Well, what is it then, brother?" she said.

He crossed his arms on his desk and leaned forward.

"I think you should go back to the ruling province," he said.

She sat still for a moment. "Back. To Silangarde? You do recall that city tried to kill me more than once."

Ricarde looked at her. "We will take precautions, but it's clear that this feud with the Sedas is escalating. It isn't just about Talve anymore. We're going to have to litigate this in the capitol courts."

She turned and looked at Kedrick. "So, you've been talking to *him*."

Kedrick smiled at her.

"You do know that he has recruited me to serve this very purpose for The Shroud," she said, turning back around.

"Yes," Ricarde said. He set his pipe down. He'd never been all that good at keeping one lit. Camorenne always thought he smoked one just because the other Olinire nobles did. "I am aware."

Camorenne narrowed her eyes. She glanced at Davo; he held up his palms in a show of innocence. She looked back at Ricarde. He looked tired, but she didn't care.

"*How* are you aware of this?" she said.

"I told him," Kedrick said. "It was always the plan. We just needed to convince you."

"*Convince* me!" Camorenne shouted. "What is this, Ricarde?"

He spread his hands, exasperated, and handed her a stack of correspondence. They were letters between himself and Kedrick. She couldn't believe it. They'd both been playing her.

"How long—" she started.

"Since you demonstrated yourself capable, worthy, and kind," Kedrick said. "We knew your brother would be interested in an alliance, but just in case, I wanted to convince you myself."

She wasn't sure if she was angry or flattered.

"Look," Ricarde said, "Talve isn't any safer than the capitol anymore. In the last few days, we've seen artifexi from the Consortium in town—several of them—and Kedrick's enemies in the Oliniron Shroud are afoot. We've had reports directly from his comrades."

It was her turn to grab the bridge of her nose. "How does any of that have any bearing on where *I* live," she said.

Ricarde and Davo exchanged glances. "There's too much to get into, but it's clear now that our feud with the Sedas is a proxy war. It's going to get bigger and bigger as the Crown itself starts fighting here to protect its assets."

"*What* assets?" she said, looking around. "It's fucking Talve!"

Somebody else walked into the room. A tall man, with bright blue eyes and a smirk. Under other circumstances, a beautiful man, but at the moment, she was after truth, not beauty.

"It's fucking Talve, all right," the newcomer said. "Now the ethnic Naredals are agitating against Seda and his Consortium pets."

She stood up. "Who the fuck are you?"

He bowed. "Carsand Raleis."

"He's being modest," Kedrick called from behind her. It sounded like he was eating something back there. "That's Marquis Carsand Raleis, son of the Duke of Westreign."

"And," Carsand continued, "you're not going to believe this, but I think there are *Olin* out in the mountains with some of the empress's men. I think they're aligned."

"To what purpose?" Davo asked.

Carsand shrugged. "My guess is to get in while the fighting is good. If there's a chance here to wedge Oliniron back out of Karlandi rule, why not go for it."

"You think they're planning a revolution?" Ricarde said.

"Wait, wait," Camorenne said. "The empress? Of Naredesh. Why would she have men *here*?"

Carsand looked around the room. "She doesn't know?"

"There hasn't been time," Ricarde said.

"Know what!" Camorenne shouted. Damned, but these men were aggravating.

They all looked at her. "Well, because she's going to invade Karlande."

Camorenne sat down slowly. "You can't be serious."

Carsand turned to Ricarde. "I came to tell you that I think Seda is planning a strike on the mine."

"What makes you say that?" Ricarde asked.

"Because there are soldiers at the mine," Carsand said. He smirked.

"War, with Naredesh?" Camorenne said under her breath.

Ricarde held up a finger to silence Carsand. "One bloody crisis at a time."

"If I go back to Silangarde," she said. "I'll be dead in a week. Or I'll get caught in some mad invasion."

"No, you won't," Kedrick said.

She whipped her head around "You—"

"You'll be perfectly safe in a manorial estate half a day from Silangarde. We have a contract with the Minassian Estate to turn the place into a fortress."

"The *what*?" she said. "Wait, an estate?"

"It's called Dovecastle Manor," Ricarde said, rubbing his temples. "It's really quite lovely. Fully staffed. Beautiful mountain views. I wouldn't send you back to Silangarde to die."

"The Minassian Estate for Mercenary Sciences," Kedrick said. "They're friends of ours."

"Of course, they are," she said.

Davo leaned over. "It really is a lovely property. I'd love to see it."

"Well, whose is it?"

"Yours," Kedrick said.

"You mean, my family's?" She looked at Ricarde.

"No, sister. Yours. You can stage any action you need in the city, either for me, or for Kedrick, and then you can retreat back out of it to live in luxury on the banks of Caldera Mere."

It took her a minute to process that. She looked at Davo. "And you? Will you go back to the city?"

He shook his head. "Absolutely not. I'll certainly go with you to Dovecastle, though. It's obviously a safer bet than Oliniron has turned out to be."

"And what about Naredesh's invasion? They'll storm right over such a place?" she said.

"No, they won't," Carsand said. She hadn't noticed him move behind her. He was sitting across from Kedrick now, arms spread across the back of the sofa.

"And why not?" she said.

"Because I asked the empress not to."

"You . . . know . . . the *empress*?"

Carsand winked at her. "She's my lover."

"The Marquis is the key to securing Westreign's loyalty so Naredesh can reclaim Nidal and use it as a staging ground into Karlande," Ricarde said.

She looked at her brother. She felt absolutely stunned by this conversation.

"Ricarde," she said, "this is a lot."

He smiled at her. "Think it over."

Camorenne jerked straight upright. She'd been sound asleep, and she wasn't sure what she'd heard, but she'd heard *something*. And whatever it was, it wasn't good. She could hear a commotion in the hallway, and as she fumbled to get her feet out from under her blankets and onto the floor, Emille busted unceremoniously through her chamber door. The girl stopped mid-entrance, holding the outer door knob in a death grip.

"What the hell is going on?" Camorenne asked. The lights from the hallway were shining behind Emille's hair. Camorenne couldn't see her face, though. She looked like a haunt, like a ghost story she might have heard once.

"I think it's the mines, milady," Emille said. "I think an attack has been sprung?"

"What kind of an att—"

"I'll go find out!" Emille said.

And then she was gone. She hadn't closed the door. It was left gaping, almost as if it were as surprised at its lack of propriety as anyone else. Camorenne could hear servants shouting at each other.

"Wait, Emille!"

She sat still for a moment, trying to hear anything intelligible.

"For fuck's sake," Camorenne said, reaching for a gown.

"I wouldn't bother."

She turned back to the doorway. Kedrick was leaning against the frame, his stiletto perched between his fingertips. He wasn't looking at her, but at the knife instead.

"Kedrick?" Camorenne said. "What's going on? What are you doing?"

The house had gone strangely silent. The light in the hallway that had made Emille look so spectral now looked occluded, like it was shining through a wall of amber. Even the details of her bedchamber had become less distinct.

"You didn't think you could just come hide in your father's house, did you?" Kedrick said.

"What? *You* made me come here."

Something was wrong in his demeanor. She felt like she was seeing yet another of his identities. And this version made her uncomfortable.

"What about Dovecastle?" she said. "What about your plans?"

"Ah," Kedrick said. "Dovecastle. Indeed."

"Emille!" Camorenne shouted. "Davo!"

Kedrick turned and clasped his stiletto behind his back. He took a step into the room. "Oh, they can't hear you. There's an attack on, after all. Everyone is quite busy. Everyone but you."

Camorenne tried to scoot back across her bed.

"Everyone always has so much to do around you—around idle ladies like you, sticking your nose into business that doesn't concern you. Creating waves. Drawing attention."

"Kedrick, stop this at once!"

Kedrick brandished his stiletto. He cocked his head to the side.

"You'll be just another casualty of war," Kedrick said. "There will be many tonight, after all."

Camorenne nearly fell over the other edge of the bed. She managed to grab it and tumble into a crouch.

"Anyone! Help me, please!"

"Too late," Kedrick said. He lunged toward the bed, but something happened. Something strange. He couldn't finish his attack. He was hung, as if someone had frozen him, off-balance, in mid-stride.

"Who . . ." he said.

Camorenne watched as some of that strange amber light began streaming off of Kedrick—like flames drawn by a wind. She could hear some of the noise in the house again.

"You," Kedrick said with a snarl.

Camorenne looked. She didn't see anyone. What the living hell was going on? Had Kedrick gone completely mad?

The odd light surged and ripped away from Kedrick like thin fabric, and suddenly there was Couran standing in her doorway, a hand held out, as if he might repel Kedrick from across the room.

Except, there was no Kedrick. It was a woman. From the Consortium. Camorenne would recognize their dark attire anywhere, especially at the foot of her bed with a knife.

Except where was the knife? The woman wasn't holding anything.

"How dare you?" the woman said to Couran.

He didn't say anything. He just stood in the doorway, hand held against her, swaying slightly. There was blood coming out of his nose and ears.

"Who the bleeding hell are you?" Camorenne said.

The dark-haired woman whipped a glance at Camorenne. "Be silent!"

And suddenly Camorenne was immersed in complete blackness, complete silence. She tried to scream, but she couldn't hear herself.

Once again, things began to tear. The darkness pulled away in shreds, and Couran was now on his knees, the dark woman standing over him, fingers extended gently, as if she might caress his forehead. She had taken off one of her gloves, and her pale hand shone in the spectral hallway light. Couran wasn't even looking at her. His strange eyes were looking at something else, somewhere else. As if he existed in a different room.

"That's enough now," the woman said softly.

She touched Couran's forehead, and he jerked, and there was a flash of powder from his palm, and the strange artifex jerked away from him like he was made of pure fire. Her scream was the loudest thing Camorenne had heard in ages. She stumbled away from him, clutching her hand.

"How could you . . ." the woman said, incredulous. When Couran got unsteadily back to his feet, shambling like a puppet, the artifex lifted her injured, bare hand once again, and the room began to bend and rotate, and Camorenne felt as if she might tumble to the ceiling and vomit.

Couran took a step, flung a fistful of his dark powder once more. It took the woman full in the face. Couran collapsed like a falling tree, stiff, as if posture were still important when losing consciousness.

There was no scream this time. The woman grunted, face smeared with what looked like soot, blood bubbling from her eyes, and then she fell. Almost as if she was simply swooning from an overtight corset and a room without enough air.

Camorenne just stared at them, crouched on the other side of her bed. She heard thundering footsteps outside her room, and then Carsand charged into the room, pistol drawn, Emille in tow. They stopped and stared at the people on the floor.

"Well, I'll be god-damned," Carsand said.

Emille ran around him, over the prone artifexi, and to Camorenne's side. She put her hands under Camorenne's arms and helped her stand.

"Who . . . is that?" Camorenne asked.

"That," Carsand said, "gesturing with his pistol, "is Moiren Sile. She's from the Consortium."

"That much I gathered," Camorenne said.

"She's one of the prime minister's bulldogs."

Carsand walked across the room and nudged her with his boot. She didn't move. He knelt down and felt for her pulse. Then he felt for Couran's.

"Well?" Camorenne said.

Carsand looked at her. "She's dead." He brandished a fingertip, but it was too dark to see what he'd found. "Blood poisoning. Looks like he got her with iron filings to the face."

"What in the hell does that mean?" Camorenne said.

"Never mind," Carsand said. "The boy's done us both a kindness tonight. Better help me get him on the bed. He's still got a chance."

"But why *me*?" she said. "The Consortium?"

Carsand grabbed Couran under the armpits. Camorenne hurried to get his feet.

"Consortium, Shroud—it doesn't matter. It's all of them. One big, old happy conspiracy. You're a liability."

They got Couran onto the bed, and Camorenne sent Emille to find Lady Challant.

"You had a pretty close call," Carsand said, arching his back. "Looks like you might be better off hiding from your enemies in plain sight."

"You mean Dovecastle," she said.

He gestured all around them. "You'd rather die in here?"

"But I don't understand why I'm *everyone*'s enemy now."

He clapped her on the shoulder, as if they were drinking buddies in some shithole saloon she would never patronize. She frowned at him, but she didn't move his hand.

"My lady," he said, "you don't get to choose your enemies. They choose you."

CHAPTER NINETEEN

Couran pulled himself from the deep dark, starting simply as an idea of himself until he had the wherewithal to open his eyes and let in the light. He felt heavy and sore—but calm. It took his eyes a few minutes to settle themselves into action, and then he could see the room around him. It looked like a servant's chamber—white walls and a simple window through which daylight gushed like it was filling a hole. Ashre was sitting in a chair to the side of his bed. She wasn't wearing her gloves or her hat or even her waistcoat—just her blouse and a pair of trousers. It was how she preferred to sleep. He'd passed a thousand mornings with her like this out in the open country.

Then he remembered. The artifex.

"I survived," he said. His voice sounded thick, and his throat hurt.

Ashre was quiet for a moment. She had her hands folded on her knee, and her hair looked like fire in the brilliant light.

"You didn't think you would?" she said.

"I didn't know."

"You almost didn't."

He paused. "Yes, mistress."

"Tell me what happened," she said. It was the same tone she used when she was trying to help him find the lesson in something he'd done—something she'd tried to teach him.

He licked his lips. "I was with you and Master Challant. We were looking at the survey maps in Lord Astafo's viewing room. Then the alarm about the invasion came down the hallway."

He stopped. There was a gap in his memory.

"Concentrate," Ashre said. "Recreate it. Build it like an interference."

He took a breath. "Then we were underground, in a . . . tunnel. We were running. Master Challant was worried about the mine. Something he'd done to it. Something we might have to undo."

"But you didn't follow me," she said.

Couran was staring at the ceiling, but Ashre's gaze had texture—heft. He could feel her studying him.

"No, mistress."

"Why not?"

"Because there was an imbalance."

"Go on."

He thought for a moment. "It was like the manor itself was calling. Something had happened to it. It was afraid for its life."

"But a manor can't fear for its life."

"I know. It was a person. The manor was scaring the person. Something wasn't right."

"So, you stopped," Ashre said.

"You weren't stopping."

"So, *you* stopped," she said.

"I had to. I just knew . . . I had to. I couldn't tell why you didn't have to, but I did. I didn't think, I just started running back."

"Then what happened?"

"I started chewing damproot as fast as I could."

"You were planning an interference."

"Yes, ma'am."

"Without my permission."

"Yes . . . ma'am."

"Go on."

"My filament woke up, seemingly on its own—"

Ashre shifted against the wall. It was the first movement she'd made since he woke up. He noted it.

"—and we followed the terror, and people were running past, answering the alarms, but they were all running the wrong way. Away from the imbalance. And then I found her."

"Moiren Sile," Ashre said.

"I didn't know who she was."

"Of course, you didn't. Go on."

"She was an Inquisitor, from the Consortium, and she was doing something to Lady Camorenne's mind. She had her trapped in an illusion, and Camorenne's body was all out of balance. The room was out of balance. Everything was. The Inquisitor was fooling Camorenne's mind into destroying itself."

"That's what they do," Ashre said. "It's their strongest attack."

"So, I undid it," Couran said.

There was a pause.

"You . . . undid it," Ashre said.

He turned his head to look at her. She didn't look angry. She looked calm, like he was telling her a story he heard at the pub. Something to pass the time on a cold evening in the middle of nowhere.

"I saw a way to knock her off balance, to disrupt. Her interference didn't account for someone pulling the drain plug at the other end. She wasn't ready for me. So, I started restoring the balance."

"She was a very powerful artifex, Couran. She nearly tore your mind apart."

"I know." He licked his lips. "I knew I couldn't beat her, not with an interference, so I improvised."

"The iron filings," Ashre said.

"I threw the first handful," Couran said. "It shocked her, and it gave us a beat, just enough time. The second time, my filament threw it."

"And she tore her own mind apart," Ashre said.

He hadn't thought of that. "Is that what happened to her?"

Ashre nodded. "And blood poisoning, of course."

He didn't say anything.

"You've never seen it before."

He shook his head.

"Never forget it."

"No, ma'am. I won't."

She stood up and looked down at him for a moment. He could see a bit of a smile. It was rare. She didn't smile often. At least, not until Sovi had joined them.

Ashre sat down gently on the edge of the bed and folded her hands in her lap.

"I'm sorry, mistress," he said. He felt like he might cry. "I should've followed you."

She reached over and brushed his hair off his forehead with her fingertips. "No, Couran. You did exactly what I've taught you to do. You restored the balance when no one else would, not even me. I didn't hear it. You did. And you nearly died for it."

"I know," he said.

She put her hands back in her lap. "That's the job, Couran. Restoration, balance, selflessness. And most importantly . . . bravery."

"I was scared," he said.

"The thing about being brave," she said, fully smiling now, "is that it's fucking terrifying."

That made him laugh.

"I think you know what this means," she said.

He stopped laughing.

"No, wait—"

"Our time together has come to end, Couran."

He couldn't stop his tears. A sob climbed right out of his throat.

"Mistress—"

"I've taught you what I needed to teach you. Your path was always up to you. You just needed to take the time to realize it."

"No, Ashre—please! I can't lose you."

She reached down and took his face in her palms. The curtain of her hair fell around them. It was something he remembered from being little. She would use her hair like that to close things off. And when the world got smaller for him, like that, he could calm down.

"My beautiful boy," she said. "You will *never* lose me."

He sobbed again. "But I don't want—"

She shushed him. "It's not about what you want. You know that. It's not about what I want either."

He took a breath. He felt a little calmer.

"Yes, mistress."

She shook her head gently. "You don't call me that anymore, Couran. You can call me 'Lady Challant,' if you want to put on airs. But it's just Ashre now."

He swallowed. "So that's it? We're just, we're finished?"

She leaned back and tucked her hair behind her ears. "I have one more lesson to teach you, and then there's something we must do together. An imbalance here in Talve we must restore."

"What is the lesson?"

"I'm going to teach you how to talk on the wind. Like I do. This is how you will call me. And when you need me, I'll come."

"Yes, mist—. . . okay."

"To find me across the spread of time and energy all around us, you have to start with a memory. What's your most powerful memory of me?"

He thought for a moment. "I was little. It wasn't long after you accepted me. We were camping on a plain, and it was windy, and cold, and you had me in your lap, wrapped in your jacket. You were singing lullabies, and it was just us and the dark. I guess you would have been about my age now."

She smiled at him and took his hands in her own.

"What's your fondest memory of me?" he asked.

She didn't say anything for a long time. It made him feel better. It was how she normally was. Quiet. Contemplative. A woman of thought, not compulsion.

"We haven't quite finished making that one yet," she said.

The smooth masonry of Astafo Manor's underground passages gave way to rough-hewn stone. The only light came from Marquis Raleis's lantern, and it was directed into the darkness ahead of them. Master Challant was following the marquis, and Ashre was behind him. Couran came last. All he could see ahead of them was the dim outline of the rock passage. It reminded him of the Tower of Te'hruz, like walking into the open maw of something ancient, something . . . hungry.

He placed his hand on Ashre's shoulder ahead of him. She did the same to her brother. They'd both been chewing *salve* for the last several minutes. Ordinarily, it was just bitter. Under the circumstances, Couran thought it tasted a little like blood, as if he'd bitten his own tongue. He relaxed his eyes and let them wander the darkness on their own. His filament uncoiled in the hollows of his mind and joined his consciousness. He felt the calm of this union roll through him. The filament knew what he needed, and it could massage Couran's brain to create a sense of calm—or, as in the case of Moiren Sile, courage.

He felt Ashre slide into his awareness.

We're no longer under the primary estate, she shared with him. *You should start feeling the Consortium's imbalances up on the surface. They're trying to find us to break the Gnostic Accords.*

He shared his understanding with her. *Artifexi at war—after so many generations of peace.*

There hasn't been any peace, she shared, *simply proxy conflicts. This is the biggest one yet. But we can't be found, and we can't let Adwar or Carsand be found. We have to get to Seda Manor. We have to undo whatever the Consortium has done to produce Moths of War.*

I'm ready, he shared. He could feel Ashre's understanding. She trusted him. She was proud of him. He'd helped her with countless restorations before, but that's because that's all he knew how to do. It was all he was capable of. Now, he was helping her because she needed him to. He liked that feeling.

He would never let her down.

They continued into the long dark, and the Consortium's inquisitions came for them. They were searching, divining—listening with their seeker minds for the vibrations of other artifexi in Talve. When they came close, Ashre began unraveling the interferences and diffusing their power through her transducer. It made the underground atmosphere feel tight. Couran wondered if it would have any effect on the stone above them.

As the inquisitions came faster, Ashre began her restorations and then handed them over to Couran. He picked up where she left off, and the carefully arranged harmonics of the inquistions came apart like threadbare quilts. He imagined that, for the Consortium artifexi creating the inquistions, these dissolutions were maddening. They had to know it was the Restoration thwarting their efforts, but they wouldn't have any way of pinpointing them. Which was the point. He understood now—any conflict with an Inquisitor had to be a game of cat-and-mouse. If they got ahead of him, like Moiren had, he wouldn't have enough remaining mind to undo their work.

Carsand stopped at a juncture at the head of their column.

We're at the Astafo Mine, Ashre shared. *We're going to have to pass through a portion of it, but there are knights from both households in here.*

They're fighting in *the mine? That's insane.*

I will keep the inquisitions at bay, Ashre shared. *Help the marquis. He's going to cover Adwar. He's going to have to create an exit for us.*

How should I help him?

She didn't know. Couran wasn't used to her uncertainty. She'd never shared it before.

He clapped her on the shoulder and squeezed his way past. Master Challant grabbed him by the shoulders and issued him forward—there was barely enough room for the two men to stand in the same spot.

Couran put his hand on Carsand's shoulder. He was as stiff as the stone around him. He didn't have a filament keeping him calm. Ashre's shoulder had been relaxed, ready. Carsand's body, on the other hand, was preparing to defend itself against . . . whatever.

Couran could see the mine ahead of them in the light from Carsand's lantern. There were wooden trusses against the walls and along the low ceiling. Gunshots rang out deeper in the mine, and the muffled voices of men shouting sounded pretty much exactly how Couran had always imagined hell might.

"We have to go deeper in," Couran said.

"Yeah, no shit," Carsand said. He hefted his pistol in his other hand. "How far?"

"Far enough," Couran said. "Don't worry—I'm going to help you."

Carsand turned and gave him a steady glare. "I don't like artifexi."

Couran clapped his shoulder. "It's mutual. Let's go."

Carsand rolled his head back and forth. "Salvation," he muttered, and then they were moving.

The din grew louder, the air got tighter, and the inquisitions kept coming. Couran doubted there were any Consortium actually in the mine. He couldn't imagine them being willing to take that degree of risk. That, at least, would give Lord Astafo's men a fighting chance against the Seda knights. Couran didn't think even someone as powerful as Moiren would have been able to create illusions through solid rock, separated by hundreds of feet from their targets.

The first patrol was just as surprised as Carsand was when their lantern beams found each other around a curve in the shaft.

"Down," Carsand shouted.

He lifted his pistol, and the bloodmetal mechanism started throwing bullets like whip-cracks at the Sedas. The first knight dropped like a sack of lead, and then powder gunshots sundered the air. They were so loud, it felt like being punched in the ears, Couran thought. Carsand was outgunned, and the mine wasn't giving them enough cover.

After a couple shots sliced past them, he and his filament formed an idea of how they moved—the degree of their arc, their rotation, even the wind resistance created by the air, which was now swirling with powder smoke. The idea seemed so simple. The bullets were unbalancing the cool dark of the mine's natural harmonic state.

When the Sedas fired again, the filament took over, layering and folding and preparing a different resolution to the disturbance, and power fell into Couran's mind, making the air itself chill and hollow around him. He felt Carsand tense when it happened.

And his transducer sent the wavelengths of Couran's interference pulsing into the gunsmoke, and they slammed and slammed in rapid succession against the Sedas' thundering gunshots, absorbing that power and shuddering it back into the stone around them. Dust tumbled from the rocks overhead, and the bullets slowed in midair and then dropped. They rolled a little when they hit the dirt.

Carsand didn't hesitate. He jumped up, charged around the curve, and shot the remaining two knights point-blank. Silence filled the mine for a moment, and Couran's ears rang. His filament quickly shushed them.

Carsand stared at him. "You can stop bullets?"

"I can stop a lot of things," Couran said.

"But, you're just a kid," Carsand said.

Couran stood up. Adwar and Ashre followed suit behind them.

"Not anymore," Couran said.

Couran could tell that Ashre was becoming tired, too. The Consortium's inquisitions were relentless, and they'd been tucked away in this corner of the mine for what seemed like hours while Adwar stared at a slender crack in the stone wall, his fingers delicately touching the opening, as if he might peel it apart.

Couran felt detached from himself as he dug into his satchel and retrieved a small jar of stimulant powder—and a handkerchief. He and his filament didn't normally stay in communion like this for so long. It wasn't an uncomfortable experience, but it was disorienting, to be sure.

He packed some of the powder under his tongue, and then tapped Ashre on the jaw. She looked slowly at him with watery eyes, and he held up the jar. She took it sluggishly, and he daubed blood from her nostrils with the handkerchief.

"How long is this going to take?" Carsand said, squatting against the wall, pistol held lazily across his knees. He kept looking in different directions down the mine, watching for more knights.

"As long as it takes," Ashre said. "Adwar created this seam by accident when he re-ordered the Astafos mine."

"*Re-ordered*," Carsand said. "That's one way to put it."

"It's the easiest way through," Ashre said.

"Through to where?"

"There," Adwar whispered. He pulled at the edges of the dark crack in the stone, and the stone peeled way like wet paper. When he had created an opening large enough to pass through, he took his hands away from the wall and folded them against his abdomen. He closed his eyes and stood there silently, breathing.

"Well?" Carsand said. "Is he finished?"

Ashre didn't say anything, and Couran had no idea.

Adwar turned and smiled at Carsand. The lantern caught the gold trim on Adwar's cassock in a little flash. "We should be going now. I don't expect any additional surprises."

He gestured to the opening.

Carsand stood up and approached the wall. He ran his fingers over the edges of the opening—stone, through and through. He took a deep breath, brandished his lantern, and stepped through.

Ashre went next—she also couldn't resist the urge to touch Adwar's infant stone on the way through. Couran followed her.

"What is this?" he asked. He could see in the light from the lantern that this tunnel was perfectly round, as if it had been chewed out of the ground by some giant worm. The walls were smooth.

Adwar followed him into the new tunnel. "It is a passageway for a transduction conveyance."

"Kam," Carsand said. "Damn, he keeps busy."

"Who?" Couran said.

Carsand smiled at him. "Kam Glimjeld, ex-Inquisitor, exiled to the Glim. Master of his own destiny and capable of pretty much anything you can imagine."

"Ex-Inquisitor?" Couran said.

"Another time," Adwar said, settling a hand on Couran's shoulder. "Let's go."

Carsand led the progression again. "Where are we going?"

"To the Seda estate," Adwar said. "We cannot allow the Consortium to refine Moths of War. We must sabotage whatever they're hiding on the estate."

The stone around them shuddered and groaned. Couran could feel a sudden swell in the imbalance of power on the surface.

"It would seem the conflict has escalated," Adwar said.

"Well," Carsand said, "let's see—you've got Seda's knights, the Consortium, and Silangarde Shroud on one side, and the Astafos, the ethnic Naredals, Olinire Shroud, and, apparently, the last of the Olin themselves on another."

He turned around and looked at them as he walked. "Honestly, I'd rather be down here with you lot then trying to fight my way through that clusterfuck."

"Keep walking," Ashre said.

They marched for hours. The further away they moved from the center of the conflict, which, Couran imagined, was the entrance to the mine and its surrounds, the less intense the inquisitions became. They were too far away now. Eventually, Couran's filament slinked away into the shadows of his mind—there was no reality for it to effect here but the reality of sore feet and silence. Adwar occasionally tracked his fingers along the edge of the passageway as they went.

"Isn't Kam going to be . . . *upset* if you sabotage whatever he's hiding," Carsand said out of nowhere. "The Consortium paid him to do it, after all."

"He was unbothered by the idea when I discussed it with him," Adwar said.

Carsand thought for a moment. "Doesn't that seem strange to you?"

"We have more pressing issues to manage than Kam Glimjeld's hurt feelings," Adwar said.

Carsand shrugged. "Seems weird."

Adwar stopped. "Here."

Carsand turned the lantern on him. Couran could just see the dim outline of what looked like a concave door.

"Ashre," Adwar said. He moved aside.

Ashre put her fingers on the stone, closed her eyes, and Couran felt power draw out of the tunnel. A mechanism clicked behind the stone, and the doorway swung open without a sound.

They all looked at Adwar.

"Even a madman like Kam knows to create secondary exits," he said.

Carsand stepped through the portal without a complaint. Couran followed Ashre through again, and he nearly tripped when his boot kicked a stair.

"Careful," Ashre said above him. "Stairs."

"Yes, mistress," he said.

Ashre turned, but he didn't need to see her expression to be able to read it, even in darkness.

"Sorry," he said. "Old habits."

They emerged into an aspen grove in a narrow valley between two slopes. The sun was still high, and it felt strange to hear only wind and birdsong. The sounds of murder, mayhem, and madness belonged to the other end of the county.

Adwar knelt and pressed his palm against the earth. Whatever interference he was performing, the draw was strong enough that it rattled the leaves in the trees. Couran glanced at Ashre, but she was staring at her brother.

"This way," Adwar said, gesturing.

"What have you found?" Ashre asked.

"Cultivation," he said, walking. "It doesn't belong out here."

Carsand stashed their lantern just inside the doorway they had emerged through. They'd wedged the stone door with a rock. Couran imagined they didn't want to be hunting for the opening when they were finished with their deeds here. If this Kam person had dug this tunnel to bring him directly to his secret operation on Lord Seda's property, Couran imagined it wasn't wise of them to hang around looking for things any longer than they had to.

They hiked through the trees in silence. The elevation was low enough here for ferns and other forms of bracken to dampen their footsteps. Adwar marched them directly to a cliff wall.

"It's here," he said.

Ashre stepped up beside him and touched the stone. She instantly jerked her hand away.

"It stings," she said.

Adwar nodded. Ashre turned to Couran. "With me."

He stepped up beside her. It felt stupid to stare at a stinging wall, but she'd asked him to do stranger things during his apprenticeship.

"Get the gingervine," she said.

He rummaged through his satchel and pulled out a reagent tin. Ashre opened it and dragged a finger through the paste. She smeared it across her gums, and then handed it back to him.

"More than usual," she said.

Couran did as he was told, and his gums burned when he applied the gingervine. They didn't use it very often. "What's the task?"

She stared at the stone in front of them. "This isn't real. It's a deflection. We need to undo it."

Couran's filament, as if it heard its own name, stirred. Ashre started drawing power. Couran wasn't sure what she wanted, so he began drawing, too, and he fed the swirling energy into the current she'd created, giving her more to work with. The trees around them bent and drooped as they sapped them of the power they needed. One snapped in half and hit the forest floor with a reverberating *thud*.

An eruption of light burst from the stone wall, and an opening appeared, a maw of roots and stone that snapped and fluttered like paper. Storm-force wind blew them all back a step as the illusory wall sprayed power like a ruptured dam.

"Go," Ashre said. "I can't restore this. It's some kind of automation."

Carsand had stopped nagging them for answers the stranger their errand became. He immediately jumped through. Adwar stepped calmly after him.

Now you, she shared with Couran.

He hurried through, and she whipped herself through right after him. The stone reformed itself immediately, and Ashre fell to her knees. Couran knelt down to help her.

"Ashre," he said. "Look."

She lifted her head, and they both stared at the field before them. It was cultivated, as Adwar had said, but there was terracework and lattices of strange vines. It looked like a process of cultivating caged animals. On the other side of the field, there was a dark timber structure that looked like a church. There was no one in sight.

Ashre got to her feet and joined Adwar where he was staring through the lattices. Carsand had taken a knee and had his pistol trained on the structure.

"The top vines," he said, "are a salt-hungry species. They draw alkalinity out of the soil. Look . . ."

Couran stepped up beside Ashre, and they followed Adwar's pointing finger. Large, feathery moths were perched on the vines everywhere, slowly moving their darkly splotched wings.

"They're eating the bark on those vines," Couran said.

"Moths of War," Ashre said.

Couran leaned closer. Under the vines, he could see delicately pruned flower beds. There were clusters of pink blossoms that looked like fingers emerging from dark fronds.

"There isn't much time," Adwar said. He stepped forward and thrust his arm between the vines and directly into the earth, up to his elbow.

"How did—" Couran said.

"Not now," Ashre said.

Nothing happened for long minutes.

"Now would be a good time to hurry," Carsand hissed.

"Ashre?" Couran said.

"Hold," she said.

Still, Adwar knelt. Unmoving, his head bowed. Long minutes passed, and then Couran heard a tearing sound coming from the ground. He peered closer at the flowers beneath the latticed vines. The sound intensified, and then, the plants fell into the earth, as if swallowed, pulled into the underworld. Couran looked around. They were gone everywhere—only the vines remained. The moths began fluttering from their perches.

"Hey!"

They all looked. There was a boy standing further into the field. Around him, other children got to their feet. It looked to Couran like they'd been lying in the field. They were all holding spades and other implements.

"What've you done?" the first boy called.

"Ah, damn," Carsand said. He started to raise his gun, but then he thought better of the move. He looked helplessly at the others.

"We grew those for Lady Fabienne!"

Another child shouted, and then another. They began popping up from their unintentional hiding spots all over. Couran saw a Salvation nun come running around the building. She stopped when she saw them and ran back the way she came.

"Adwar," Ashre said, "we have to go."

"That's a lot of kids," Carsand said. "Are we just going to leave them here?"

Adwar stood up. "We have no choice. Let's go."

A Seda knight came running from behind the building, nun in tow. He shouted something, and then lifted a powder rifle and fired. The shot slammed into the dirt a few feet in front of Couran.

"Couran," Ashre said, hurrying after the others, "come on!"

Couran stood. He stared at the kids, and they stared back at him. The knight took another shot, and Couran heard Carsand's blood-metal pistol whip-crack another bullet across the field. Couran thought about the Consortium. He thought about their tests and his eyes and Ashre holding him on a windy plain. He thought about being unwanted . . .

"Couran!" Ashre shouted.

He turned and ran. Ashre was struggling to run with her limp. Couran got her arm up over his shoulders, and they hobbled along as quickly as they could. More shots followed them.

"We can't abandon them," he said.

Ashre gasped for breath. "You won't."

"We got everything we could," Camorenne said, handing the satchel over to Ashre.

"Thank you," Ashre said. They couldn't go back to Astafo Manor—it would too much effort to keep fending off the Consortium's searches. She turned and handed the satchel up to her brother. He situated it on the saddle behind him and began tying it in place.

Ashre squinted into the sun. It would drop below the ridgeline soon. Nightfall seemed to come early in the mountains.

She extended a hand to Camorenne, and they shook. "Travel safely."

Camorenne smirked. "With your bullet-stopping protégé in tow, I think I'll sleep a little easier."

Ashre took her hand back. "Do what he says now. Couran knows the backlands. If any of those three can get you to Dovecastle in one piece, it'll be him."

Camorenne bowed her head. For once, she bit her tongue, and moved over to join Kedrick and Davo. Ashre and Couran were alone while the others made their preparations.

"Keep an eye on her," Ashre said. "She's important to the balance of things, and she can help you get the word out about the children on Seda's property."

"Yes, ma'am," he said. "I will."

"Don't take any unnecessary risks," Ashre said. "And don't let the others walk you into a bad situation. If something stinks, turn around."

"Yes, ma'am."

"Contact me tomorrow night. I want updates on your progress."

He took a step closer and pulled off his gloves. He extended his palms to Ashre. "You know I will."

She looked at him for a long time, then she took off her own gloves and took his hands in hers.

"I feel like maybe I didn't say it enough, but I hoped you always knew."

She turned her head. He didn't try to stop his own tears.

"I knew," he said. "I love you, too."

She pulled him into an embrace, and the wind whipped her hair against his cheek. It stuck there, held fast by the rivulet of tears.

"Ashre," Sovi called. "We have to go. We're losing the sun."

Ashre pried herself away from him, and held him by the shoulders. "We've got to get Carsand to Levuwes. He's crucial to all these politics."

He sniffed. Neither one of them had ever held much interest in politics. "Go on, then."

She nodded and limped her way to her horse. Carsand helped hoist her into the saddle.

"Let's go, Couran" Camorenne called. "I'm about ready to be looked after by all you *men*."

That made him laugh. He liked Lady Astafo. He'd keep her safe. When he mounted his horse and turned back, Ashre and her party were already riding—due west to Naredesh, straight at the sun atop the peaks.

He heard an explosion in the distance. The proxy war was still raging at Astafo Manor.

He nudged his horse into place beside Camorenne. She extended a hand and smiled at him.

He put his gloves back on before he took her hand.

CHAPTER TWENTY

Fabienne swirled her fingers through the steaming water. Rose petals, and lily petals, and all kinds of fragrant herbs were floating around her. The water felt perfect against her skin, like an incubation—an embrace that was keeping her safe and comfortable against the whole of the universe. She swam slowly through the massive bath. Marble arcades ringed the place, and servants in white gowns carried trays and prepared massages and otherwise waited for her to emerge from the water for some new luxury. In the distance, the ocean shimmered, and it looked like sunlight on beaten metal.

Someone cleared their throat behind her. She turned. Kam stood at the edge of the bath, Aisabelle at his side in a silken gown. She no longer had Kam's device implanted into her forehead.

"Oh, hello," Fabienne said, distracted by the swirling flowers. "It's nice of you to come."

"Who am I speaking to?" Kam said.

"To whom am I speaking," Fabienne said, "is the correct question. And don't be silly, it's me."

"Who is me? Fabienne or Communion?"

"Fabienne, of course," she said. She laughed.

Kam looked around the steaming chamber. Aisabelle stood demurely at his side, eyes down. "And where are we?"

"Would you like to join me?" Fabienne said. "The water is perfect."

"You're having a swim?" he said.

"What else does one do in a bath?" she said.

He smiled. "Of course. A bath. Communion is keeping your mind comfy indeed—I can only imagine the power of the illusion you're seeing."

"Why have you come if not for a bath?"

"Because Adwar has done as we expected."

"He stole the flowers?"

"He pulled them into the bowels of the earth."

"*All* of them?"

"Every one," Kam said. Fabienne wondered why he and her sister weren't hot in the baths, wearing all those clothes like that. They weren't even sweating.

"How impressive," Fabienne said.

"You promised me more," Kam said.

"Oh, Communion will have to take care of that," she said.

"Yes, well," he said, "I was hoping I'd be speaking to Communion."

That made her laugh. "How could you speak to Communion while you're speaking to me?"

"I want those flowers, Fabienne," he said.

"I'm busy," she said, swimming away from him.

"Your sister—"

"Is no longer your prisoner," Fabienne said. "She doesn't have the device. You've either charmed her or broken her. Either way, do with her what you will. I've already done away with her somewhere else."

"I was never going to hurt her," he said. "I just needed to get you to this point."

"And you never realized that here was exactly where I wanted to be."

"We had a deal," he said.

"Oh, very well. Fine!"

Everything vanished, and Fabienne dissolved into nothing.

Streamers of black muslin whipped against Fabienne's face as she stomped into the wind, desert sand blowing all around her. The sky looked like blue fire, clouds streaming like smoke. Kam and Aisabelle were set up at a tea table atop one of the dunes, he in a coat and tails, she in a ball gown and tiara. It took Fabienne a while to climb the dune, and when she got near enough, Kam finally noticed her and turned his head. He stood up abruptly.

"Fabienne?" he said.

"Yes," she said, drawing the muslin away from her face, "it's me."

He waited, and she stomped across the sand and took his hands in her own. When she pulled away, she had left a handful of *delirium shade* in his palms.

"Where did you get it?" he said.

She twirled, arms extended. "From the neighbors."

"The neighbors?"

"The realities next door. Communion took us there, and we stole it."

"This isn't enough," he said.

"Don't worry," she said, letting her arms fall. "There are many worlds to burn."

AFTERWORD

This book is a story unto itself. It's been almost twenty-five years since I typed word one of this story that would consume most of my adult life. There are many people along the way who helped it see print, which is why its story is worth sharing.

Bloodmetal is based on a Dungeons and Dragons campaign. When I was sixteen, I was DMing a campaign with my fellow loser buddies, and at the core of the adventure was a field full of unwanted children cultivating an arcane crop. Hijinx ensued, dice were rolled, hours of sleep were sacrificed to completing the adventure in my parents' basement.

At the time, I had only recently begun showing interest in writing. I had joined the literary magazine staff in school, and those same loser buddies and I were experimenting with bad poetry and short stories. So, this adventure in the Olinire mountains stuck with me. I chewed on it and chewed on it, slowly drawing out a novel-length plotline and the capers to fill it. At around eighteen, I started writing *IMMORTAL MADNESS*, which was the first godawful version of this novel's name. I worked on it dutifully for three years, and I finished the first draft only a day or two before my twenty-first birthday (which had been the plan).

That book was awful. It was 300,000 words long (the version you're holding in your hands is about 75,000, by way of comparison). I was reading enough books on How to Be a Writer that I knew what had to be done. I threw it away and started over. Same story, same characters, a few plot tweaks. I had to do better.

That took another two years. At that point I realized that only *half* the book sucked. So, I did it again. I threw away another 150,000 words (yes, I seemed to have been stuck at that 300,000-word length, for whatever reason), and I rewrote them.

At this point, the book was no longer terrible—it just needed professional help. I was fortunate to land my long-time agent, Kristopher O'Higgins, with this version of the book, and he got to work on some edits. We threw away half again, and I fixed everything, this time, inspired by the confidence of a literary agent and the exciting world of the publishing market. We got the book into shape, Kris got to work shopping it around, and life went on.

And something changed. I'd been living with this story for so long, I thought it would be all I ever wanted to work on. But, in 2007, I finished graduate school, and my wife and I moved out of state. I had a freshly minted Ph.D., no job, and no friends. And between 2007-2008, the economy imploded. So, money was tight, too. I broke up with this story.

My first published novel, *Noise*, came together in only about six months. It was short, mean, and perfect for the collapsey zeitgeist of the time. Critics liked it, I got good reviews, and my peers seemed to think it wasn't total trash. That's an intoxicating mixture. *Noise*, and the other two books of the Dystopian Cluster, *Chimpanzee* and *Totem*, are nothing like *Bloodmetal*. They're aggressive, experimental, and cerebral. Sure, there are plenty of explosions, but they each had a thesis they were trying to convey. They weren't just stories for story's sake.

So, after *Noise* sold to Juliet Ulman at Bantam Spectra, I became hooked on apocalypse. An offer of publication came through for *Bloodmetal*, in its old form. There it was—the dream. Something I'd been working toward, at that point, for ten years.

I said no.

I explained to my agent how I needed to write these apocalypse books, how I thought they would define my voice as a novelist. I didn't think I could do fantasy anymore, so we passed on the offer, and life went on.

Except, *Bloodmetal* just wouldn't. let. go. It stayed in the back of my mind, hibernating in the dark, not unlike a filament. It was this alien thing that was a part of me, and I couldn't excise it. But I knew I couldn't move forward with the manuscript as it was. The book just wasn't where it was supposed to be.

I rethought the magic system, re-did the characters, changed motivations—some things are still original to the first draft, but those are stories for another time. And then, you guessed it, I threw the old book away. Again.

So, this is the fourth time I've written this book. In 2020, I realized I wanted to tell this story, finally. I was done writing dystopias. I love them, but they're emotionally draining to work on, and who in 2020 had the spirit to read another dystopian book, let alone write one?

As you can imagine, 2020 unfolded the way it did, and 2021 wasn't much better. I signed a deal with Underland to deliver this book by the end of 2020. That absolutely didn't happen. I had to do my time in the desert like everyone else. I lost family members to COVID. I lost beloved friends. I lost what I thought was the job of my life. We had to involve anti-depressants and anti-anxiety medication and exercise and diet and meditation and every trick we were all using to try to get through the global pandemic. So, I wasn't writing. *Bloodmetal* was in limbo again.

But, and here's where the acknowledgements begin, Mark Teppo (my publisher) and John Klima (my editor) and I started meeting up every couple of weeks on Zoom. Ostensibly, we were doing so to talk shop, but those sessions came to be more like therapy, and it is because of those two men that this book exists. They dragged me kicking, screaming, and crying with virtual hugs, toasts, and messages of hope until I finally finished the story.

Then there's my wife, Rima Abunasser, who went through every agonizing thing with me along the way. From those lonely depths of 2007 to the agony of 2020, she's always believed—and she's edited more than one version of this book!

And of course, my agent, Kris O'Higgins, who managed to sell the damn thing *twice*. I know many writers change agents like socks—I've never had a reason to consider it, so here we are, eighteen years later, still raising hell.

We all had families, either by blood or adoption, that helped us get through the darkness of the last few years. My parents, Layne and Jayme Bradley, steered an isolated (and separated) family with grace, and my sisters, Kristy and Sharee, managed by sheer force of will to keep our family's spirit alive. But my adopted family, my quaranteam, has been my everything. Virtual Christmases and birthdays and movie screenings and long conversations through webcams got us through shared trauma. Andy and Christi LaViolette, Scott Porter, Aaron Anderson, Ashley Bender, Aaron Leis—you're a buncha goddamn rocks, and now you're stuck with me forever. My friends Craig Williams, Ryan Crowder, Brian Carlson, and Kip Nettles played that D&D campaign, lo, those many years ago, and Maxwell Cozad was a fixture during my early edits. Love and light to you all, old friends.

So, what's the punchline? I'm not sure there is one. When a younger version of myself set out to be a career "writer," I had no idea what that meant—I had only the fantasies I'd created about the profession. I idolized other writers and how I imagined their lives and careers were unfolding. But what I've learned is that their way was never going to be my way. Things unfold the way they do, and if you're reading this and wondering about your own way, remember that. My way is not your way. *Bloodmetal* is a book about adventure, about friendship, love, and hardship, and I cherish everything that tempered this teenage dreamer to finally share his grand adventure twenty-five years later. Embrace your own way—you only get the one.